Meet the
NIGHT ANGEL 9:

Stephanie Savage
Compassionate and overzealous, this firefighter-paramedic's attitude usually locks horns with those of her coworkers. But as a divorcée who struggled to make ends meet to help her son enter college, she had to be tough-as-nails.

Abdullah "Abe" Kashmiri
A rookie EMT, this young Pakistani-American is quick on his feet and good at his job. Despite his shy, timid nature, his colleagues believe he has great potential—if he can only convince himself.

Isabel "Izzy" Vivas
A firefighter-paramedic and the single mother of a little girl with whom she spends every free moment. She finds it difficult to separate her emotions from the patients she treats, but keeps a tight rein on her temper—except when dealing with her ex-husband.

John "Doe" Smith
Originally from Dallas, Texas, this firefighter-paramedic likes to live fast—both on call and with the ladies. But despite his carefree attitude, he doesn't want to grow old alone.

Dr. Joanna Boccaccio
The base hospital physician of San Fernando Medical Center. She's a real professional, and a workaholic with no time for a social life . . . but plenty of time to dream about it.

Charti Darunyothin
A mobile intensive-care nurse who operates the radio, provides medical control, and directs paramedic squads as necessary. Ordered, precise, and quiet, he harbors a less-subdued lifestyle outside of work—and remains haunted by a childhood tragedy.

Don't miss the first novel in the series . . .
NIGHT ANGEL 9

"So realistic, I felt I was actually there."
—Leonard S. Goldberg, author of *Lethal Measures*

"Peter Telep's skills shine on every page."
—Don Donaldson, author of *Do No Harm* and *In the Blood*

Playing with Fire

NIGHT ANGEL

9

Peter Telep

B

BERKLEY BOOKS, NEW YORK

This is a work of fiction. Names, characters, places, and incidents are either the product of the author's imagination or are used fictitiously, and any resemblance to actual persons, living or dead, business establishments, events, or locales is entirely coincidental.

NIGHT ANGEL NINE: PLAYING WITH FIRE

A Berkley Book / published by arrangement with
the author

PRINTING HISTORY
Berkley edition / May 2001

The Penguin Putnam Inc. World Wide Web site address is
www.penguinputnam.com

ISBN: 0-425-17958-3

BERKLEY®
Berkley Books are published by The Berkley Publishing Group,
a division of Penguin Putnam Inc.,
375 Hudson Street, New York, New York 10014.
BERKLEY and the "B" design
are trademarks belonging to Penguin Putnam Inc.

PRINTED IN THE UNITED STATES OF AMERICA

10 9 8 7 6 5 4 3 2 1

This one's for Mom...

Acknowledgments

As with the first novel in this series, I received help from many wonderful and giving individuals.

Fire Service Technician/Paramedic Michael A. Scott, Lieutenant Mike Hammonds, Lieutenant Michael Johansmeyer, Lieutenant Steve Jones, Fire Service Technician/Paramedic Kevin Welday, and FSTs Dennis Miller, Eric Borns, Christopher Cahill, Heath Gifford, Ed Michalowski, Wayne Bernowska, and David Scott, all from Fire Station 35, Seminole County, Florida, answered many of my pesky questions and were extraordinarily helpful in the creation of this series.

Jim Newberger, a full-time Nationally Registered EMT-Paramedic working out of North Memorial Medical Center in Minneapolis, Minnesota, and a fine writer in his own right, once again brought his twelve-plus years of working the streets to this second manuscript. His contributions were many, from scene ideas to technical advice to suggestions for the next novel. Jim and I chatted daily during the writing of this novel, and his on-the-spot criticism and willingness to listen to ideas repeatedly left me in his debt.

Thanks to my editor, Kim Waltemyer, for her encouragement and keen editorial advice, and to my agent, John Talbot, for his humor and continued support.

Author's Note

The Valley Police Department and Fire Department, as well as San Fernando Medical Center, are products of my imagination. They are in no way meant to represent the actual police, fire, and medical services presently available and operating in the San Fernando Valley. The EMS system in this book is based on a number of different organizations, some located in Los Angeles, one in Florida, one in Minnesota, and one in New Mexico. Logistics and creative freedom informed this decision. I received my hands-on training in Florida, gathered notes from my consultants in Minnesota and New Mexico, and relied on materials from several West Coast organizations. Those who work in EMS will tell you that all systems have basic similarities; much of what you'll read here could very well occur. The procedures and protocols of the wonderful folks working in Los Angeles are, in some cases, different from those described in this novel.

1

The row of abandoned stores jogged back into the rainy night's swelling gloom. Sheets of warping plywood hung over shattered windows and bore the blood red curves of territorial graffiti best translated by gangbangers or police officers. Above this ramshackle file rose a thorny cluster of dilapidated apartments whose paint peeled in long lashes. Duct tape spanned many of the tenement's broken windows and formed a loose gray web that settled over the building.

"What a shithole," muttered Firefighter-Paramedic Abe Kashmiri as he came around the rescue truck. "How do people wind up in places like this?"

Stephanie Savage regarded the skinny rookie for a moment, his dark skin paling in the flashing lights, his black crew cut glazed by drizzle. She wiped her eyes and shrugged. "Fitzy'd tell you that the government wants them here. Doe'd tell you that they're all just lazy F-in' crackheads and deserve to lie in their own shit. But I don't know. Guess I've stopped wondering. Come on. Code 4. We're good to go in."

At the corner ahead, two Valley Police Department

cruiser idled, lights wheeling. A third car from VPD's Special Gang Unit rolled to a squeaky halt. Whether the anonymous emergency call involved gang activity Savage wasn't sure, but she felt more comfortable with two more officers on the scene. Only two weeks before, she and Abe had responded to another anonymous emergency call at an apartment building. A resident had mistaken them for home invaders and had exercised his right to bear arms. Thank God he'd been a poor shot. At least this time law enforcement had arrived first.

"Somebody up there made the call," said one of the cops, a middle-aged black man with biceps large enough to warrant a second look. "No one's coughing up an admission. Got a little boy who looks sick. Mom says she didn't call."

"Yeah, we heard the update," Savage replied.

"Goddamn," said the cop's partner, a square-jawed military type with sooty eyes too small for his shaven head. He smirked at the tenement. "Guess they don't validate parking. Franco? You got a quarter for the meter?"

Savage rolled her eyes at Abe. She didn't have much patience for glib cops. The rain had something to do with that. Damned rainy nights. Always made her blonde hair go frizzy. Always reminded her of that dark Friday when Tim, her ex, had wrapped their Ford Escort around a lamppost and had walked away without a scratch. In truth, he hadn't walked away, but had been hauled off in cuffs and charged with DUI.

Rainy nights in Los Angeles. Had to hate them. Always set off her trick knee and made the arthritis in her back act up. Always increased the number of MVAs because Angelinos did *not* know how to drive on wet roads. Always made the job harder when you were husky, over forty, and responsible for the field training of a rookie medic doing his three-month probation. Way it was. Accept it or get out.

They mounted a rickety outside staircase and ventured up toward a hallway between units. For a second, Savage thought the staircase might pull away from the wall and send them toppling to the pavement. Her paycheck failed to compensate for this brand of shit.

A pair of beer bottles sat on the landing, collecting rain through their open tops. Muddy footprints crossed empty condom wrappers and cigarette butts that had fallen out of a black garbage bag piled with a dozen others along one wall. If the hallway had any lights, they didn't work. A chute of darkness lay before them until the big cop pierced it with his Mag light. The powerful stench of cigarettes and piss and something gone bad in the trash had Savage grimacing as they moved deeper into the hall. She ran her gloved hand along the rough wall, then rubbed paint chips between her fingers. Although no rats darted away from the big cop's light, they undoubtedly lurked in the crevices, sniffing, waiting.

"Manager says every unit's got a good view," said the comedian cop. "You can see right down into the Dumpsters out back and plan your dinner."

"Don't laugh," Abe said. "Bet that ain't far from the truth."

"There it is," sighed the big cop, focusing his beam on a wooden door whose metal number had long since fallen off, revealing the dirty outline of a 5 broken by nail holes. Hip-hop music thrummed from inside, and Savage wondered why the cops had not turned it off. First thing you did when entering a residence was silence those damned TVs and stereos.

The big cop lumbered in, followed by Abe, Savage, and the comedian. A narrow foyer led to a filthy kitchen on

the right and a living room ahead that was jammed with
two frayed and stained sofas and a battered oak veneer
coffee table supporting a trio of heavy glass ashtrays overflowing with butts. Several gaping holes had been
punched in the Sheetrock to Savage's immediate left, just
beneath a large wooden cross. The rest of the decor sug-
gested contemporary ghetto garage sale, with chairs, artwork, end tables, and lamps cracked or mismatched or
hanging at tremor-inspired angles. Two Hispanic men in
their early twenties occupied one sofa. Both were heavily
tattooed and wore green knit caps, white T-shirts, baggy
pants, and canvas shoes—this year's spring fashion line
for gangbangers. Bright gold earrings dangled from their
ears as they nodded to the music, the rhythm establishing
a barrier between them and the authority figures milling
about. A third man—white, gaunt, perhaps thirty, with
matted brown hair and the hazy gaze of an addict—sat
on the floor and leaned back against the other sofa. He
tugged violently at the collar of his faded black T-shirt,
then unabashedly scratched his crotch through worn-out
boxer shorts. Above him sat a bony black woman of about
the same age, her hair heavily beaded in varicolored
strings, her glare as heated as they came. She wrestled
with the five-year-old boy on her lap. The kid's cries
broke into a spasm of coughing.

Savage crossed to the boom box on the floor near the
sofas. She punched a button.

" 'da fuck you do that for?" cried the gangbanger with
the snake tattooed over his left brow.

"We keep turning it off, and they keep turning it on,"
said a young cop who came from a hallway that appeared
to lead to the bedrooms. "*Don't* turn it on again. Hear
me?"

"Don't fuck wit' my jams," said the banger, his lip

twitching as he bolted from the sofa toward the boom box.

Abe moved faster. With one powerful stroke, he ripped the power cord from the back of the boom box and threw it at the guy, then thumbed open a panel to check for batteries. None there.

The bug-eyed *cholo* waved the power cord, which had frayed. "Yo, you broke my fuckin' radio!"

Abe nodded. "The county will pay to have it fixed."

Savage grabbed Abe's arm and pulled him up and away, toward a window. "What're you doing?"

"I got a thing about hip-hop music. I'll tell you about it sometime."

Swearing under her breath, Savage headed back to the mother. She introduced herself, then said, "Your son sounds sick. Can we check him out?"

"I'm goin' to the clinic tomorrow. Nobody called 911. This is my apartment, and I want y'all to just go 'fore I sue your asses for trespassing."

"What's your name?"

"None of your business."

"Her name's Shonica," said the junkie in an eerie lilt as he placed a hand on her knee. "And she's got her mind made up. You won't change it. She'll go to the clinic. Now, if everyone would just stop watching us and giving us the third degree and get the fuck out, we'd be happy." He closed his eyes, and his jaw jerked involuntarily.

"Shonica, are you sure you don't want us to check out your little boy? Only take a couple of minutes."

"You listening? I'm goin' take him to the clinic tomorrow. I don't know who call 911. Wasn't us."

Savage leaned closer to the woman and locked gazes. "You sure? Really sure? We're talking about your little boy. He could have a respiratory infection. Lot of that going around. If he has epiglottitis, it could be life-threatening. Seen a lot of kids with that."

"He ain't got that, and I didn't call. I don't want your help. Leave."

"Okay. You just have to sign something."

The mother gritted her yellowing teeth. "If it'll get y'all out."

Savage glanced at Abe; he would handle the refusal-to-be-treated form.

As she turned away, the big cop gave Savage a resigned look. "She says these other two traveling salesmen are her friends. Show me those caps and those tattoos, and I'll show you two crack dealers. But I don't know these guys or their colors. Must be a new set in town."

"So who made the call?"

"Dispatch couldn't get an ID."

Savage frowned. "The call came from this apartment?"

"Yeah. Phone's right there."

"What's that?" Savage asked, spotting the leg of a doll sitting on the kitchen counter. She crossed to the toy—a Barbie in full beachwear. "Hey, Shonica, does your little boy play with Barbies?"

"That's my daughter's doll."

"Where's she at?"

"She's down the hall at my sister's apartment. I signed your form. Now get out."

Abe walked up to Savage, the two bangers glaring after him. He cocked a brow and held up the refusal form. "Ready?"

Savage looked to the big cop. "We're out of here."

"What kind of a mother refuses care for her sick kid?" Abe said as they headed for the door.

"I don't know," Savage groaned. "But I've seen a lot of them. Couple more years of this, and maybe you'll stop asking that question. Maybe you won't even care why they refuse. You'll just want that signature so you can leave."

He opened the door, paused, looked back. "So how come you're not that cold?"

"Who says I'm not?"

"You? I'm surprised you didn't give her a sermon on motherhood. Probably too busy thinking about your vacation. Just a few more hours, and it all begins." He flicked on his flashlight and slipped into the hall, the dispatcher's voice echoing from his portable.

As Savage followed, a tingle rose from the nape of her neck. Were those footfalls behind her? "Abe? Hold up."

His light shone past her to reveal a nine- or ten-year-old black girl cowering against the wall. Bare feet pushed out of grimy corduroys, her soiled purple shirt had a tear in one short sleeve, and a daisy patch hung limply at her shoulder. She pulled nervously at the patch.

"Hey," Savage called, "it's all right."

The girl lunged forward.

Savage stood there, stunned, as the child dropped to her knees. "Please take me with you. Please." She clutched Savage's leg.

With a growing lump in her throat, Savage stroked the girl's hair, wincing at the dirt and tangles. "Easy. What's your name?"

"Keesa. Can I go with you? Please?"

"Where do you live?"

"Here. But I don't want to anymore."

"Do you live in apartment 5?"

"Yes."

Savage locked looks with Abe, who then stared somberly at the girl. He crouched to meet her gaze. "Your mom's in there."

"I don't care."

"You have to go back inside." Savage tensed and shifted her leg. The girl clung fiercely. "Weren't you at your aunt's apartment?"

"I was there. She finished drinking and fell asleep. I want to go with you. Let me go with you. Please." She sobbed into Savage's leg.

The comedian cop trudged down the hall. "Looks like you got a growth." His tone softened as Savage fixed him with a hard look. "She belong back there?"

"Yeah," Abe said.

"Please don't take me back."

"Sorry, sweetheart." The cop slipped his arm around the girl's waist and pulled her swiftly from Savage's leg. She kicked. She screamed. Tears glistened in the flashlight's thin beam. Unfazed, the cop hauled her back toward the apartment.

"Jesus Christ," Abe said through a sigh. "I bet she made the call."

Panting, thoughts birthing, colliding, dying, Savage could not bring herself to move as the cop rounded the corner and the girl released a final wail before entering the apartment. That little face burned so brilliantly, so painfully. . . .

"Steph?"

Savage held out a hand. "Don't talk. Don't say anything."

They remained there for a long moment, Abe fidgeting, Savage trying to exhale her anger. She wanted more than anything to march back into that apartment and tell that poor excuse for a mother that she was ruining her children's lives, that her babies deserved better than this, that she needed to get help, that she needed to find some way, any way, to get out of this hole. But that wasn't Savage's job. No more strays. No more other people's problems.

To hell with it. She rushed for the door, but Abe latched onto her wrist with a remarkable grip. "Unh-unh. Forget it. Let HRS do their thing. Maybe they'll get her out of here. Cops inside got it covered. Mom's getting her lecture, trust me. She doesn't need one from you."

Damn, the rookie had her. She jerked once more, wasn't going anywhere. "I can't shove my morals down other people's throats. No shit. But when it comes to kids . . . fuck! What is she thinking?"

"Who knows. But I'm thinking we get out of here. Now." Abe gave the steely glance of a man twice his age.

"Okay. Okay. Know what? I'm sorry. That was totally unprofessional. I'm supposed to be your FTO, for God's sake. I'm okay now. I'm okay."

He raised his brows and increased his grip. "You'll be okay."

She closed her eyes, tried *not* to see that little girl. "Maybe I'll start my vacation early. . . ."

"Engine Twelve, Rescue Ten. Engine Twelve, Rescue Ten. Code 3 to an MVA northbound Van Nuys Boulevard. Cross street Burbank. VPD on scene. Report multiple victims. Time out: twenty-two thirteen."

John "Doe" Smith tossed his *Sports Illustrated* swimsuit issue onto the end table and hoisted himself from the recliner. He felt a decent adrenaline rush as he hustled out of Fire Station Ten's day room and onto the apparatus floor, where Isabel Vivas climbed into the driver's side of their rescue. She had been restocking a few supplies, and you didn't get in the big Latina's way when she did that. Lives depended on their making sure the equipment functioned and that supplies were well stocked. She performed the task like an artist who would not suffer interruptions or criticism. So be it. She kept the rescue more organized than Doe ever could, despite his "senior medic" status. One peek at his dresser drawers would confirm that. He was the only person he knew who stored ratchet sets beside underwear. (Don't ask.)

"Done drooling over your magazine?" Vivas hollered as he vaulted into the cab, assuming his usual spot in "the seat."

He wriggled his brows, flashed deep blue eyes, then slipped the headset over his ears, muffling the siren and rumbling diesel engine. "You know, there's a woman in there who looks a lot like you," he said. "All that long, black hair tied back. Nice chocolate skin. Big eyes."

"And a big, fat ass, too?"

"Your ass ain't big," he said in his best politician's tone, then lifted the rescue's microphone. "Rescue Ten responding."

"Rescue Ten," acknowledged the dispatcher.

"You know, I'm pretty much blown away," Vivas confessed, guiding the rescue away from the fire station. "For the past two weeks you're not as nasty and you're not complaining and you're even telling me that I don't have a fat ass when you, me, and Jenny Craig know that I do."

"All right. So you got through to me. All that stuff you said about me being a cold bastard and treating patients like hunks of meat? I thought a lot about it. I'm a changed man." The lie warmed Doe's cheeks.

"What's her name?"

"Excuse me?"

Vivas grinned crookedly. "You heard me. You're trying to impress her, and you're practicing on me."

He squirmed. "There's no woman. I just, uh, wanted to stop being such a prick. I don't take too many things very seriously. I figured I'd better start working on myself or no woman will ever want me."

"But now I don't like you anymore. I've created a monster. I need you to go back to your old ways. I want you to be a whoremonger and a sexist pig. I want you to bitch and moan about every call. I want you to look dying people right in the eye and think only about what's for lunch or whether or not you'll have that sexy little bystander's ankles in the air by midnight."

"What?"

"I want you to start smoking again. Wear T-shirts and roll a pack of Marlboros in your sleeve. Treat me like shit. That's what I want."

"You'd better lay off that Slim Fast. It's going to your brain."

She chuckled. "Whatever it is, I'm glad you're . . . let's say, a little more sensitive."

"Ouch. Not used to hearing that. Not sure if I like hearing it. And her name's Geneva."

"I knew it."

"You're the only one who knows. Swear to God you won't tell anybody."

"Why the big secret?"

"I don't know. I just don't want everyone knowing my business."

"You mean you don't want to ruin your playboy reputation."

Why it came out so suddenly, Doe didn't know, but it felt awfully good to tell someone. The pressure had been building for two weeks. "We're going to have a baby."

"Oh, my God. Really? You were just telling me how your sister's always bugging you to settle down. Congratulations."

"Aren't you going to ask the question?"

"What?"

"If we're going to get married."

"Are you?"

"Don't know yet."

Vivas narrowed her gaze in thought. "How long have you been with her?"

"Little over six months now."

"What? Six months? And you've been cheating on her left and right?"

He sighed. "All those dates I told you about? Lies. I've only been with her. Brace yourself. I've been faithful."

"Let me guess. You found out about two weeks ago that she's pregnant. That's why you were so distant. I get it now. Man, you should've told me. We could've talked." Her expression grew long.

"Don't be pissed, Izzy. This is all just screwed up, and it caught me way off guard. I mean, *me* a *dad*. You tell that to people who know me, and they'll laugh."

"Doe, a one-woman man," she said, testing the sound of it. "Know what? I'm not laughing."

"Yeah, you're like me. Crying over my lost freedom."

"You're growing up, Doe. You're growing up."

"Maybe you're right. Only took thirty or so years. I'm like fine wine."

She made a face. "Cheap champagne."

He shook his head as the light ahead abruptly turned green under the electronic persuasion of the Opticom unit mounted atop the rescue. He wiped condensation from the window and reported all clear to the right—his job during code 3 driving.

Two cross streets later, they pulled ahead of the accident, a three-car fender bender, with all vehicles pulled to the curb and the three drivers near their cars. VPD cruisers sat at the front and back of the line, and Engine Twelve rolled up behind the twinkling parade as Doe and Vivas gloved up and leaped down from the rig. Vivas went for the long backboard and c-spine bag. Doe caught the attention of a tall, heavyset sergeant, a gray-haired Hispanic woman named Ramirez who looked less than thrilled to be out in the rain. "Hey, Juanita. Haven't seen you. Figured you pissed off somebody again and got transferred."

The sergeant rubbed the small of her back. "Nah, I finally got that operation. Six weeks out. First week back. Still hurts like a bitch. Maybe even more than it did before the surgery. But I played. Now I pay."

Like Doe, Ramirez was a big-time dirt bike enthusiast who had taken one too many spills. She and Doe had gone biking together on several occasions, and the sergeant had taken risks that made even a veteran cyclist like Doe cringe. "So what do we have?"

"Got that old lady up front who the gay guy behind her says jammed on her brakes for no good reason. Got this little Dodger fan in the back who couldn't stop in time and skidded across the wet road. They were all out of their cars when we got here. Jimmy's over there with a c-spine on the old lady. The other two claim they're okay, but now they're starting to rub their necks. Acute checkbook pains, eh?"

Doe shrugged. Two weeks ago he would have nodded. "Thanks." He looked back to Vivas and thought of taking the most seriously injured patient for himself, but in deference to her, he opted for the other two. "You got the lady. I got these guys." He lifted his chin toward a young man with a sunken chest and a spike cut dyed blond and a much shorter man of about forty with a beer gut and a Dodgers cap sitting high on his balding head.

The three firefighters from Engine Twelve strode toward the scene as Doe approached the shorter driver.

"How you doing, sir? I'm John Smith. I'm a paramedic. Can I check you out?"

The diminutive sports fan cupped a hand over his cell phone. "Just give me a minute, will ya, buddy? I got a pizza in my oven that's gonna burn if I don't get my neighbor to take it out."

Though he wanted to smirk, Doe simply nodded and turned his attention to the spike-haired man Ramirez had assumed was gay. The guy did not exude masculinity, but neither was he flamboyant about his sexuality. "Hey, sir. I'm paramedic John Smith. You all right?"

"No, I'm not all right," the guy snapped, then smashed a fist on the window of his brand-new Volkswagen Beetle, crunched both front and back, banana yellow paint flaking onto shattered taillights. "Look at my car. I'm freaking out."

"Forget your car. And do me a favor. Don't move your neck. You might've injured your spine." Doe ran a finger over his own c-spine. "We'll put a collar on, just to be sure. What's your name?"

The guy *tsk*ed. "My name's Liga Thomas. I'm sure my lawyer will be glad you treated me."

"Here's your collar," came a familiar voice.

Doe glanced over his shoulder and nearly lost his balance.

Nicole Cavalier had materialized from the rain. A dozen shades of short blond hair framed her narrow face. Hazel eyes widened with intensity and excitement. Lean, muscular curves begged for exploration.

It was her all right, Nicole Cavalier, the district's most notorious femme fatale, a woman who snared you in her claws of whimsy and rough sex, bled off her thrills, then tossed you into the gutter like so much roadkill. Somehow, she had picked up Doe's scent and now howled at the moon.

"So you're back?" he asked, dumbfounded, as he accepted the collar. "What happened to New York?"

Her lips grew pouty. "It's still there."

Doe had to look away. He began fastening the collar. "Okay, Mr. Thomas. This will feel a little uncomfortable. Do you have pain anywhere else?"

"I got a headache."

"Did you hit your head?"

"No, this is definitely stress-related."

"Are you allergic to any medications, and are you taking anything right now?" Nicole asked, diving right into the primary assessment.

The guy flinched as Doe finished with the collar. "I'm not allergic. I'm not taking anything."

"Do you have any history of illness or major surgeries?" asked Doe.

"Nope. Had my tonsils out. That's about it."

Nicole lifted her voice over the roar of a passing truck. "When's the last time you ate something?"

"I don't know," the guy said, growing pissed. "All I know is my car is fucked! How am I gonna get to work tomorrow?"

Doe shrugged. "Maybe your insurance company can get you a loaner. Why don't you tell us what happened?"

"Because I already told the cops. You guys are just medics."

Nicole brushed past Doe, trailing a wave of expensive perfume. Doe's heart sank. She came in tight on the patient. "We just want to figure out what we call the mechanism of injury," she explained. "Just tell us how you moved inside the car when you got hit."

"Like I remember? It all happened in like a couple of

seconds. I hit that dumb old bitch, and I get thrown forward, then Danny Devito over there hits me, and I get whipped back. And you know what? My neck is really starting to hurt now."

Doe nodded and pulled out his portable. "Valley, Rescue Ten."

"Ten, Valley."

"Request second rescue unit to this location."

"Copy, Ten. Requesting second unit your location."

"Sir, come back to our ambulance." Doe looked to the other guy in the Dodgers cap. "And you, too, sir. Just need to check you out."

The guy removed his cap and palmed his head. "Whatever."

"You're going to transport that lady," said Nicole. "Mind if I ride along?"

"I don't need any help."

"I've been meaning to call you."

"How long you been back?"

"About a month. But it's been insane. You know, the move. Settling in. Fighting to get my job back. For a week there, I thought I'd have to go private. Wind up getting used and abused with all those EMTs fresh out of school. Man, that would've sucked. But I just went in there and told them point blank what I'm about. I'm a kick-ass paramedic. A goddamned medical machine. I've run more calls in my six-year career than some of these lazy farts have run in their whole lives. No one can touch my skills. Even the guy who thinks he's the best in this district."

"I don't *think* I'm the best. I *am* the best."

"I was talking about Troft. You're just a standard-issue trauma monkey with decent hands." She grabbed his wrist. "Good. No rings yet. Then again, there never will be, right?"

They reached the rescue, and that saved Doe from having to answer. The old lady had already been lowered onto the long backboard, her head placed between the cushiony Head-Ons, her extremities secured by straps. Two firefighters lifted the board onto the stretcher, then guided it into the ambulance.

"Let's get vitals on these gentlemen," Doe told one of the firefighters who had loaded the stretcher. Then he re-garded Vivas, who sat inside the rescue with her patient. "Oh, sorry. Isabel Vivas, Nicole Cavalier."

They traded polite grins, then Vivas gave Doe a sus-picious look before refocusing on her patient.

Nicole leaned in close. "You fuck her yet?"

Doe frowned.

"Why not? She's got nice tits. Big ass, yeah, but I'm sure you'd give her a good drilling. Damn, I remember how you used to do me. . . ."

"I got a patient," he said, warding off the chills. "Izzy? You need any help back there?"

"No, I'm good."

Doe gazed restlessly between Nicole and the driver's side door. "You heard the woman. I have to go. Good luck, I guess."

"I'll ride up front. My lieutenant's pretty cool. He won't mind."

"Mine's not. She will. So, I'll see you." He lowered his head and got out of there.

"Hey, you still hang out at Tuba's?"

He froze, didn't look back. "Sometimes."

"We're on the same schedule. Maybe I'll catch you there."

"Yeah, maybe."

Back in the rescue, Doe slipped on his headset, tapped on the siren, then pulled cautiously onto the road.

"Doe?" Vivas asked in a strange tone.

"Yes," he answered, matching her.

"You never told me about Nicole. I'm thinking ex-girlfriend?"

"You're thinking too much."

"I'm thinking you've insulted me by keeping this secret. And I'm getting a weird something from her. Just be careful. You listening, Doe? You listening?"

2

Isabel Vivas gazed across the table and scarcely recognized the man seated there. Gone were Manny Nuva's familiar stubble and the smirk on his narrow face. Her ex had even put makeup over the tarantula tattoo on his neck. Sure, you could still see the crawling spider, but Manny obviously—and surprisingly—was striving for a conservative look. He had shaved his head about two weeks ago, and the hair was growing in to cover the three small scars where he had been slashed during a gang fight. You might mistake him for a thirty-year-old stockbroker in a dark suit instead of a Sears auto mechanic who had once sported the knit cap and baggy pants of his set. He had cautiously placed the red cloth napkin on his lap and had arranged his silverware with a precision that made Vivas conscious of her own movements. She could not remember a time when they had been together and had acted so formally, so gracefully.

He leaned over his water glass. "Izzy, you look beautiful."

She glanced past him to the ornate brass railing and the clusters of candlelit tables below. He had taken her to one of the most exclusive and expensive Italian restaurants in the Valley, and he had booked one of the three balcony tables. You climbed a narrow spiral staircase to get to the balcony, and were served by your own private waiter. If the heavenly scents rising from the wood-burning ovens did not overcome you, wine from Angelino's world-renowned wine cellar might do the trick. Never mind the seven-piece band and amazingly talented singing waiters who delivered their songs with enough eye contact to make you blush. Vivas knew all about the restaurant and could pitch it to her colleagues at Fire Station Ten as though she were reading the advertisement. Manny had taken her here on the night he had proposed.

The moment was perfect. Perfectly wrong.

Why had she let it go this far? She had sworn to herself two weeks ago that allowing him to have Sunday dinner at her apartment was where she would draw the line. But at that dinner Manny had said all the right things, and Consuela had seemed overjoyed to see her parents seated at the same table. Then the bastard had called her, had taken her to lunch (fast food, yes, but for some reason that didn't matter), and they had met twice more for lunch. Then he had hazarded a dinner invitation, refusing to say where they were going until they had pulled up to Angelino's valet stand. She should have refused to go in; she should have ordered him to take her to another place.

"I said, you look beautiful."

Vivas clutched her plunging neckline. "Manny, this is nuts. We know we can't get back. We're just torturing ourselves."

"We're just having dinner."

"So why couldn't we go to Taco Bell?"

"I put on a suit to go to Taco Bell?"

"This isn't right. I don't want to ruin this place. Why

can't you just leave the memories alone instead of spending two hundred bucks to make it worse?"

He leaned back, glanced away, shook his head a fraction. "I wanted to come here *because* of those memories. I don't think we appreciate them. I know I took us for granted. But it can't be too late. It just can't."

"I don't want to fight, but this is too much right now. I should have said something outside. I know you'll lose the deposit. I'll pay you back."

"It's not too much. We have to do this. We know what it's like to be without each other. We need to look at what we threw away. I don't want to find anybody else. That's it."

She had to smile. "For once you sound like you know what you want."

He set his elbows on the table, his expression growing intent. "Your mother helped me realize that what I want is you. She was the one who first said coming here would be a good idea. I wasn't sure, but. . . ."

Vivas gripped the edge of the table. "I told her not to talk to you. Why can't you leave her out of this?"

"Because she knows you better than anyone. You'd probably do the same thing if you. . . ."

"Not with your parents, I wouldn't. God, no." She clenched her teeth. "Listen to me. I don't want you talking to my mother about us. Don't say another word. I don't want to hear her bullshit. She lived with a man she didn't love for her entire life, and now she wants a medal because of that. God forbid I do the same thing."

"If you're saying you don't love me, then you're lying."

"I don't know what I'm saying anymore."

"All right," he said, throwing up his hands. "It's not like I can talk to my mother about us."

"And there's the whole problem."

Jamaal, a handsome young black man (an aspiring actor, of course), gently set down their plates of lasagna and tortellini, refilled their glasses, then rushed off to sing.

"This looks really good," said Manny. "And no chicken nuggets."

Vivas smiled inwardly at the joke. No matter how nice the restaurant was, if they brought Consuela along, they always ordered chicken nuggets. "So, do your parents know we're here?"

"It doesn't matter."

"Have you even told them we've been to lunch? You figure out if you're a man yet?"

"I'm a man. But we can't fix this problem with my parents overnight."

"Well, if they died. . . ."

"Oh, that's cold, even for you," he said, wincing. "We've managed not to talk about them for the past two weeks, and it's been really good. I've been feeling really happy. Why do you have to talk about them now?"

"Because you want them in your life, and they don't want me in yours. How can you not get that? If you plan on pursuing us, then you know what it'll come to, right? There won't be some agreement. It's them or me. That's the choice they want you to make, so they won't feel guilty. They can say, 'Yeah, our son chose to go back to his wife, the dyke fireman. He chose her over us. Not our fault. He's the bastard.' See, they just want a clear conscience because they're selfish."

He huffed and rubbed his eyes. "Forget all that. I'm asking you right now—do you think we'll ever get back?"

She stared at her food. "I don't know. When it comes to your parents, I don't see how, because you won't hurt them. They were the ones asking you to make the choice, not me. For five years I tried. I listened to your mother and father beat me into the ground, and I said nothing. Now it's my turn. It's them or me. You can't have your cake. So I'd think about that the next time you decide to spend two hundred bucks on a meal."

The music suddenly rose, the lights dimmed, and a spotlight picked out Jamaal. He stood in the middle of the restaurant and began a sweet, sad melody, uttering the Italian as though it were his native tongue. He shifted through the tables, his white uniform flashing as he sang a line to a pretty blonde, another to a heavyset tourist from someplace like Topeka. He reached the wall below the balcony and, to the audience's gasping delight, mounted a wooden trellis, ascending some fifteen feet while gripping his wireless microphone. His head suddenly popped over the railing, and Vivas felt the blood rushing into her cheeks. Manny raised his glass and toasted the waiter, who grinned as he sustained a magnificently long note, turned back to the tables below—

And slipped from the trellis.

"Oh, my God," Vivas gasped, then sprang from her seat toward the railing.

Jamaal lay supine on the parquet floor as patrons murmured their surprise and concern. A few people nearest him left their tables to hunker down.

High heels notwithstanding, Vivas practically dived for the narrow spiral staircase behind their table. As she hit the first step, Manny cried, "I'm right behind you, Izzy."

"Call 911."

After nearly falling, Vivas reached the ground floor and hurried toward Jamaal. "Excuse me. Please, get back. I'm a medic. Everybody please move back. Let me through."

A few of the more attentive patrons yielded, but as usual, a few were mesmerized by the grim spectacle. She shoved her way to Jamaal and dropped to her knees. The young man groaned softly and rubbed his right wrist, which was beginning to swell. His eyes remained closed, and he grimaced as he shifted his head.

"Jamaal, this is Isabel. You were waiting on me up there. Do you understand?"

"Yeah. I'm sorry. I'm really sorry. Guess I blew my tip."

"That's all right," she said with a mild grin while checking his respiratory rate and depth. "Believe it or not, you just rescued me. You'll have to trust me on that." She gently squeezed his good wrist to get a radial pulse, which would also give her an estimate of blood pressure. "Did you black out?"

"No, I remember everything."

"Know where you are?"

"Angelino's."

"Good. You know the date?"

"Yeah. It's February twenty-first. My wrist is killing me. Damn!"

"Used it to break your fall, huh?"

He swallowed. "I think so."

"You probably fractured it." She guided the hand onto his chest. "Just set it down here. Don't move it. And don't move your head or try to get up. You hurting anywhere else?"

"I'm getting a nasty headache. And my back hurts now. Smacked 'em pretty good."

"I saw the whole thing," said another waiter, a woman of about twenty with a mop of curly hair pulled into a bun. "His feet hit, then he fell forward, tried to stop himself with that hand, then fell onto his stomach and rolled over. Looked like he hit his hand really hard."

Jamaal's wrist was the last thing Vivas was worried about. She focused her attention on potential internal injuries, knowing that rapid deceleration causes many organs to be compressed, displaced, or twisted. She also worried about his neck and head. He could have a cervical spine injury and/or a fractured skull. No opens wounds were visible on his head, though she felt some swelling on the left side. She checked his ears for cerebrospinal fluid, saw none, but knew she would have to be on the lookout for it. A glance back revealed only unfamiliar faces. "Manny? Manny?"

Her ex knifed his way between a girl with a bad boob job and a wizened sugar daddy. "Rescue's on the way."

"Outstanding. Give me some help with a c-spine. You remember, don't you?"

"You kidding? I bet I can pass those exams, too. I'll keep his neck immobile. I know what to do." He knelt behind Jamaal's head and held the waiter's neck steady with both hands.

In the second that she watched him, Vivas remembered all those nights of him posing questions from the study guides or pretending to be a patient and her feeling ecstatic that he took an interest in her job. He had seen her through every step of her training, and when she had passed the National Registry exam, he had thrown her a surprise party to end all surprise parties.

"Everybody, please return to your seats," came the strong but polite voice of a gray-haired man in a tailored suit. "The ambulance has been called. Please return to your seats."

"Manager," said Manny. And as he spoke, the band struck up a lively tune.

"How you doing, Jamaal?" asked Vivas.

"Okay. Head's starting to throb. Goddamned wrist. My back. Shit. Sorry I ruined your dinner."

"Hey, forget about that. Just relax and think about your

breathing. You're doing okay. Can you open your eyes?"

He squinted against the light.

"That's good. Can you move your feet?"

"Yeah, but that hurts a little."

"Hurting or not, that's really good." She rolled up his pants and pinched his leg. "Feel that?"

"Ouch!"

"Very good. What's your name?"

"Jamaal West."

"Excellent. Just keep talking. Know where you are?"

"I'm at work, where I just did something so stupid that I'm gonna get fired because my boss's insurance will go up, and he'll find a way to fire me. See how it works?"

"That won't happen," said Manny. "They already got singing waiters. That's boring. They'll bill you as the flying waiter. Probably draw big crowds. Probably make a bad TV show about you. You could even talk to Izzy about that. Her brother's a TV star."

"No shit, really? Who is he? You think I could talk to him?"

"I'll set you up," said Vivas, "but first let's get you better."

She made more small talk, observed his vital signs, and got a medical history as they waited for the medics of Rescue Eight to arrive.

Once they did, Vivas updated the senior medic, an FF-P named Julie Addix. How Addix managed to balance a career as a medic, a husband, and six kids Vivas did not know, but she would pay to learn the secret. "This is Mr. Jamaal West, a twenty-four-year-old male who took a fall from the top of that trellis. Landed on his feet, then fell forward. Possible wrist and skull fractures. Possible lumbar injury. Pulse is 60 palp. Respiration's 20. GCS is 15. He says he didn't black out and remembers the whole thing. No prior medical problems. No meds. No allergies."

"Thanks, Izzy." Addix blew a wayward wisp of gray hair from her eyes, then gaped at the restaurant. "Wish I could get Tommy to take me to a place like this." With that, she introduced herself to Jamaal while her partner lowered a long backboard to the floor.

"Where's Isabel?"

"I'm right here, Jamaal. Don't worry. You're in good hands."

"Okay," he answered weakly. "Thanks."

"Excuse me," said the manager, gently touching Vivas's shoulder. "I can't thank you enough for helping out."

"Don't worry about it," said Manny. "She lives for this. Just doing her job."

"Well, we're lucky you were here," the manager replied with a wan grin. "Your meals are on the house. And the next time you come, I'll comp those dinners as well."

"You don't owe us anything," said Vivas.

"But that's really nice of you, and we'll take it," Manny corrected.

The manager extended his hand. "I insist."

Vivas shook hands, then stood back as Addix and her partner carried Jamaal out of the restaurant.

"Well, you can't say I don't plan an exciting evening," Manny said as they mounted the spiral staircase to return to their meals, which the manager had ordered replaced. He turned back. "That was . . . really cool." He came close, seized the back of her neck.

"Manny. . . ." She had meant to utter his name in a warning tone, not in a gasp of desire.

It had been too long since she had kissed a man, and her surrender felt agonizingly good.

• • •

Most of Stephanie Savage's colleagues frowned over her decision to stay home during her two-week vacation. She wouldn't be jetting to Florida to check up on her son? No. Donny was in the middle of a semester at the University of Central Florida. He could live without a nit-picking mother rearranging his furniture and filling up his refrigerator. That Savage had come to this conclusion less than thrilled her. In recent weeks she had been contemplating the growing distance between herself and her only son. A phone call had triggered that excruciating reality.

"Listen to me. You'll have a lot of time in your life to do a lot of traveling. I don't feel comfortable about you packing yourself into a truck full of college kids and driving all the way to Miami at night."

"And I don't feel comfortable about you sticking needles into AIDs patients and working on the side of the road where you can get run over. But I don't ask you to stop, do I?"

One of Donny's friends had even called her a loon for being so worried. Donny had survived the Miami joyride, and he would probably survive many more. Savage had to keep telling herself that wherever he went, all of her mothering went with him. She had produced an amazing child who had weathered a divorce with strength and wisdom beyond his years.

Nodding to herself, she moved her glance from Donny's high school graduation picture, hanging prominently in her living room. She finished opening the boxes of Chinese food and breathed in the beef and broccoli, fried rice, and egg rolls. She dished a healthy portion onto a plate, snatched up a fork and napkin, then plopped down on her sofa. She ate off a rickety folding table as she watched a tape of *West Hampton*, her favorite daytime soap opera. She had spent most of the day shopping for a new car and, thank God, had remembered to set the VCR. Her old Toyota pickup was about to die after 221,000 thousand miles of faithful service. Drooling salespersons had tried to sell her on lease programs, but she had owned only four cars in her entire life, and had driven each of them from five to ten years. Something about owning and being faithful to a vehicle made her feel secure.

Her door buzzer sounded. She went to the intercom. "Who is it?"

"Ma, it's me."

"Donny?"

"Yeah. Surprise! Buzz us up."

She frowned and hit the buzzer. What the hell was he doing in Los Angeles? She trembled, darted around the living room, fixed a few pillows on the sofa, stacked some newspapers, thought of doing something about the dishes piled up in the sink, thought about rushing out to meet him at the elevator when the doorbell rang. *Oh, God.* She answered.

His blonde hair was much bushier than she remembered, his jeans were torn at the knees, his Nikes were unlaced, his white tank top was giving up too much chest hair. Donny smiled. "Hey, Ma." A bulging duffel bag hung from his shoulder. Was that a tattoo on his arm? And who was the bimbo cracking gum?

"Ma, this is Tina. She came with me and Eric and everybody else down to Miami."

"Hi," said the thing, her eyes shaded by a tremendous mane of strawberry blonde dreadlocks unacceptable even on a Muppet. She wore a skimpy blue top sans bra, jeans as torn as Donny's, and a pair of Birkenstocks that exposed rings on at least three toes of each foot. Had she not pulled self-consciously at her navel, Savage might

have missed the ring there, and had she not been chomp-
ing on her gum, Savage might have missed the tongue
piercing as well. "I'm like really nervous. Sorry."

Though Savage's voice failed to function, she at least
remembered to move and allow them inside.

"Smells like Chinese food," said the thing, setting down
her own duffel beside the sofa.

"I was just, uh, just having dinner." Savage closed the
door, opened her mouth.

"Ma, before you say anything, let me talk. Okay?"
Donny didn't wait for an answer, and worked his mouth
like a machine gun. "So we got together while we were
driving down to Miami, and I don't know what it was,
but it was like I finally understood what I want to do with
my life, and getting a business degree ain't it. Tina was
doing the same thing, and we both figured out that where
we really wanna be is here, and what we really wanna do
is go to school here and try to figure out what our majors
should be. Her parents live in Canoga Park. That's not a
coincidence. It's fate. So when I told her that you lived
here, we just knew that we knew, and we didn't want to
ignore the signs, and that's why we just came as fast as
we could. All right, so I lose a semester, but I'm gonna
transfer here. Maybe Pierce or even UCLA or USC. It's
not about greed anymore. It's not about going through the
motions to get a degree that's supposed to get me—
quote—a good job. Because you know what? A good job
is the one that's gonna make me happy, and sitting in a
windowless conference room with a bunch of business
majors who got ulcers and nervous tics and gray hair at
twenty-five because the next class of graduates is threatening to take their jobs is not what I call happy. This is
what we want. This is what we're gonna do. And you'll
get to see me a lot more. It feels right to be home."

Savage crossed to the TV and switched it off.

"Mrs. Savage, you look really mad," said the thing, sounding a bit breathless, if not stoned. "This might seem sudden, and I know my parents won't be happy either, but sometimes you just have an epiphany, you know? And you gotta listen to it. Because when you're eighty years old and looking back on your life, do you want to say 'I should have done this,' or do you want to say, 'I did that, and I changed my life for the better'? You can't live in fear. You gotta go for it."

Donny flipped hair out of his eyes, went into the kitchen, found a fork, then stabbed the beef and broccoli. "You listening to that, Ma? I don't want to become a pissed-off old man like Dad." He raised his chin to Tina. "Sweetie? Want some?"

The thing nodded, and they plopped onto the sofa. Donny fed Savage's dinner to the thing. After several forkfuls, he finally looked over. "Ma, you there?"

"I'm here. Just thinking about all those years I sacrificed so you could have a college education."

"See, I told you," Donny muttered to the thing.

"Tina? I wanna talk to my son in the bedroom." She marched toward the hall. "Donny? Let's go."

"She can listen to this, Ma."

"Oh, no, she can't."

"Once you start yelling, you think these walls will help?"

Savage swung around to glower at her son. "My place. My rules. You know that drill. Get in the bedroom."

Swearing under his breath, Donny dragged himself from the sofa. She followed him into her modest-sized bedroom, then shut the door.

"I know what you're gonna say."

Savage cocked a thumb over her shoulder. "You got a

little taste of that inside and let her talk you into this?"

His lip twisted. "No. This is *my* decision."

"Bullshit. I know you, Donny. She wanted to be here, and spread her legs, and you just yessed her to death without thinking. Where'd you find her? In a strip club?"

He spun away and drifted toward the window. "I knew you'd be pissed off, but why are you blaming it all on her? I decided to do this first. I talked her into coming."

"Look at me and say that."

Their eyes met. He ground out each word: "It was my decision."

She studied him a moment more, tightened her lips. "Bull . . . shit."

"Jesus Christ, Ma. You're gonna need to deal with this, 'cause it ain't gonna change. I'm here."

"Yeah, until I get you on a plane. You'll go back to school and tell your professors that you had to visit your sick mom in LA. I'll get you a note. And I'll pay for the ticket. That's what *you're* gonna deal with, 'cause *that* ain't gonna change. As far as your little tramp in there is concerned, let her parents deal with her."

Donny threw his hands into the air. "Ma . . . hello? I'm a man. I can do what I want. I just came here because I knew it was a good week and you're on vacation, and I wanted to let you know what I was doing. I don't want any advice, because everything you say is what you want me to do, not what *I* want to do. You don't help me make my decisions—you try to make 'em for me. And that doesn't cut it anymore."

Grabbing him by the shirt collar was probably a bad idea, but she had him in her grasp before reason took over. "Listen, you ungrateful bastard. There are kids out there living in slums with parents who are junkies and don't give a shit about 'em. They'd fuckin' kill somebody to have a mother like me. But you? You think you can listen to some fuckin' tramp, and everything's gonna be okay. How do you plan on supporting yourself? Who's paying for your school? You think you're gonna walk right into another scholarship? You think all of your courses will transfer okay? They won't. You haven't even thought about this. You're gonna fall flat on your ass, and I'm trying to tell you that. But advice from Mommy doesn't cut it anymore. That's fine. You go ahead, go listen to your little slut in there with her pierced tongue. Let her lead you around on her leash. But when the whole fuckin' thing falls down around you, DON'T COME RUNNIN' TO ME."

He tore himself away. "I'm gone. Tina? Tina? C'mon. We're going."

"Where are you going, Donny?" Savage called after him. "That's the real question."

"Yeah, and *I'll* answer it, not you." He spoke in hushed tones to the thing as Savage stood panting in her bedroom.

The front door slammed shut. Silence.

Savage dug fingernails into her palms. "God damn you, Donny. And you, you fuckin' tramp . . . you think you're gonna mess up my kid? You don't know who you're dealing with."

Still out of breath, she paced the room. What to do next? How to get him back on the right course? How to get rid of the slut? He'd go see his father in Calabasas. Had to get Tim on the right side. She shot to her nightstand, fished out her phone book, thumbed through the pages to find Tim's number. She hoped the loser hadn't moved again and forgotten to give her the new listing.

"Tim? Yeah, it's me. We got a problem."

"Donny there yet?"

"He just left."

"So he told you."

"He told you?"

"It's what he wants. We have to back him."

"Are you fuckin' kidding me? You're telling me you think it's okay that he drops out of school?"

"Steph, I'm telling you that I don't agree with what he's doing, and I told him that. But he's made up his mind, so the only thing we can do now is support him on this. If we help him, he'll be all right."

"I don't believe this."

"Look, I'm a little busy right now. I'll call you in a day or two. We'll talk about him some more. But you gotta support him. If you don't, you'll alienate him and be miserable."

"If you don't tell him that he has to go back to Florida and get back into school, then you're helping ruin the kid's life. Think about that when he comes to you for *help*." Savage hung up, then stomped out of the bedroom and into the kitchen. She wrenched open the refrigerator door, seized a beer, then backhanded a tear from her cheek. With a screaming headache coming on, she popped open the can and downed half in a single pull.

3

M edic Abe Kashmiri stepped tentatively onto the apparatus floor. Out near the rescue stood an imposing figure all but consumed by the driver's side forward bay. "Are you Rasso?"

No answer.

The guy's salt-and-pepper crew cut gave him an air of menace that prevented Abe from asking again. The big guy slammed the bay door shut, brought himself to his full six feet and four inches, then palmed sweat from his pate. Finally, his arctic gaze lowered to Abe. "You the kid?"

"I'm Abe Kashmiri."

Ignoring Abe's hand, the veteran medic turned back to the second bay, yanked it open, then crinkled his pug nose. "Where you from, Abe Kashmiri?"

"From here."

Rasso rifled through equipment in the bay. "I don't believe this guy. You look just like the jockeys my brother was popping during Desert Storm. Raise your hands above your head."

"Excuse me?"

His tone sharpened. "Raise your hands above your head."

Abe complied.

"Yeah," the guy said with an ugly smile. "You look just like those guys." He snorted. "This is gonna be fun."

Gripped by disbelief that someone would make such a comment, Abe lowered his hands. He thought of a comeback, then just squared his shoulders and tapped a knuckle on the bay door. "I got here at seven and already went over everything. Logs are signed. We're all set."

Rasso chuckled under his breath. "You think I'm going out after some rookie checks my gear? Son, go back inside until we get a call. And when we do, you do whatever I say—that way I won't have to fuck with you, and that'll make us both happy. Trust me. I'm good people, once you get to know me, but if you start toying with me, this'll be the longest two weeks of your life. Do we understand each other?"

Abe's eyes burned. He made a face, nodded, then shuffled back into the day room, where Fitzy sat in a recliner and greeted him with a coy grin before burying his graying red mustache in a mug. "So you met old Rasso," the firefighter said, then smacked his lips. "I bet Station Seventeen's glad to get rid of him for a couple of weeks. What's the matter? You don't look too happy."

"Why didn't you tell me?"

"See, now, there's no real way to describe that boy."

After sighing in disgust, Abe dropped into his own recliner. "How long has he been with us?"

Fitzy squinted into an estimate. "Oh, I think about ten years, last five or six at Seventeen." He tossed Abe a devilish grin. "Sounds like he just flew in from the Bronx, eh?"

"He says he's good people, whatever that means."

"It means that if he likes you, he'll take care of you. But if not, then. . . ." Fitzy shook his head.

"Well, it's only two weeks."

"We'll put that on your tombstone."

"Hey, numbnuts, you checked this tank?" cried Rasso from the doorway. He hoisted a heavy air tank, the one he would use should they be called to a fire.

"I checked that one. It's full."

"Yeah, it is, but you didn't strap it in right. Could be rattlin' around inside the bay and get damaged. If I were you, I'd take a little bit more time checkin' out my partner's equipment. If this is the way you're gonna watch my back, then shit, you still got a lot to learn."

"Hey, Ras, take it easy on this kid. He's our big TV star," Fitzy stated, doing a lame job of trying to lighten the mood. Two weeks prior, Abe had given an interview regarding a car wreck, then he had been taped pulling a little girl from a burning house.

Rasso smirked at the tank. "Tell you what, I can see Savage has been working with the kid. She's this sloppy, too."

"Hey, now," Fitzy warned, "his team of lawyers will sue you for harassment."

The medic forced a smile, erased it as quickly, then spun and bounded back into the garage.

"What's his problem?" Abe asked, dumbfounded.

Fitzy raised his recliner's footrest and groaned softly. "Don't matter. He's a hardcore asshole. And the only way to shut up a hardcore asshole is to be a bigger hardcore asshole, which you ain't. Maybe he was a good guy when he was your age, but I think four bad marriages and a son who died from cancer made him just a little angry at the world."

Abe snickered. "Just a little?"

Before Fitzy could respond, the alarm sounded. First call of the shift. Chest pain. Assisted living facility. Abe made it to the rescue in under seven seconds. Rasso, who had already climbed into the cab, scowled at him and spoke through clenched teeth. "Don't let me make you nervous."

ED Attending Physician Joanna Boccaccio had not heard from her mother in two weeks, despite having left numerous messages on the woman's answering machine. Mom had returned to Las Vegas after a brief and admittedly strange visit during which she had announced her affair with Drew, a greasy flirt half her age. She had sported trashy clothing and plastic surgery that had turned her into a pathetic cliché of a woman, a woman in serious crisis who had refused to discuss her problems with her daughter. Boccaccio had, she thought, really tried to get through to her mother, but the woman had been much too irrational. Even Dad seemed at a loss, and as he picked at his macadamia nut cookie, he repeatedly glanced out the hospital cafeteria's windows.

"I know you're worried about her, Joanna," he eventually said, removing his glasses and rubbing the bridge of his nose. "But this is the game she wants you to play. You leave lots of messages, and she'll call you at her convenience, not yours. You may be in your thirties, but she still wants to have some control over your life." He replaced the glasses, then eyed her, his expression full of compassion and a strong dose of melancholy.

"She's really in trouble. I know that. And I can't get this off my mind. I kept telling her I couldn't handle it, and she kept saying that I didn't approve of her happiness. I mean all of that—the boob job, the boyfriend—she's just crying out for help. And I ignored her." Boccaccio tightened the band around her mane of curly black hair, then shook her head and pulled at the corner of her napkin. "If her boyfriend doesn't get her any help, then we have to do something. I mean, the woman is not thinking straight. She's telling lie after lie. She's believing the lies. One minute she's laughing, the next she's hysterical. Whether it's bipolar or whatever it is, she needs help."

"You know, when your mother and I got divorced, I knew I'd never get her completely out of my life."

"Because of me," Boccaccio added grimly. "And I'm sorry, Dad. All I've been talking about is her, but you coming here to have breakfast these past two weeks has been the best. Really, it's been the best. You know, you grow up, and that whole father-daughter thing goes away because some of us are so busy. I never realized how much I miss just talking to you."

He gave a slight nod. "Even though we talk about her. You know, I used to think staying away from your mother was the right thing for me. And I thought it was best for you, too. Ever wonder why I wanted you to apply to med schools so far away?"

A chill woke between Boccaccio's shoulders. She remembered the nights he'd spent urging her to go east for her education. "You mean you pushed me to go out there just to get me away from her? It wasn't about the school?"

"That's right," he answered, unable to meet her gaze. "I just wanted you away from that woman. I thought that if you had some distance, you'd do much better. And you did. And I'm sitting here and I'm wanting to tell you to look for a job back east. I want to tell you to just get away from her. But it doesn't work. I tried to do it myself. . . ."

"When you moved to Vermont."

"That's right."

"You said you didn't like it there."

"I didn't, because I was too far from you. Trade-off is that when I'm near you, I'm never too far from her. So you're right. Neither one of us can run."

"So what do I do now? Because I know if I stop calling her, I'll get a phone call and she'll be screaming at me and telling me I'm a bitch for not calling, and she'll lie about her machine not taping the messages. See, that's the crazy part of it. I know just how her mind works. So what do I do?"

He half-shrugged. "Maybe when you get some time off, you go out there. Do some kind of an intervention or something. I don't know."

"Yeah, but all those years of therapy you forced on her didn't work."

"Because she won't take the medication. She keeps trying to get back this lost childhood, and the older she gets, the more she knows she can't have it—and that makes her even nuttier. If there was some way to get her the medication without her knowing. . . ."

"Drug her cornflakes," Boccaccio said with a wry smile. "You'd have to be living with her to. . . ."

"The boyfriend," Dad concluded. "If she's living with the guy, you talk to him, get him to do it."

"But she still has to see a doctor, get diagnosed, and get the scrip. How do I pull that off?"

"You go out there, give her a shot of something to knock her out, then you call 911 and get her transported to a hospital," he said, then nonchalantly finished his cookie.

"Dad, that's kidnapping. I could lose my license."

He winked. "I didn't say there wouldn't be risks."

"C'mon. We need something better than that."

"Maybe you can get a doctor to go there, pretend she's somebody else, and get the diagnosis. Then we work on the boyfriend to get her the drugs."

Boccaccio straightened her shoulders. "That's a little better. I'll make some calls. Maybe I can reach somebody out there who'd be willing to help. I'll also talk to the people here. Get a few tips. I just hate telling people in this hospital my business. Even if I say I have a patient who blah, blah, blah, I think they'll see right through me."

"Don't worry about it. I bet half those shrinks have problems bigger than their patients."

"You're probably right."

"You sound better." He looked at the pager beside her coffee mug. "And that thing hasn't gone off once. I bet you'll have a nice, easy shift."

Boccaccio seized the newspaper at his elbow, unfolded it, then thumbed to the weather page, where she examined the phases of the moon. "How much you wanna bet?"

By 8 P.M., Abe Kashmiri found himself staring longingly at a gun shop on the corner of Westland and Sherman Way as he and his temporary Field Training Officer Vincent Rasso headed back to the station. Rasso had been on a rampage of criticism that had started with that unsecured air tank. During that first chest pain call—which would have been a fairly routine transport of an elderly woman— the veteran had twice snapped at Abe in front of the facility's staff, thoroughly embarrassing him. "C'mon, man! You're as slow as some of these old fuckers. I've never seen anybody take so goddamned long to get a pressure. Strap on the cuff and pump it up. Jesus Christ! Give me that fuckin' thing. Give it to me right now!"

If Vincent Rasso had any patience, he had exhausted it at that nursing home. He was all about doing it fast. Abe understood that, but he wanted to do things correctly because, excuse me, lives were at stake.

Not that Rasso really gave a shit about anyone but himself. Anyone could figure that out five minutes after meeting him.

"You brake like a pussy, man. The light turns, and you apply the brake. Apply it. You're tapping it like you wanna sleep with it."

The man thought he was pretty clever. He occasionally commented on his wit, frequently laughed at his own jokes, and repeatedly condemned nearly everyone he spied through the windshield. "See that poor bastard over there?" he said, hoisting a thumb toward a hunchbacked homeless man dragging a rusty old kid's wagon. "If we hit him just right, the impact would tear his aorta. No one would miss him. The people he pisses off would be like, Hey, cool, that fuckin' pain in the ass is gone." Then Rasso laughed and told Abe that he was just fucking with him, and wasn't serious. Abe suspected otherwise.

"That's better," Rasso said at the next light. "And you know, you're really starting to piss me off."

Abe kept his gaze forward. "Starting? I thought that happened when you decided I look like an Iraqi, even though my parents come from Pakistan."

"Nah. I'm an open-minded kinda guy. 'Course my brother and his buddies would call all you people sand niggers. They'd rather quit than ride in an ambulance with you. No, what's pissing me off is the fact that I've been dishing it out for twelve hours, and you've been just taking it. I mean, I never seen anybody play dead like you."

"Stephanie is pretty hard on me."

"Not as hard as me."

"No, not as hard as you." Abe cleared his throat. "So how am I doing?"

"You fuckin' suck. Your heart ain't in this. And let me tell you, kid, I've been a street medic since I was your age, and you gotta have a gut—I mean a *real* gut—to do it that long. You'll burn out in a couple of years. Maybe you think you wanna be a doctor, and you're just doing this to warm up. You'll think that for a while, until you realize how much crap you gotta go through. Then you'll wash out. Maybe get a job in retail or driving a truck for FedEx or somebody. Then you'll get married, have a couple of kids, and realize that now you can't change what you're doing and you'll stay there until you're in your fifties and hurt your back. Then for ten years you'll be filing workmen's comp claims and wearing a back brace and bitching about how all the young guns don't know fuckin' jack about your business. Then one day, while you've got your ass planted on a toilet, you'll feel a sharp pain in your chest and think, *Fuck, I'm gonna die on the toilet, just like Elvis Presley*. And you will. And that's that."

Abe stole a wary glance at the man. "Does this stuff just come to you, or do you write it down first?"

"Engine Nine, Rescue Nine. Engine Nine, Rescue Nine. Respond code 3 to possible overdose. One-six-nine-seven-two Lankershim. Apartment three-one-four. Cross street Riverside. VPD on scene. Time out: twenty-twenty-three."

Rasso grabbed the mike. "Valley, Rescue Nine responding."

"Nine, Valley," acknowledged TRO Six.

"Clear right!" announced Rasso as he flipped on the siren.

Skirting around a line of parked cars, Abe careened onto Woodman Avenue.

"That's right, asshole," Rasso yelled at the driver of a

silver Lexus ahead. "When an ambulance comes up behind you, slam on the brakes. That's right, asshole. Plant
your fat car right in our way."

"He's moving," Abe said, as the driver found an opening and yielded. As they passed the Lexus, Abe added,
"You said you've been doing this since you were my age,
and you still let this crap get to you?"

"What can I tell you? I'm a sensitive guy. Tell you
another thing: common sense is unbelievable. When you
see it, you don't even recognize it because you're expecting people to do the stupid thing."

"Steph was telling me about how you get cynical or
find religion in this job. I think if you lose faith in people,
that's when you bottom out."

Surprisingly, Rasso had no insights. He gazed blankly
ahead, then checked the next cross street. "Clear right."

After a few more blocks, Abe hung a hard left onto
Riverside and took them down to Lankershim. They rolled
up beside an upscale apartment complex encompassed by
an eight-foot-high wall with wrought-iron gates. A second
VPD unit, the sergeant's cruiser, was already on scene,
and an officer stood vigil at the open gate.

As Abe gloved up, Rasso groaned his way down from
the rescue and humped over to the officer, a white female
no more than thirty with dark hair and a nice complexion.
Tensing over the fact that his partner wouldn't give him
a hand, Abe fetched the drug box, airway bag, and long
backboard as Rasso stood flirting with the cop. Equipment
in hand, Abe lumbered toward them. "What do we got?"

"Ah, fuckin' guy's depressed. Locked himself in the
toilet," Rasso answered. "Fuckin' coincidence. I was just
talking about dying on the bowl. I'm telling you, I got
something. ESP or what have you. And put all that stuff
back. What do you wanna do? Set up an ER in there?

Just take the airway bag. That's it—*rookie*."

Abe gritted his teeth and complied.

The cops had propped the main door open by folding over the entrance mat so Rasso and Abe could avoid the delay of being buzzed in. They took the elevator to the third floor, then thumped across marble tile to apartment 314, whose door stood ajar. Tinny voices echoed from police portables inside. Rasso beat a fist on the door, pushing it out of his way. Abe shifted clumsily behind him, banging the airway bag on the wall before getting inside.

Two cops stood in a living room sparsely decorated with Southwest art and bric-a-brac. One, the female, spoke quietly with a very scared-looking girl, maybe nineteen or twenty, dressed in a flowing black nightgown and matching slippers. Abe chanced a second look at her long tresses and remarkably blue eyes. If she wasn't an actress or a model, she should be.

"We'll set up over there," Rasso said, looking toward a spot near a pickled oak coffee table. He gestured to the girl. "Get the skinny from her."

"No shit," Abe wanted to say, but simply nodded.

"Hey, Jackie Chan? Where is he?" Rasso asked the female cop's partner, an Asian guy in his thirties who bore little resemblance to the Jackie Chan who starred in all those martial arts films.

"He's down the hall with the sergeant. Second door on the left. And my name's not Chan."

Rasso smiled crookedly, then went for a look.

"Sympathetic partner you got there," said the officer, hunkering down to watch Abe open the airway bag. "And he'll get fired with a mouth like that. By the way, I'm Billy Chang."

"Abe Kashmiri." He glanced to the hall. "He's just relieving my FTO. She's on vacation for two weeks."

"Yeah, being a rookie sucks. I remember those days. I think I've only seen that guy a few times."

"He's borrowed from Seventeen. So what's up in there?"

Chang frowned. "Girlfriend says she woke up, found the bed empty, found the bathroom door locked. Called. He answered. Said he wasn't coming out. Wouldn't say why. And he took all the keys to open the privacy locks. He hasn't threatened to kill himself, but the girl got scared. According to her, nothing bad happened to him recently. They both moved here from Nebraska about a year ago. He's the actor. Works part-time for Ralph's. She's the singer. Works at the California Pizza Kitchen. He didn't lose a job or anything. She says they're not on drugs. No E-T-O-H. No history of mental problems. He's not taking psych meds. They don't have any weapons, but you know how creative some of these people are. He could fill up the tub and drop in the blow-dryer. I don't know if this is true, but a medic from Station Ten, guy named Doe—maybe you know him—he was telling me about how sometimes you won't get electrocuted too badly if the breaker goes off right away. That true?"

Abe shivered inwardly at the morbid thought. "I don't know."

The sergeant, a thickset black man graying at the temples, and Rasso appeared from the hall, wearing dubious expressions.

"Will he come out?" asked the girl.

"No. Won't say why. And we're just pissing him off," answered the sergeant.

"And he's just pissing me off," mumbled Rasso.

"Can I try?" Abe asked, intrigued by the possibility that he could talk the guy out of the bathroom and have at least one triumph he could fly in Rasso's face. Then again, that was a selfish reason. He was supposed to think about the patient's welfare. All right. He would have his triumph *and* help the patient.

"I don't think that's a good idea," said the sergeant. "I couldn't make a connection with him, and I'm the easiest-going guy I know. We'll just force entry and Mace him. You guys can transport him to VGH for a psych eval."

Rasso, his gaze intent on Abe, raised a finger to silence the sergeant. "You think you can talk him out?"

Abe raised his brows. "Maybe."

"Twenty bucks says you can't."

"I don't wanna bet."

Rasso folded his arms over his chest. "For a medic, you sure *don't* like to take risks."

"All right. Whatever. Twenty bucks," Abe said, then looked to the sergeant.

"Well, it won't be pretty if we gotta take him by force. I'll give you five minutes. Either way, if I say you're out of there, you're out of there."

Abe stood. "What's his name?"

"Brian."

"Sarge, can we get someone to bring up a board?" Rasso asked.

"We won't need it," Abe said.

"Sarge, we'll need that board."

With a sigh, Abe entered the hall and found the bathroom door opposite the bedroom. He glanced at the queen-size bed and pine furniture. Nothing there spoke of Brian's personality or depression. Abe knocked gently on the bathroom door and, as always, kept himself to one side for safety. "Hey, Brian? This is Abe Kashmiri. I'm a paramedic."

"Go away. I just wanna be alone. I don't know why

she called the police—and now you guys. This is ridiculous. I just wanna be alone."

"Can you do that in the bedroom? There are four cops out here who gotta take a leak."

"You hear me laughing? I'm not laughing."

"So what's going on? Why do you need to be alone?"

"Because I do."

"Your girlfriend's worried."

His voice grew faint. "I know."

As the sergeant and Rasso took up positions in the hall, Abe continued.

"I could tell you a story about the time I locked myself in the bathroom, but you wouldn't believe it. You'll think I'm making it up because I want to understand what's going on in there. But I don't wanna lie to you. I mean, I got no reason to lie. I'm guessing you're just really stressed out, right?"

"Good guess. *Duh.*"

"Everybody gets stressed out, but not everyone wants to kill themselves like you."

"I didn't say I wanted to kill myself."

"But you do, right?"

"I don't know."

"How 'bout we make a deal? You don't kill yourself for a couple of minutes, and we'll just talk. I mean, what's a couple of minutes if you're going to be dead anyway?"

"I said I want to be alone."

"Your girlfriend has no idea why you want to kill yourself. How come you didn't tell her?"

"Fuck off."

"It's okay. You don't want to tell her. It would hurt her. I get it. But you know what? If you told me, it wouldn't matter, because I'm just a guy out here—just a guy like you."

"Why should I tell you?"

"Because maybe you haven't told anybody, and it's like this pressure builds up inside. It happens to medics all the time. We got these things we call Critical Incident Stress Debriefings so we can vent about shit that's happened to us. Like a couple weeks ago we pulled this nice little family out of a really bad car wreck. So what I did was I imagined that all of my stress was, like, sitting there in my stomach, and when I talked about it, the sounds came out, and when the sounds came out, the stress was gone. It actually left my body. It's a physical thing, and you can cut it loose by talking. I swear to God it works."

"Where's Kady?"

"That's your girlfriend? She's in the living room with the cops."

"Okay. You just tell her I'm sorry. And you know, Abe, there's another way to get rid of stress. And I swear to God it works, too."

"Brian?" called the sergeant.

Abe froze. "Brian, what are you——"

A gunshot rang out, rattling Abe to the marrow.

"Aw, fuck," the sergeant cried.

Abe gasped.

The sergeant pulled himself against the opposite wall. "Get back!" He threw himself at the door, right shoulder first. The wood splintered as the door swung open and banged against the wall.

Brian had been sitting cross-legged on the tile. He had removed all of his clothes except for a brown cowboy hat, and had jammed the muzzle of a .45 caliber pistol into his mouth. He had made a perfect "stem" shot that had killed him instantly. He now lay slumped beneath the toilet, the hat blown off and behind him, his head an awful lump of shattered flesh, the gun still in his grasp. A huge spray of blood, skull fragments, hair, and gray matter dripped down the walls and toilet tank.

"She said he didn't have a gun," hollered the sergeant as he slipped on the gore.

Kady screamed from the living room.

Abe just stood there, trembling.

"This guy I like," Rasso said softly. "If you're gonna do it, do it right. I hate when they miss."

Kady continued wailing, and the cops inside tried in vain to calm her.

"Abe, get out of here," Rasso said disgustedly.

"Okay. I'll, uh, I'll go hit the girlfriend with some nitrous. Calm her down."

"If it makes you happy." Rasso unclipped his portable. "Valley, Rescue Nine."

"Nine, Valley."

"Yeah, we got a single victim of a gunshot wound to the head. Patient has expired at this time. No rescue required."

"Copy, Nine."

In a haze, Abe found himself squeezing out of the bathroom and into the living room. Billy Chang asked him something about where the guy got a gun, but Abe just looked at him.

"No! I want to see him! I want to see him!" Kady yelled as the female cop strong-armed her out of the apartment.

"Hey, guy, you all right?" asked Billy. "What the hell happened? What the hell did he say?"

Abe closed his eyes, took a long breath. "I don't know. I don't know." He stumbled toward the front door, and once out in the hall, he glanced sidelong at a half-dozen neighbors standing near their doors.

"Yo, man, was that a gunshot?" asked a short, muscular man with a remote control tucked under his arm.

"Go back inside."

"That was a shot I heard," he argued.

"Just go back inside." Abe shifted past the guy, hurrying for the stairwell door. He reached it just as his cheeks sank. He fought against the urge, fought as hard as he could, bent over, gripped the wall, held on, held on, then emptied his stomach. "Oh, God. Oh, God."

"You puking or having sex?" came a horribly familiar voice. Rasso's stubbly head eclipsed the hall light.

"Sorry," Abe managed. "I've never seen—"

"Well, now you have. And it cost you twenty bucks to boot. Maybe I oughta get that hysterical girl out here to help *you*."

Abe gritted his teeth. "Just give me a second, all right?"

Rasso smiled crookedly. "You take all the fuckin' time you want. We'll let the cops help her. And I'll call for another rescue. That one'll be for you."

Wiping his mouth on his sleeve, Abe ripped himself away from Rasso, opened the stairwell door, then hustled down. "I'll get the nitrous."

"You'd better," Rasso cautioned. "If you can't think straight, then you don't belong here. And by the way, if you haven't figured it out by now, I'm not here to make friends. Just doing the job—like you should."

The medic's voice rang hollowly through the stairwell.

"**W**hy are you pulling over?" Isabel Vivas asked.

Manny gave her a reassuring look. "This will only take a second."

"Mommy, I want to go to Magic Mountain," whined Consuela from the backseat of Manny's '77 El Dorado.

"We're going, honey, we're going. Daddy just has to make a quick stop." Vivas grabbed his wrist. "What's going on?"

"Nothing. I just gotta drop off some parts for a guy I work with. Take a second." With that, he climbed out, opened the trunk, and removed a cardboard box that, judging from his expression, wasn't light. He hauled it across the sidewalk toward the entrance of a condo complex whose gate was shadowed by twin clusters of palm trees. He set down the box, dialed a number on the intercom, spoke a few words, then turned back and waved.

Manny Nuva looked quite the family man in his blue cargo shorts, crisp white T-shirt, and brand-new K-Mart sneakers. Vivas had little trouble imagining him smiling and walking around the amusement park. The whole day would, she hoped, turn out perfectly because they had not planned anything. Manny had called at 7:30 A.M. to say that he wanted to use one of his sick days to take Consuela to the park. Vivas had the day off anyway, and she had planned to run a few errands and to leave Consuela in day care for at least four hours. Manny's call had set her pulse racing. She and Consuela had quickly dressed and scarfed down a couple of bagels, then had sat around waiting impatiently for Manny to arrive. Mama had the day off as well, and she had spent the morning going on about how Manny wanted to change his ways, about how he made a good father, and about how Vivas was doing the right thing by spending time with him. Maybe they would get back together, maybe not. Vivas still wasn't sure how she felt about him. Yes, she felt a longing and loved their shorthand, but close friends shared those things, too. What was it that made their marriage compelling? What was it that made getting back together much more than trying to provide a stable home for Consuela? Did she want to try it again just for her daughter's sake, or was something really there, something still burning that would die only when she did? There had to be a real reason. She shook with the desire to find it.

"Mommy? What's taking so long? I wanna go to Magic Mountain." Consuela slammed a fist into the leather seat.

Vivas switched on her mother glower. "If you keep whining and hitting that seat, we're not going anywhere."

"But I wanna go."

"Patience."

Manny stepped away from the gate as a Hispanic man in a black tank top, pecs swelling above the low neckline, appeared. He slapped hands with Manny in a gesture used by some gangs. Vivas stiffened as the guy eyed the scene, then shoved a wad of cash into Manny's hand. Manny pocketed the money as the guy picked up the box and vanished behind the gate.

"Here comes Daddy," cried Consuela.

With a broad grin plastered on his face, Manny loped back to the car, got in, then craned his head to Consuela. "We all ready back there for Magic Mountain?"

Consuela wrestled against her seat belt. "Yeah! Yeah! Come on, Daddy, let's go!"

"Turn the car around and take us home," Vivas said.

"What?"

She faced forward. "Take us home."

"Why?"

"What was that about?"

He grabbed her chin, forced her to look at him. "What was what about?"

"You gave him the parts. He gave you money. Who is he? And where are you getting these parts?"

"What do you think? You think I'm stealing them or something? You think I'd risk my job over something like that? I've been there for ten years. You think I'm that stupid?"

She knocked his hand away. "I don't know what to think. You're not telling me anything."

"I told you everything. That's Paco. I work with him. I had some old carburetor parts, couple fuel pumps, and a battery I bought when I was fixing up this car. Some of them I don't need anymore. I was telling him about 'em, and he said he'd buy 'em. His cousin's got an old El Dorado, too."

"Pull out that money in your pocket."

"Why?"

"I wanna see how much he gave you."

He swore in Spanish, then tried to stare her down. She

didn't flinch. He cursed again, then pulled out the money: a wad of fifties.

"You're just like Ricardo. He used to lie so much that he believed the lies. The day he killed that guy, he lied to me about that, too."

"I'm not your brother. I don't plan on spending my life in jail like him. I'm telling you—I'm not lying."

"How much you got there?"

"Daddy? Why aren't we going?"

"In a second, honey."

"No! Now!"

"Consuela, shut up!" screamed Vivas.

The five-year-old's face screwed up into a knot. She tucked her chin into her chest, then bawled loudly.

"Oh, Jesus," Manny groaned. "You gotta yell at her like that?" He leaned over the seat and stroked Consuela's cheek. "It's all right, my baby, it's all right. Mommy didn't mean to yell. And we're going now. We're going."

Vivas tore the money from Manny's grasp and began counting it. "What do you got? Couple grand here? I didn't realize auto parts were so expensive."

"I loaned him some money, and he just paid me back. The parts were three hundred."

"So now you're making loans?" Vivas sighed heavily and tossed the money onto his lap. She faced the window, stared at the curb. "I didn't know you had money to spare. All I hear is how they keep raising the rent on your apartment and how you can barely make the child support."

"The guy was in trouble. I helped him out. He'd do the same for me." He threw the car in gear and peeled away from the sidewalk.

"You're taking us home, right?"

"You don't trust me?"

"Manny, I know you too well. Every time you lie to

me, you're fighting off a smile. Why can't you just tell me the truth?"

He braked hard at a red light. "Maybe I'm smiling because you're making me feel guilty over something I didn't even do. Why can't you believe me?"

"Because I remember how it was when we were dating. I won't go through that again. You promised me a long time ago that you were done running with those people."

Manny broke into rapid-fire Spanish: "Oh, I forgot. Paco's young. He's Hispanic. He must be in a gang. I must be stealing the parts from work and selling them to him and his gang buddies so they can fix up their cars and do their drive-bys in style."

Vivas glanced back to Consuela, who returned a woeful stare. "You'd better be telling the truth."

"I am. Think about it. Why would I bring my wife and kid along if I was doing something illegal? You think I'd want my daughter to see that?"

"I guess not. And I'm not your wife. At least not anymore."

"You know, I don't even feel like going now."

"But Daddy, you promised to take me to Magic Mountain."

Manny threw his head back, then slowly nodded. "Yeah, I did. And it's a beautiful day out." He leaned toward Vivas. "Let's not waste it."

"Daddy, when we get there, I don't want to go on the roller coaster, because that's scary and only for big kids and mommies and daddies. But they have rides for little kids, right?"

"Yes, honey, they do."

For the next forty minutes Vivas barely uttered a word. She suddenly felt very much married again and contemplating a divorce. It was a strange feeling, having to remind yourself that you didn't own any of this pain; that it fell on a dead relationship; that there was absolutely no reason to be upset. And that's when she realized that there was something beyond their daughter; something that kept her linked to Manny; something she wanted to call love, though that word seemed wrong. She and Manny knew each other, really knew each other. Not a lot of couples could say that, and it felt incredibly reassuring to be around him. She rested both easily and excruciatingly in their history. And she did own the pain, owned it because she had not lost hope.

If John "Doe" Smith had his way, visitors to his two-bedroom palace of hedonism would find themselves greeted by two brawny Roman soldiers. (You know, like those guys they got at Caesar's Palace in Vegas.) A third guard standing in the anteroom would announce your arrival as you padded across white marble and into a great hall, where you would find the man himself, clad in a glittering white toga and seated on a throne shaped like the back of a fire truck. He would wave you in as those *Sports Illustrated* swimsuit models he lusted after in his magazine fanned and fed him Beer Nuts. "Enter, my most welcome guest. Yes, enter." He would gesture to one of six purple beanbag chairs, then make you wait several minutes while one of his overphotographed nymphs kneaded a kink out of his neck. Finally, he would spare a glance in your direction, remember you were waiting for him, then ask in a booming baritone that had once made James Earl Jones clutch his throat in envy, "Wuz up?"

But Doe had rarely had his way, and now that he had committed himself to Geneva, and might even ask her to marry him, he felt a pang of guilt over having such thoughts. As Vivas had said at the end of their last shift, he could read the menu; he just couldn't order. Of course, he could read the menu only when Geneva wasn't looking.

Doe shoved the key in the lock, opened the door, then keyed off the alarm. Geneva followed him inside and, with a terrific sigh, lowered herself onto his black leather sofa. "You know, every time we go to that place for dinner, I say I'm going to order light. And every time I walk out of there, I feel like a blimp."

"You're pregnant," Doe reminded her, then tossed his keys on the kitchen counter.

"What's that supposed to mean? I'm not even showing yet. Unless you already think I'm a blimp."

Damn, he had to watch himself. Anything he said could be used against him in her court of law. "No, I mean you can't expect to feel normal, right?"

"Yeah, but I don't buy that whole 'I'm eating for two' business. That's why so many women get so fat while they're pregnant. They use pregnancy as an excuse for gluttony. You're supposed to exercise. You're not supposed to park close to the supermarket in one of those expectant mother spots. You're supposed to park far and walk. I refuse to get fat. I absolutely refuse."

"Sounds good to me," he said, glancing at the kitchen clock. Good. Only six-thirty. Going for an early dinner had been a great idea (not his, of course). They now had plenty of time for a movie before he conked out on the couch and Geneva bitched at him for falling asleep on her. He didn't want to do that, but working in EMS meant that you slept wherever and whenever you could. Most of Doe's ex-girlfriends had difficulty with that. He had once fallen asleep right in the middle of a dinner conversation. He had caught major hell for that one. He knew he would have an easier time staying awake if they watched something that interested him.

And now came the most difficult part: convincing her to watch the action/adventure flick on TBS, though he knew she wanted to see one of those romantic comedies with Julia whatever her name was. He crossed to the coffee table, picked up the remote, and thumbed on the TV. "There's a really good one on tonight," he said. "I think TBS."

"No, you mean on HBO One. That movie I've been telling you I really want to see? I checked the *TV Guide*. It's on tonight. But I think it already started." She rose with a slight wince. "Be right back."

Doe switched to TBS. His movie was already in full swing. Twin explosions filled the screen as a big-breasted woman jogged away from the chaos. Doe grinned and thought, *Bombs. Beautiful women. What more could you ask from a movie?* And hey, the woman looked familiar. Maybe he had seen her on the wrestling channel.

"Honey? Your machine's blinking," Geneva called, then shut the bathroom door.

"Probably the damned credit card people," he muttered. "I get one more call from those idiots. . . ." He popped off his sneakers and carried them into the bedroom. The machine flashed a number 1. He hit the play button:

"Hey, Johnny Boy, it's me. God, did I have a hard time getting your new number, and I know you'll have a hard time listening to this. I just took a shower, and I'm lying here, naked and all wet—"

Doe banged the Stop button. Silence. The toilet flushed. He stuck his head into the hall, wondering if Geneva had heard. Probably not. He slipped back into the living room and dropped onto the sofa as she returned.

"Who was it?"

Moment of truth—or not. Lie to her and let it go? Tell her that Nicole was back in town and pestering him? His reward for being honest might be a really pissed-off girlfriend. He had told her all about his relationship with Nicole, how he had thought she was the only girl for him, how she had dumped him, how he had been hurt so badly by her that he had decided to go on a dating rampage, one that only Geneva had stopped. He just wanted to have a nice night with no bullshit.

"Oh, it was just credit card people," he told her. "They wanna sell me life insurance. Some kind of crap."

"That's weird," she said, snuggling up next to him. "My friend's a telemarketer, and her company doesn't want them leaving messages on people's machines. They want you to talk to a real person, so they can get you to buy right then and there. Can you put on HBO One?"

"Yeah." He switched the channel.

She suddenly pulled away. "You're heart's racing."

"What?"

"I just had my ear on your chest, and your heart's racing. What's the matter with you?"

Time for that innocent look. "Nothing. I'm just . . . I don't know. It's caffeine or something."

"Come on, I know that face. Why are you so nervous?"

"I don't know. I guess I just want everything to go right. That's all. I keep thinking that I'm going to screw up, and that makes me nervous."

"That sounds really nice," she said, smiling for all of two seconds. "Of course, it's bullshit. But it sounds really nice. Who was on your machine?"

Time to really turn up that innocent look. "I told you."

"Mind if I go listen?

"You don't trust me?"

"Think about it. You listen to a message, I come back

from the bathroom, and now you're all nervous. Doesn't take much brains to figure this one out."

"It's just crap. Forget about it."

"Doe, I'm giving you a chance to tell the truth. We can't build a relationship on lies."

"I know that. You don't think I know that?"

She slid away from him. "Then let me listen to the message."

"Is this how it'll be? You'll have your finger on every little part of my life? Gotta listen to every little message, know exactly where I am every second of every day? I mean, I'm a bit of a control freak, but I know when to let go."

She rolled her eyes. "Don't change the subject. I don't want to control your life. I just want to listen to one message, one message that includes the word *naked*—or at least that's what I thought I heard." She started for the bedroom.

Doe sprang from his seat and cut her off. "All right. All right. Let me just tell you something before you hear it."

She swore. "Why didn't I see this coming? Who is the slut?"

"The other day I ran into Nicole Cavalier. She moved back to L.A. I swear to God I blew her off. She must've got my number."

Geneva's lower lip trembled, and the tears came on as she whirled toward the kitchen, scooped up her purse, then bounded for the door. "Fuck you, Doe."

"Geneva, just listen to me!" He scrambled to block her.

"It's my fault. This is all my fault." She shoved him aside. "I believed that an asshole like you could actually have a relationship. I don't matter. The baby doesn't matter. Nothing matters to you but fucking around." She opened the door and rushed into the hall.

"But if you listen to the message, you'll see that she just got my number. I haven't done anything wrong!"

"Yeah, right," she called back as she reached the elevator and punched the button.

He gripped her shoulders. "Where do you think you're going?"

"I'm going home. I don't care. I'll take a bus. I'll walk. I can't believe what an idiot I am."

When Isabel Vivas stepped into her apartment after spending an exhausting day at the amusement park, she was surprised to find paramedic Stephanie Savage seated at the dining room table and having dinner with Mama, who wore her bright green apron like a uniform of authority.

While Consuela rattled off her adventures to Mama, Vivas took a seat and breathed in the heavenly scent of chicken fajitas. "Hey, Mama. Hey, Steph. What's going on?"

Savage lowered her fork. "I stopped by about an hour ago to drop off those tapes you lent me."

Vivas smiled knowingly, then raised her chin at her mother. "And she wouldn't let you leave without feeding you and talking your ear off."

"I'll never turn down a home-cooked meal. Beats Chinese takeout and fast food any day."

"You didn't have to bring back the tapes. I told you, you could keep them as long as you like."

"I watched them. I just can't get into exercising with a woman who's like four or five sizes smaller than me. She just ticks me off."

Vivas chuckled. "That's why I can't watch them either.

And I can't watch the ones with all the really fat women. We gotta find a tape with husky women."

"I'm going to give this one a bath," said Mama, gripping Consuela's shoulders and raising her graying brows at Vivas. "Had a good time, no?"

"Yes, I had a good time," Vivas groaned. "Thanks for giving her a bath."

"She's been riding all those filthy rides all day," Mama said, then *tsk*ed. "I'll kill those germs. And remember, Isabel, you have to drive me to work tomorrow."

"I'll get you there, Mama."

As the woman guided Consuela toward the hall, Savage said, "Your mother was going on about her job at the market. She was telling me how it's a lot like what we do. She never sees people at their best because they're parting with their money and that gets 'em mad."

"She's been working at the same Ralph's for a really long time. Probably too long."

"So I heard you were up at Magic Mountain. How'd that go?"

Vivas swiped a piece of chicken from Mama's dish. "Really good, which is really bad."

"What do you mean? Sounds like he's really trying."

"He is."

"So?"

"So you know what the problem is."

Savage nodded. "You marry the man *and* his family. Most men don't have the guts to stand up to their mothers—except for my little bastard. I tell you he shows up at my door with some little pierced slut? Tells me he dropped out of school and wants to transfer here?"

"Whoa. When did this happen?"

"The other day. I think he's either staying with her

parents or his father. I've been trying to get a hold of him all week."

"What are you gonna do?"

"I'm going to put that ungrateful little bastard on a plane and ship his ass back to Florida. No way will I let him chuck all that work. He says he doesn't even want to major in business anymore. His little slut girlfriend has him brainwashed."

"Wow, I'm sorry." Vivas sat there a moment. Something nagged at her, something familiar about Savage's situation. "Are you sure it isn't Donny's decision?"

Savage snorted. "His decision? Not my Donny. He didn't come up with this on his own. He's always let people sway him this way and that. That's why I've always had to stay on him. I don't care what his bimbo does. He's going back to Florida."

"Steph, we've known each other for a pretty long time, and I'm gonna say this because you need to hear it. You sound just like my ex-mother-in-law. She thinks I'm a bitch and brainwashing her son. You don't want to do to your kid what she did to Manny. You don't want to do that. Don't make him choose. Maybe he loves this girl. You don't know."

"I know my kid. If he does this, he'll fall on his face, then coming running to me. But by then it might be too late. He's going to lose time and money. I can save him a lot of headaches right now."

Vivas softened her tone. "Or you might be the one causing the headache. I don't want to take his side. But you have to look at this through his eyes."

Savage wiped her mouth, then stood. "Tell Mama thanks for the dinner. And Izzy, I appreciate that. But I have to do this my way. Like I said, I know my kid."

"Maybe you should get to know his girlfriend before you condemn her."

"I met her. There isn't much to know." Savage reached the door. "I thought I taught him better than this. And it's really killing me. Damn, I got a lot to do, and now I gotta go teach a class. Take it easy. I'll give you a call."

5

D oe rushed into the elevator before Geneva could stop him. She reached for the panel of buttons, but he shoved himself in the way. "Let's go back inside. You need to hear that message."

"Get out of my way."

"Look at what you're doing. You're just running. You're not giving me a chance."

She backhanded a tear from her eye. "I've given you a million chances. I'm tired of it. You lied to me about the message. You got something to hide."

"I just didn't want to get you upset. That's why I lied. I figured you wouldn't believe the truth anyway."

"So you thought lying was better?"

"No, I just . . . I don't know."

"You don't really care if I'm upset, you just wanna have the best of both worlds. You don't want to feel guilty, so you're trying to make me feel better."

"What are you talking about?"

"Forget it." She pushed him aside and stabbed a button. They descended toward the garage level.

"Okay, you want to go? Fine. But I'm driving."

"I'm not riding in the same car with you."

"You're carrying my child. I should have a say in how you get home. You're not getting on a bus."

"I'll call a cab."

Doe closed his eyes. "Geneva. . . ."

"How could you do this? You told me you thought we could be a family. You told me you'd give it try."

"And you said you knew I wouldn't change overnight."

She pushed him against the wall. "So that gives you an excuse to screw your ex-girlfriend?"

"I didn't screw her. There's nothing going on. She's a crazy bitch. She's just messing with my head."

"Like you're messing with mine. I don't know what to believe anymore."

"Why don't you come upstairs and listen to the fuckin' machine! She says she just found my number. That should tell you we haven't been doing anything."

The doors opened, and a cool wind blew through the parking garage. Doe shuddered. Tires screeched in the distance.

"Just take me home." Geneva stormed onto the concrete. "My mother was right about you."

"What'd she say? They come in from Tahoe, and we treat 'em like a king and queen. What'd she say?"

"She said I'd have to watch you."

"I thought she liked me."

"She likes you, but she knows your kind. Never wanna grow up. Live for the moment. Never think about the consequences of anything you do." She reached his vintage Corvette, tried the lock, then banged the window.

Doe reached into his pocket. "Shit! My keys are upstairs. Why don't you come up? You can listen to the message."

"No." She flicked her gaze to the exit door.

He frowned. "You won't wait for me, will you?"

She shook her head.

"Geneva, I love you."

"You love yourself." She pulled out her cell phone. "I'll take a cab."

"Let me get my keys."

"I'll be gone when you get back."

He sighed in disgust, then folded his arms over his chest and waited as she got Information, muttered the number, dialed, then finally ordered the cab. They walked in silence through the exit door and onto the sidewalk. One by one the streetlights switched on, and more light from thousands of windows traced the distant mountains. A relentless flow of traffic whipped by, and Geneva gripped her arms against the chill. Doe slid an arm around her, but she pulled away.

"This is stupid," he finally said.

"Yeah, it is. Maybe I should've had that abortion."

"Don't say that," he snapped. "Don't ever say that."

"What'll it be like with a kid involved? How do I tell my kid that Daddy is cheating on Mommy?"

"It'll never come to that."

She gave him a look.

They stood a few moments more. The cab finally arrived. She got in without looking back. He opened his mouth, wanted to say something, as the cab sped away.

Most first responder classes were about forty hours long and met for four hours, once per week. They covered the basics of emergency care: trauma, medicals, splinting, basic airways, use of oxygen, scene safety, CPR, and usually included one ride-along shift with paramedics and one to three "clinicals" in an emergency room. Cops, basic firefighters, state troopers, Highway Patrol personnel, and safety people working in industry were generally required to take First Responder and receive their certification, though anyone could take the course. It served as an excellent introduction to Emergency Medical Services.

Stephanie Savage had served as an assistant FR instructor for the past two years and helped with hands-on skills training and testing. She had developed a reputation with three main instructors who taught courses at several local hospitals and community colleges, and she often provided her skills for twenty-five dollars per hour. Sometimes Savage had to turn down offers to assist because the street simply wore her down. Now, with two weeks off, she had plenty of time to teach, and welcomed any distraction. Donny's insane decision to return continued burning in her gut, and the conversation with Vivas had only fueled the fire.

She stepped self-consciously into the college classroom, finished chewing her breath mint to kill the stench of beer, and caught Tony Wilsa's attention. He had already dragged in the mannequins and other equipment they would need. That was Tony for you. Fifty-seven years old, hernia that always acted up, and tattoos of military insignia on his forearms. He wore one of his trademark photographer's vests (he had a thing for pockets) and scowled at you from behind thick bifocals. Tony had retired early from Valley Fire Department and supplemented his income through teaching. "Glad to see at least one of you hired guns showed up," he said, digging out a sign-in sheet from his briefcase. "Troft said he'd come. Called the last minute. And Tenpenney stood me up last week."

Savage forced a cheerful tone. "How're you doing tonight, Tony? You sound good. Really good."

"Don't give me that shit," he said distractedly, scratching his ivory-colored crew cut. "You know the drill. Help me hand out stuff. Kick back for the intro, and after the break, you got CPR."

"Hey, Tony. *I* showed up."

"Yeah, yeah. You want a fact? I'm not asking those people anymore. You got one shot with me now. You no show, you go."

"You want a fact? I'm not sure they care. Sad but true." Savage picked up a stack of syllabi from the desk and faced the class.

Typical bored-looking bunch. You could spot the young cops and firefighters a mile away, with their tight T-shirts, bulging muscles, and mouths working overtime to snap gum and yak at each other. Your safety people from industry had loosened their ties and probably wouldn't bother to turn off their cell phones. One woman seated in the back caught Savage off guard. She had to be in her seventies, with white hair died the barest shade of pink and bound in a hair net. Her simple blue dress, black purse, and stockings made you want to help her across the street. What was her story? Maybe she was just curious. Maybe she had lost someone because she didn't know CPR.

Tony introduced himself, told a few of his corny jokes, then went over the syllabus. Savage sat in the front row and pretended to pay attention. Tony wanted you to model correct behavior for the students. Problem was, some people taking the course had not been in a classroom in years, or had just finished a lot of training and could barely stand yet another class. People got up and left, came in late, and caused other distractions you might find in a middle school class: falling out of or scraping their chairs, tripping, banging the door shut, and chattering. Undaunted, Tony described exactly what first responders are, what they do, and how long the class would take. He told several of his own adventures, and Savage leaned back for a good thirty minutes while he shared the tale of the great building fire on Ventura. She had heard the story at least a dozen times, and occasionally caught herself mouthing along. That done, Tony fielded several questions, then dismissed the group for a fifteen-minute break.

Savage went into the hall and shoved a few quarters into a coffee machine that had to be twenty years old but produced a brew that rivaled even 7-Eleven's. She spent the entire break leaning on the machine, sipping her coffee. She cried inwardly over her son's foolishness. She played out a dozen conversations with him, convinced him to go back to Florida in one, listened to him curse her in another. God, she didn't have that much in her life. Just her job. And that kid.

With her head hung low, she returned to the classroom as the others settled in. When she reached the desk, an eerily familiar voice struck her rigid. "Hello, Stephanie Savage."

"Oh, no," she whispered, then turned around.

George Solaris beamed at her from his front row seat. The young man wore a blue T-shirt with the Valley Fire Department logo on the breast, jeans, and pricey sneakers probably bought with his mother's fortune. The classroom's fluorescent light made him seem paler than usual, and a brush had not met his shaggy blond hair or a razor his face for at least a couple of days. He looked like a surfer bum, junkie, and frat boy rolled into one. In truth, he was the most famous frequent flyer in Savage's district, a hypochondriac par excellence who had been in the back of her rig so many times that he could tell you where extra 4×4s were stored. "Surprise, surprise," he said. "Saw your name on the list. Couldn't resist."

"George, get out."

"I paid for the class. It's open to the public. I have every right to be here. I wanna be a CFR instead of always being the victim."

"Where'd you steal the T-shirt?"

"It was a gift."

"We're not supposed to give those out."

"Who knew?"

Savage hunkered down beside him. "Listen to me, you little shit, you pull anything here. . . ."

"You kidding me, sweetheart? You know I live for this stuff. Mommy taught me well. And I wanna stay here as long as I can. Oh, yeah. Sorry I was late. Had to leave VGH AMA."

"You left a hospital against medical advice? I don't believe it."

"Regina and all those nurses applauded when I left."

"They weren't clapping because they were glad to get rid of you. They were just clapping for your performance."

"That's right," he said. "That's right."

Only two weeks prior, Savage had found him lying on the sidewalk in front of a newsstand.

"Why don't you tell my new partner how you grew up watching your mother perform on that hospital show? And while you're at it, why don't you tell him how you developed a fetish for ambulances and hospitals?" George had continued to fake having a seizure. *"Looks like you need some Narcan. And Abe's got a 14-gauge catheter with your name on it. Course you'd just like that, wouldn't you?"*

To an outsider, the kid's problem seemed as weird as it was amusing. But George's fetish controlled his life and, unfortunately, kept him in Savage's. "Here's the way it goes, George. You shuddup and listen. No wiseass remarks. No fake obstructed airway or MI or tuna dance."

He tried to form a wounded boy's expression, but his gaunt face just didn't cut it. "You're like a mother to me."

"If you were my kid, I would've kicked your ass a long time ago. Course your mother's too busy doing her infomercials, right?"

"Don't talk to me about my mother."

"You know this student?" Tony asked impatiently. "Maybe you guys can catch up *after* class."

Savage sent a threatening look at George, then returned to the desk as Tony took a seat and gave her his own evil eye. She introduced herself and mentioned that she had been a CPR instructor for the past few years. "Tonight we'll go over the basics of one-person, adult CPR."

6

D r. Joanna Boccaccio nearly missed him. She hurried into the Galleria as one of his buddies was locking the adjacent doors. "Excuse me, ma'am. The Galleria's closing now."

"Yeah, I know. I'm looking for Santiago. Is he working tonight?"

The gangly, pimple-faced guard gave her the once-over and, suddenly nervous, unclipped his radio. "Yeah, he is. Want me to call him?"

"I don't want to get him in trouble."

"It's no problem." The kid stared at Boccaccio's chest. Maybe her blouse was a little too tight, and maybe she should have zipped up her leather jacket. "The boss already went home. What's your name?"

"Joanna. He'll recognize me when he sees me. I hope. Just tell him we met here about two weeks ago."

The kid spoke quietly into the radio, then said that Jose would be right over.

Boccaccio glanced at a few shops, feigning interest in some furniture and artwork. She knew the young guard was staring at her, trying to figure out why this woman in her thirties with all that curly black hair had taken an interest in his buddy.

Footsteps echoed through the empty Galleria, and Jose Santiago double-timed down the corridor. His gaze lit. "I remember you."

"Hi. I was hoping you were on tonight."

"I am. But we're closing up. I know you like to hang around here."

She blushed. "Only when I'm trying to escape my mother. She came for a visit, and I wasn't in the mood to go home."

"I know how that is. So what's up? You need our help with something?"

"I feel like a jerk. I came here on the spur of the moment. I don't even know you, but I just was wondering if you're hungry, if maybe you'd want to go grab something."

"Serious?"

Of course I'm serious, she thought. *I've had some pretty vivid fantasies about you. Do you have any idea how lonely I am?* "I was thinking we'd go over to Jerry's Famous Deli. You like that place?"

"Yeah," he gasped. "I just have to finish up here and make a call. Um, my car's messed up right now."

"I'll drive."

"Okay. So where will I meet you?"

"I'm parked downstairs. It's a Grand Cherokee, right by the elevator. I'll wait."

Still dumbfounded, Jose nodded. "I'll be there. See you in a couple of minutes."

She smiled, then turned for the doors. Sensing the skinny guard's gaze, Boccaccio smiled politely and thanked him, then hastened for the exit. Despite her nervousness, she made it back to her truck and leaned on her door, breathless.

She wondered what she was doing. The guy was like ten years younger than her. He was a kid. And as "Bones" from *Star Trek* would say, "I'm a doctor, Jim, not a cradle robber." Boccaccio knew better.

But the "kid" wasn't a teenager anymore, and he wasn't one of those pompous asses from the hospital who would take her out and spend the whole time talking about how many medical awards he'd won. The kid didn't see it as a competition. And sure, he would want sex. They all did. But if he just listened and tried to understand who she was, then that would be enough.

Feeling as though she were being watched, Boccaccio climbed into her truck and locked the door. A notepad lay on the passenger's seat. She had scribbled a list of phone numbers on one page, and now the pad had her thinking about her mother, about how the woman still refused to return her calls. Boccaccio had even contacted Bally's Casino to reach Mom's boyfriend. According to one manager, Drew now worked at another casino. The manager had not been sure which one, and after trying a half-dozen, Boccaccio had given up. She considered calling the police to go check on her mother, though she feared what that might do to Mom's fragile mental state. She had found a good psychologist working at Valley General (she had not mustered the nerve to speak with her colleagues at SFMC), and he had given her the numbers of some colleagues in the Vegas area. Still, Boccaccio had not followed up. She really needed to talk to Drew, then take it from there.

A tapping came from the passenger's side window. She jolted. Jose Santiago widened his eyes. "Sorry to scare you."

She hit the power lock button and waved him in. "Seems like I'm always a little tense. It's not you."

"To be honest, I'm a little tense myself. I've never done anything like this. And I'm really, well, surprised."

She started the truck. "Please don't think I go around doing this. It's not like I have a thing for security guards and hit all the malls. Okay, this is impulsive. But I don't know . . . it just feels fun."

"You sound like you need a little fun."

She slumped. "No, I need a lot of fun."

"So your name's Joanna," he said, searching for his seat belt. "Joanna what?"

She paused. Oh, it was probably all right to tell him. Her number was unlisted anyway. "Boccaccio."

"Italian girl. I'm one-quarter Italian. The rest is Mexican and Cuban, with a little Filipino in there somewhere."

They left the parking garage and turned onto Ventura Boulevard. She glanced at him a few times and caught him glancing back. "If you weren't with me, where would you be tonight?"

"Home. Watching *Cops* or something."

"Where's home?"

"Sun Valley. Since my car broke, my mom's been driving me to work. You think you could give me a lift home?"

"I don't know. Gas prices are pretty high."

"I'll pay you."

She punched his arm. "I'm only kidding."

"So what would you be doing?"

"Probably watching TV. Or I'd be writing. I have so many papers to write."

He ran fingers over the dashboard. "Nice truck. You must have a pretty good job."

"I'm a doctor."

"Serious?"

"Yeah. I work in a big hospital."

He shook his head, amazed. "You look so young."

"But I feel so old. Anyway, I love my job, even though it takes so much from me. Most of the people I meet are sick or in trouble. It's like you have to give them some of your happiness. Sometimes I worry that I'll run out."

"So you're a doctor. Probably got a place up in the hills. What do you want with me? I'm making a little more than minimum. I don't even have a degree. Unless you want me for something else?"

"Like what?"

"I don't know. Are you recruiting people for a test or something? Need a guinea pig?"

"No," she said, holding back a laugh. "You're not my science experiment. We met. We talked. I thought this could be fun. So here I am."

"Why'd you wait two weeks?"

"I've been busy, and I guess I had to get up the nerve. This seems pretty reckless."

"But here we are."

"Yeah, here we are."

She turned into the restaurant's parking lot and found a space in the boondocks. Jose pulled off his security guard shirt to reveal a white T-shirt and a magnificently narrow waist. As they headed inside, she chanced a look at his butt. Definitely cute butt.

A hostess with a diamond stud in her nose took them to a corner booth. The place was usually jammed, weeknight or no, and Boccaccio whispered a silent "thank you" that the booth had so conveniently opened up. She told Jose to order anything he wanted. He said he didn't want to take advantage of her. That was the whole idea, but she simply nodded.

Yes, I'll feed this boy, then I'll take him home for some very serious sex.

Oh, my God. What am I thinking? Why does it feel so good to be with this kid?

She ordered a chicken Caesar salad and a glass of wine, and he took on a massive burger, fries, and shake. They didn't say a word until the drinks came. He took a sip. "Mmmm. Know what? I feel like I won the lottery. I never come here. It's too expensive. I usually go to Carl Jr.'s or El Pollo Loco or someplace."

"I've only been here a few times myself. I'm a take-out kind of girl. And at work, it seems like I eat nothing but junk food. If I wasn't running around so much, I'd really pack on the pounds."

"I still can't believe you're a doctor. That's so cool."

"The people I fix up think so. Course there's always a few that don't want to be treated: the martyrs and the war heroes who want to take the pain. Then there are the, shall we say, youthful neighborhood representatives and unlicensed pharmaceutical distributors, who tend to be very combative."

"Wanna hear something funny? I've never been in a hospital. Except when I was born. Guess they scare me."

She adopted his word: "Serious?"

"Unless you're having a baby, you go there because something bad happened."

"Depends on how you look at it. I know some people who met their husband or wife in a hospital. I also know some people who figured out what they really wanted to do with their lives by working in a hospital. It's weird, but it all goes on there. Life. Death. Everything in between. It can be depressing and it can be really exciting. And like I said, it always wears you out."

"I hope this doesn't sound stupid, but can you say

something like a doctor? I just think that's so cool when the doctors rattle off all that stuff."

God, he's so young. Are you sure about this, Joanna? Really sure?

"They make it sound pretty dramatic on TV. Thing is, when you have an emergency situation, everyone has to remain calm and think clearly. When I'm in a trauma bay, there are all kinds of sharp instruments being passed around. You don't want to get cut or stabbed. You don't want someone's blood contaminating you. And you don't want to miss anything on your patient. If you're shouting and rushing through it, the chance of mistakes increases. I've been in some EDs where that kind of controlled chaos occurs, but if you train your residents right, you shouldn't have that. Sorry, I'm suddenly venting, and you don't need to hear this. You just wanted me to say something cool, like 'Get me four units of O-neg and a chest tray.' "

"Sorry I got you started. Damn, I still can't believe I'm here with you. And I just remembered that I'm off the clock, and I can tell you that you look really good without getting fired for harassment."

"So do you."

They nursed their drinks and passed a few moments in silence until the food arrived. The small talk returned, and Boccaccio's anticipation neared the breaking point. She devoured her salad, drained her wineglass, then watched him finish his burger.

"You must've been hungry," he said.

"Very."

The waiter asked if they would like dessert. Jose declined. Boccaccio requested the check.

"So what now?"

"Do you have to get up early?"

He shook his head. "There's a couple of good movies we could see."

"I was thinking we'd hang out at my place."

"Serious?"

"Unless you feel uncomfortable. . . ."

"No. Maybe we can rent a tape. Or just watch what's on."

She narrowed her gaze.

He drew back from the table. "Oh. I wasn't sure that . . . well, I didn't think you. . . ."

"I'm not a slut, Jose." She closed her eyes. "I'm definitely not a slut."

"Neither am I."

"And I'm not just some horny older woman." She looked at him.

He wriggled his brows. "Neither am I."

One of the cable channels—Abe Kashmiri forgot which one—was showing an exposé on hospitals. The report focused on a nationwide nursing shortage, which Abe had experienced firsthand. Nurses at several California hospitals said that three beds did not always equal three patients, that sometimes two or even three other patients were placed in temporary holding areas and were all waiting for that one bed. In the meantime, all of those patients still needed care. If that wasn't stressful enough, some hospitals were issuing electronic bands to track the movements of their nurses, many of whom were overworked, underpaid, and now feeling mistrusted. On the other hand, hospital administrators stated that some nurses would deliberately position their patients away from call buttons and sometimes leave meds on the table without knowing if their patients actually took them.

Problems with patient care did not end there. Experienced RNs and Certified Nursing Assistants were being laid off or fired and replaced with "patient care associates" and "nursing assistants"—unlicensed caregivers with sometimes only three weeks of training. These PCAs cost a third as much as registered nurses and were often recruited from the hospital's cleaning service or from prisons with work furlough programs. That's right, prisons. The PCAs were supposed to perform "routine care," but were regularly given more complex responsibilities like drawing blood and initiating EKGs. One PCA said that she didn't feel ready to make independent decisions and that the "see one, do one" training just didn't work. A charge nurse supported the young woman's claim with a very telling fact regarding the PCAs in her hospital: "They don't know what they don't know." She told several stories of patients being left in the hands of poorly trained, unsupervised PCAs. She added that the confusion regarding titles was intentional. RN, PCA, aide, assistant . . . administrators wanted you to think they were one and the same.

"You believe this?" Abe said, waving a hand at the television and sliding his pillow a little higher.

"Believe what?" Lisa Margrove looked up from the bookstore's sales report. She had pulled her red hair into a ponytail and had washed off her makeup. She looked like a nineteen-year-old lying next to him, and Abe suddenly cursed himself for being so moody with her.

"These administrators are screwing over the public."

"Sorry. I wasn't paying attention. I'm supposed to read this damned thing, but it's so boring. Look at us, Abe. Dating two weeks and we're like an old married couple, lying here in my bed, watching TV. So . . . are you going to tell me what's bothering you?"

"I'm looking at this, and I'm wondering if the county

might get the same idea. You know, cut back on paramedics and just use lots of EMTs. Then force out as many of the experienced and higher-priced people as they can. We'll be like the worst of the worst private ambulance company. Most people don't even know the difference between a paramedic and an EMT anyway. We're all just ambulance drivers, and I bet that's fine with the administrators."

She studied him. "Did you sleep when you got home this morning?"

"I got off really late. Went to a debriefing. After that I tried, but I couldn't."

"So that's why you're so cranky."

"I'm not good company." He lifted the sheet, slid out of the bed.

"Where are you going?"

"Home. I just don't feel good."

"Why?"

He drew in a long breath. "Don't know."

"Abe, the thing that really attracted me to you, the thing that made me jump on you the first time you came here, was the way you just opened up. Women don't find that very often. I mean, when you told me about the first time you lost a patient, and how you remembered that boom box and that hip-hop music, and how you can't listen to that music anymore, I thought, 'My God, I've never heard a man be so open.' "

He pulled on his boxer shorts. "Yeah, but I didn't come here to whine about my problems and cry on your shoulder. I just wanted to see you."

"Well, you've been seeing me for the past four hours now, but you haven't really seen me. When we were having sex, you were definitely not here."

"It's just. . . ." Out of nowhere, a surge of anger coursed

through him. He picked up his jeans, rolled them into a ball, then threw them on the floor. "Fuck!"

"Whoa, whoa, whoa." Lisa climbed out of the bed, donned her satin robe, then came up behind him. She massaged his shoulders. "What happened last night?"

"I screwed up."

"And so you're mad about it. That's all right. You just need to talk."

"That's what I told him."

"Who?"

"Nobody." He picked up his shirt, put it on, started buttoning. "I tell you I got a new partner? Just for two weeks, while Stephanie's on vacation."

"So how's that going?"

He snickered. "Great."

"You want to talk about that?"

"I'll just go home. Try to get some sleep."

She grabbed his shoulders, turned him around. "Don't go. Please. Let me help you."

"This is just . . . don't think it has anything to do with you. It's just stuff I really don't want to talk about."

"Maybe if I tell you all about the stress on my job, that'll help you with yours."

He unrolled his jeans and hurriedly slid them on. "I'll call you tomorrow. Don't worry about me. I'll be okay. It was just a bad shift."

"I don't believe you."

He stroked her cheek, moved in for a good-bye kiss. She grabbed his head, pulled him back near the bed so hard that he had to tug away. "Lisa. . . ."

"I'm sorry. I thought that, well, you're so good for me. I want to be good to you. And right now I can't. I guess I'm an overachiever, even in relationships."

"That's okay. I'm a little like that too, which is why I

don't want to get you down. Now c'mon. Lock the door behind me."

The sex was good. Jose had no problem using protection. He would have worn a stainless steel condom if it would get him in bed with her. Boccaccio lay back on her pillow, letting the sweat trickle down her forehead. Her arms and legs still trembled. He lay beside her, breathing quietly, stroking her hair. "Thank you."

She looked at him. "For the sex?"

"You buy me dinner, take me home, we do this. Sounds pretty stupid, but I'll never forget this for the rest of my life. And I hope this isn't a one-night stand."

"I don't think so."

"That's good. Because you're the best woman I've ever had. I never knew about some things."

"I'm not that good."

"You're better than all the girls I know. And you're smart. I guess the only stupid thing you've done is be with me." He looked past her to the framed photos on her dresser. "Who's that? Your mother?"

"Yeah, that's her. I should've turned the picture around. I feel like she's watching."

"You look like her."

Boccaccio shuddered. "Yeah. I guess so."

Abe spent thirty minutes driving around in his Jeep Wrangler. Though the temperature had dropped to about fifty degrees, he didn't bother to put up the soft top. He kept asking himself why he had not told Lisa about the suicide call and about working with Rasso. Was he embarrassed? Or did he want to protect her from the seedier side of his job? He had already shared some grim stories. Why did

telling her not feel right? Maybe she wasn't the one who
needed to listen.

He found himself cruising way up Van Nuys Boulevard, away from his apartment. The dashboard clock read
11:47. Two elderly women wearing heavy wool coats sat
beneath a covered bus stop. One checked her watch. A
girl of maybe twenty, with stringy brown hair and a T-
shirt cut just above her navel, walked barefoot toward a
corner. She looked like a drifter, though there was a def-
inite purpose in her gait. Two gangbangers with those
familiar green knit caps suddenly darted across the street
and vanished down an alley. A Valley PD unit approached
from the opposite direction. As the cruiser passed, its
lights and sirens came on. The sidewalk tables of a coffee
shop just ahead were unoccupied, and dim light filtered
through the shop's windows. Somewhere up in the mountains, thunder echoed. You didn't hear that very often in
the valley, and Abe could smell the dampness of ap-
proaching rain.

He drove on.

Twenty minutes later, he pulled behind Fire Station
Seventeen. He went inside, spoke with the lieutenant on
duty, got the information he needed.

The trip took another fifteen minutes, and then ten more
to find a parking spot. Abe wound up walking two blocks
to reach the apartment house, a teal-colored, five-story
relic that had probably been renovated a half-dozen times.
He mounted a long staircase and, at the top, found the
intercom and scanned the list of names for the code. He
dialed. Listened to the ring.

"Yeah?" came a groggy voice.

"Rasso? It's me."

"Who's me?"

"Abe Kashmiri."

"Abe who?"

"Abe, your partner for two weeks."

"You? What do you want? What time is it?"

"Buzz me in. I want to talk."

"Whattaya, nuts? Go away."

Balling his hand into a fist, Abe slammed the intercom. "Listen to me, you fucking old man. You buzz me in right now, or I'm gonna break down this door and come up there and kick your fucking ass. Got it?"

The door buzzed. Abe jerked it open, marched to the elevator, and rode it to the fourth floor. When he reached Rasso's door, the medic was standing there in his underwear and scratching his pot belly. "You're gonna kick my fuckin' ass? I don't think so."

"Just let me in," Abe said, softening his tone. "I don't want to wake up your neighbors."

"How considerate of you. Don't care if you bother me, though." Rasso stumbled back into his apartment. You could smell the whiskey on his breath from ten feet away.

Abe closed the door and got his first look at Chateau Rasso. The furniture and framed art could've been lifted from a budget motel room. In fact, it had probably come with the apartment. An empty whiskey bottle lay on the coffee table beside a bowl brimming with peanut shells and a roll of paper towels. A nineteen-inch TV flickered with a late-night talk show, and atop the TV sat a VCR and three videos—episodes of the kids' show *Barney*. Weird. Perhaps a thousand stains had been rubbed into the beige carpet, and thick cobwebs hung from the ceiling corners. How anyone making a decent salary could live in such filth was beyond Abe. He thought of that tenement house last Sunday; Rasso would easily blend.

The stench of something recently burned came from the nearby kitchen, where a trash can overflowing with dirty paper plates and beer bottles sat on the countertop. Rasso padded into the kitchen and drew a smoking bag of popcorn from his microwave and poured the contents into a bowl. "Shit! You made me burn it."

"Have you ever cleaned this place?"

Ignoring the question, Rasso came into the living room with his bowl of burned popcorn and a bottle of beer. He thrust the smoldering kernels at Abe. "Want some?"

Abe grimaced and stepped back.

"Huh." Rasso dropped onto the sofa, which creaked loudly. He ate some popcorn, then found the remote and channel-surfed.

"Why didn't you come to the debriefing?" Abe asked, checking the stability of the love seat before he sat. "Martinez wants to know."

"He wants to know, let him ask me."

"Do you have to chew so loud?"

"What the fuck? You come here in the middle of the night to insult me? I didn't ask for company. But if you wanna try to kick my ass, that might be fun. And did you get to the bank machine yet? Where's my twenty bucks?"

Abe fished out a bill from his wallet, gave it to him. "You should've come to the debriefing."

"It didn't help you."

"How do you know?"

" 'Cause you're here"—he made a sissy voice—"and you wanna talk. You wanna express your feelings because some fuckin' idiot got lead poisoning on your shift. Well, *partner*, turns out the kid was dicking his actor buddies and got AIDs. Probably couldn't handle telling his girlfriend and his family he was bisexual and diseased. Happens all the time. Get over it, you fuckin' wimp. Or quit."

"I didn't come here to talk about that. I came here to tell you that if we're gonna get through next week, I have to get a little respect. I busted my ass as an EMT. I passed the National Registry exam. I'll get through this probation. Believe me, I will."

Rasso laughed so hard that he choked. "Oh, kid. You're killing me. Oh, Jesus Christ. A little respect? Oh, Jesus Christ. Fuckin' twenty-something snot nose wants a little respect. Fuckin' Rodney Dangerfield over here." Without warning, he threw the bowl of burned popcorn at Abe.

As the popcorn fell, Rasso bolted from the sofa and went to an end table. He scooped up his wallet and pulled out a photo. With a deranged glimmer in his eye, he came at Abe, waving the picture. "You want a little respect? You don't deserve it, motherfucker. I've lived more than half my life. I've *had* a life. Jobs. Marriages." He thrust the photo of a seven-year-old boy in Abe's face. "I spent three long years watching my son die of cancer. You don't know about pain. You don't know about anything except you got your feelings hurt. Respect? You want respect, *boy*? You've earned nothing from me. And you won't. Not in two weeks. A month. A year." Rasso's whiskey breath came raggedly, and spittle flew from his lips. "And what is it with you foreigners? You think the world owes you a fuckin' living?"

"I'm going to ask Lieutenant Martinez to get me another FTO," Abe said, brushing off the popcorn.

Rasso staggered back toward the end table. "Do whatever you want."

Abe muttered a curse and headed for the door.

"Hey, kid, wanna know something really scary?" Rasso leaned against the wall, the bottle of beer in his grip. "Look around. I'm your future. Maybe if I convince you to quit, I'm saving you from this. I'm a goddamned Good Samaritan."

"Yeah, that's you." Abe opened the door and, without looking back, slipped into the hall.

7

"So I was off yesterday, and I couldn't stop thinking about what happened, so I went to her job," Doe told Vivas as they wound their way through the canyons, having just come from a fender bender involving two businesswomen who had both refused transport.

"You two have a fight, and the next day you show up at her job?" Vivas asked. "Typical male."

"I thought she'd be glad. I told her I was sorry."

"This goes way beyond sorry."

"She thinks so, too. She told me to go."

"Because you were embarrassing her. She's a hair-stylist. Every woman in that place was listening."

"There were a lot of dryers going. It was loud."

"Not that loud. So let me guess. She tried to kick you out. You wouldn't leave. Then you figure if you tell her you want a haircut, then maybe she'll let you stay and you can all pretend that you're just there for a haircut and there's nothing going on."

Doe touched what was left of his hair. "Yeah. She whipped out the razor, mowed a line right down the middle before I knew what was happening. Had to shave it all off."

"You're lucky she only cut your hair."

Doe brought his legs together.

"So how'd you leave it with her?"

"I told her I liked the haircut."

"Another lie."

"She put some powder on my neck, then said that if I didn't leave, she'd call the police."

"And you told her that wouldn't work because you know most of the cops in this district."

"Nah. I just told her I'd call her that night, which I did. I know she was home, but she didn't pick up. So what do I do now?"

"I'd talk to this Nicole Cavalier person, who, by the way, I already hate—and you should've told me about her, you bastard. You go tell the bitch that you're involved. You tell her to leave you alone."

The mention of Nicole's name sent a chill through him. "That's the thing. I don't want to deal with her. There was a lot of stuff between us, and a lot of it hasn't gone away. I don't want to be around her. . . ."

"Why? Because you won't be able to help yourself? I thought I was riding with Doe Junior's daddy."

"That woman knows things about me that even you don't know. She knows every inch of my body. She knows way too much."

"She knows things I don't know?"

"Aha! That's jealousy. Right there on your face. Roll down the window. Look in the side mirror. There it is. Right there! I told you. You stick a man and woman in a rescue truck and if they're not too ugly, things happen."

"Doe, if you were the last man on Earth, I'd be a lesbian."

"So you're curious about being with women?"

"Shuddup, pig."

"Hey, maybe I'll get Nicole's number and just call. Tell her to stay away. That's good. I can do that."

"Unless she starts trying to have phone sex."

"That could happen."

"If you do call her, you'll be smart and write down her number on a piece of paper that you keep at work. But knowing you, you'll put that paper in your wallet. Then you're pulling out money at a restaurant or something, and the note's right there, and Geneva asks What's that? And you're back where you started. See how I look out for you?"

"Thanks. Knowing me, I'd do that." The whole subject made him restless. "So you hear about those guys up north who got caught with a prostitute in their firehouse?"

"In the firehouse?"

"Six guys involved. They were paying her fifteen bucks each. Guess they saved up a little lunch money."

"Right there in the firehouse? How stupid is that?"

"Yeah. Guess who caught 'em? Not the lieutenant. The battalion chief."

"That makes me so mad."

"Why? You think their wives should've caught 'em?"

"No. It's stories like that that get all the publicity, so everyone thinks firefighters are a bunch of lazy, drunken whoremongers."

"Some of them are."

"Yeah, but you got lazy, drunken whoremongers in every profession, including the presidency."

"And on that note, you hear the other story about the guy who went on a rampage and killed six firemen, including his lieutenant?"

"That one I read. Don't remind me. It'll wind up on

some TV show. They've already shown us looting the dead. What's another rampage? These are scary times. Really scary. Makes me want to protect my daughter even more."

"So how is she? I haven't seen her in months."

"She's fine. Seeing a lot of her daddy lately."

"And you're okay with that?"

"*I've* been seeing a lot of her daddy."

"Oh, no! Your mother's finally won. Thought it would never happen."

"All right, so I hate his parents. But the son of a bitch is really trying. We went up to Magic Mountain on Thursday."

"There's an idea. Maybe I'll take Geneva up there. Have some fun."

Vivas shook her head. "You'll never learn how to listen. And you don't just take a woman to an amusement park and make her better. You should move slow."

"But it worked for your ex."

"I didn't say it did."

"You didn't have to."

"Engine Ten, Rescue Ten. Engine Ten, Rescue Ten. Respond code 3 to a dog bite at West Valley Animal Hospital. Nineteen-fifty-one North Holly Vine Avenue. Cross street Oxnard. Time out, thirteen-ten."

"Engine Ten responding," Doe said. "And let there be lights. And sirens." He threw the switches.

Four police cruisers and two unmarked vehicles surrounded the animal hospital. Yellow police tape festooned the entrances. Traffic on Holly Vine had slowed to a crawl.

"VPD's either really slow or this ain't no dog bite," Doe said, then jumped down from the rescue. He wasn't surprised the call was different from the dispatcher's description. It happened a lot. A chest pain could be anything from a patient who was actually having an MI to a fat guy with belt rub. In the heat of the moment, callers often gave inaccurate information or deliberately lied to the dispatcher, hoping an ambulance would come sooner.

Doe met up with Sergeant Cortez, a big Mexican-American who spoke evenly and without the irony or cockiness of his younger colleagues. "Two perps. One armed. They went in back and got the doc to hand over the ketamine. They pistol-whipped her and took off on foot. The kicker is that when she fell, she scared the Doberman she was treating. The dog nipped her arm."

"Why didn't the dog bite the perps?"

"I'm not sure. Maybe he's a guard dog and recognizes weapons. We'll have to talk to the owner. And you know, this is the second vet robbery this week. They don't even go through the hassle of breaking in. They just pull them off around lunchtime. I was talking to one detective from the Special Gang Unit. He thinks there's a new set moving in. They wear these green knit caps. The leader's got a tattoo of a snake on his eyebrow. They got a meth lab somewhere nearby. Guess they're adding Special K to their menu."

Ketamine, aka Special K, Vitamin K, or KitKat, was a powerful, relatively low-cost anesthetic available as a liquid, white powder, or pill, and was used mainly by vets during surgery and when putting animals down. Human users injected, snorted, or swallowed the stuff, which they said made them feel like their minds were being separated from their bodies. The drug's effects lasted anywhere from one to six hours, though you needed a couple of days to recover fully. Low doses between 25 and 100mg produced quick psychedelic effects. Larger doses could result in vomiting, convulsions, and oxygen starvation of the brain. A full gram would kill you. Doe had treated at least a half-dozen teenagers who had experimented with the drug. A few had suffered permanent brain damage. One had died.

Vivas, who had listened in, went back to the rescue for the trauma bag, stick box, and long backboard while Doe went with Cortez. They ducked under the tape and crossed through a waiting area that smelled like dog. There, two witnesses, an elderly man with a black poodle and a young Hispanic woman with a multicolored kitten, were being questioned by detectives. They passed an exam room where another witness, a middle-aged black man who fought to restrain the Doberman, hollered, "When can I leave?" over the barking.

"We'll get you out of here soon," Cortez assured him.

The doctor, a trim brunette with a distinct streak of gray in her wavy hair, sat on a stool in the next exam room. She winced and rubbed the back of her head. She had removed her jacket, and a 4×4 piece of gauze had already been taped to her left forearm. A young man no more than twenty-five, presumably her assistant, stood opposite her with a VPD officer. "Hey, how are you?" Doe said. "I'm John Smith. Friendly neighborhood paramedic. Or in this case not so friendly neighborhood."

"Victoria White," she said. "Combative patient who can't afford to reschedule her appointments."

"Well, for someone who's just been robbed, you sound pretty brave."

"I feel like bashing in someone's skull right now."

Doe knew the enormity of what had happened would hit her later. "Just want to get your pulse," he said, taking her wrist. "So this bastard hit you in the back of the head?"

"Yeah. It's still sore."

"Try not to move your neck. Any dizziness? Nausea?"

"No. And no LOC, either."

Doe grinned. Victoria White knew the drill. "Can you tell me where you are?"

"Yes, and I know the day, month, and year. Who's president, blah, blah, blah."

"Mind if I take a look at your arm?"

"It's just a little pinch."

As he carefully lifted the tape, Vivas came in with the board and other equipment.

"Oh, you're not taking me out on that."

"Of course not," Vivas said. "This is my son's boogie board. I didn't want to leave it outside. It might get stolen." She opened the c-spine bag and selected a collar as Dr. White smiled. "Seriously, we'll let you walk out if you want."

"Well, this doesn't look too bad," Doe said, covering the wound. "But when it comes to punctures like this, you're better off having it checked out. Not much external bleeding, but you never know what's going on underneath."

"I know that."

"So I guess I don't have to remind you about a tetanus shot, either."

"I'm a vet. I've been bit before. My tetanus vaccination is current."

"I don't think you've been pistol-whipped before," Vivas said as she finished putting on the collar. She gently examined the woman's skull. "You've got a nice bump here. Better off getting a CT to make sure there's no fracture. Are you allergic to any medications?"

"No."

"Are you taking any meds now?"

"Just Serzone."

Doe nodded. That drug was an antidepressant pre-scribed in cases of moderate to severe clinical depression. "Any past medical problems we should now about? Sur-geries?"

"No."

"Good." He went on to ask her when she had last eaten, then had her briefly describe the events leading up to the injury. Eventually he asked her which hospital she wanted to go to, then motioned for them to leave.

"I don't want you carrying me out of here," she said.

Doe eyed Vivas, who nodded and gathered up the gear. He helped Dr. White to her feet, then braced her shoulders and guided her out of the exam room. She fired off some orders to her assistant, who said he'd meet her at the hos-pital.

Within a minute they had the doctor back in the rescue. Vivas climbed into the cab and reported their status to the dispatcher while Doe called ahead to San Fernando Med-ical Center. Medic Controller Charti Darunyothin an-swered the call, and because Doe didn't need a doctor's consult, he followed with his report:

"En route to your facility with a thirty-six-year-old white female, BLS stable. Patient was found A/O times four after being struck at the base of her skull with a pistol and bitten in the left forearm by a large dog, a Doberman. BP is 98/70, pulse is 90, respiration is 16. GCS is 15, with no LOC. Patient's neck has been immobilized with a cervical collar, and her wound has been bandaged. ETA code 1 approximately seven minutes. Copy?"

Charti acknowledged the report and would pass it on to the ER staff.

"Copy that. We'll update en route if any change." Doe

clipped in the mike, then faced the doctor, whose eyes had filled with tears.

"I can't believe this," she said, wiping off a tear. "Fuckin' bastards." She began to sob.

Doe took her hand. "Hey, it's okay."

"It was like a movie. Nylon stockings over their heads. Guns. I really thought he was gonna shoot me."

"It's no fun having a gun pointed at you. Believe me, I know. But you'll be all right. I'll tell the doc to hook you up with someone you can talk to about this. I'm not big on counseling myself, but they tell me it works."

"I'm sorry I'm putting you through all this trouble."

"Would you believe I hear that all the time? Pick up a guy who's near death, and he apologizes for bleeding all over my ambulance. It's okay. I'm just glad you're all right."

"Wow. That almost sounds sincere."

He grinned. "You know it yourself. Work with the public long enough, and you start to get numb to all the bitching and moaning. I'm trying to . . . I don't know . . . learn how to care again. I have to. I'm going to be a daddy."

"Really? Congratulations. That's a lot of responsibility."

"Yeah. But first I have to get my girlfriend to stop hating me. . . ."

"What happened?"

"Long story."

"No, really, tell me. It'll take my mind off this."

Doe checked her pulse again. "Well, it all hit the fan when my ex-girlfriend moved back to LA. . . ."

Manny Nuva finished his last car, scrubbed his hands as best as he could, then said good night to his buddies at the Sears Auto Center. He worked every third Saturday and didn't mind working weekends so much. Most customers were happy they could get repairs done, and usually left their cars for the entire day. Manny could, for the most part, set his own pace, so long as he completed his list. He liked his new manager quite a bit. The guy didn't pressure the salespeople and had been a mechanic himself. The old manager hadn't known a water pump from a fuel injector.

Manny's El Dorado sat at the far end of the Galleria's parking lot. He liked to keep his pride and joy away from the door dingers and sadistic keyers, though he could do without the five-minute walk after a twelve-hour day. At about twenty yards from the car, the distinct rumble of Flowmaster mufflers drew his attention. Up rolled a black lowrider pickup with two *cholos* in the back, two in the cab. They all wore green knit caps, white T-shirts, thin belts, well-ironed baggy pants with split cuffs, and canvas shoes. Manny recognized the driver, but the passenger and the *vatos* in the back were obviously new to the set. All three young men had black eyes and bruised cheeks from the severe beatings required for jumping in with the gang.

The pickup's owner, a twenty-four-year-old banger named Ruiz who went by the name of "Slip," slammed out of the truck's cab. The snake tattooed above his left eyebrow reared up as his face knotted with rage, and his right arm bore the gang's *placa*: a massive spiderweb with a cross in the center. "Yo, *vato*! I wanna talk to you!"

Manny's neck tingled, but he tried to look bored, even mad. He spoke deliberately in English to distinguish himself from the bangers, though the slang was hard to avoid. He had been a *cholo* himself for too many years. "What up, Slip?"

"You know what up."

The other three circled Manny.

"No, I don't. And don't be hard-looking me."

"Don't be dissing us!"

Manny glanced at the others, noting their positions. "I'm not dissing you."

Slip widened his eyes and stepped closer. "Paco boned out."

"His choice."

"Who convinced him? Who loaned him money? Who's been helping him out?"

"He doesn't want to run with you anymore. I see you got replacements. Formed a new set. What's the problem?"

"You're the problem, *vato*."

"No, I'm not a *vato*. I'm a man. I'm not in the set. I'm not kicking it with anyone anymore. You're looking at a *jefe*, and I don't want my daughter seeing this."

"So you think you can talk people out of my set? Dis me and my *cholos* like that, and go home?"

The other three closed in.

"Paco made a decision on his own," Manny said, trying to keep the tremors from his voice. "I just loaned him some money and helped him get a job. It's time for him to grow up. Time for you, too."

Slip brought his face within inches of Manny's. "Paco's not doing anything anymore. Somebody smoked him."

Manny lost his breath. "You. . . ." He broke into a string of epithets in Spanish. He whirled, searched for an opening, ready to sprint. One *cholo* grabbed his wrist. As he struggled against the banger's grip, another grabbed his free arm.

"You're an old *cholo*, Manny. Go way back. Nobody would wanna smoke you. They say you got friends all over. But you know what? I don't care."

"You're selling wolf tickets," Manny said, using an old

prison expression to accuse Slip of not backing up his threats with violence.

"You're wrong. You're jacked up. You don't even know it."

Pouring all of his strength into his legs, Manny bolted. He made it all of two yards before the *cholos* dragged him to a halt, slammed him onto the concrete, then hauled him to his feet.

Slip drove a fist into Manny's abdomen.

The others unleashed their kicks, keeping their hands locked on his wrists.

"You've been out of the set a long time," hollered Slip. "Now we make you remember what happens when you disrespect us and the neighborhood."

The punches and kicks kept coming.

Manny tried to turn, couldn't move.

A blow to the chest stole his breath.

Hands found his ears, pulled until he felt excruciating pain.

A fist connected with his jaw. Another. Another.

Warm, sweet blood pooled in the back of his throat, and he fell to the ground.

A kick to the head left him dizzy. The dark faces grew blurry; the shouting, indistinct. Hands reached into his pants, found his wallet, took it.

His head banged once more on the concrete. Hands again on his head, taking it and banging it, banging it, banging it on the pavement.

Then . . . nothing.

"*Vamos!*"

He gasped. Suddenly, it hurt to breathe. His head throbbed. He thought he felt blood on his neck.

He rolled onto his side, saw his wallet lying on the pavement, a picture of Consuela hanging from it. . . .

A gunshot blared.

"*Vamos*!"

The lowrider roared away.

Manny reached for the picture, felt the sharp pain in his chest, and. . . .

8

Stephanie Savage had spent the entire day watching TV and drinking beer. She had cracked open her first can at 9 A.M., and all of a sudden the sun had gone down. What time was it?

Her pathetic excuse of an ex-husband had finally gotten in touch with her to say that he, too, hadn't heard from Donny all week, but he figured they were staying at Tina's parents' house. No, he didn't have that number, the bastard.

The phone rang. Donny? She sprang from the sofa, tripped, and fell on her drunken ass. If she didn't get to the receiver by the fourth ring, the damned machine would—

"Hello?"

"Hello, Ms. Savage?" came a male voice.

"Who's this?"

"Don Michaelson from Reseda Ford. You were here yesterday, looking at the F-150s. Sorry to call so late, but we just got three more in. Thought you'd like to come down and have a look. They've also made some changes to the lease program that I know you'll like."

Savage sighed heavily.

"Ms. Savage?"

"Yeah, I'm here."

"If you'd like, I can take your credit card number and we can put a deposit on one. I know you wanted white, and we didn't have any. We have one now."

"Careful there, buddy."

"Excuse me?"

"Careful, you're drooling into that receiver. You'll ruin it." She hung up.

Time for another bathroom run.

The doorbell rang. Had to be her pain-in-the-ass next-door neighbor, a middle-aged woman who was divorced and manic depressive, and would plop her butt on Savage's couch for no good reason but to talk and talk and talk. "C'mon, Eve. It's like ten o'clock," Savage said as she pulled open the door.

"Hey, Ma. Sorry I haven't called. I've been trying to work this out." Donny walked by her, took one look at all the empty beer cans on the floor and sofa, then shot her a stunned look. "You're drunk."

"You're damned right I'm drunk. This is what you do to me." Savage stuck her head into the hall. "Where's your little slut?"

"She's at her parents. And she's not a slut, Ma. She's my wife."

"What?" Savage closed the door on her finger. Swore. Shut it again. "What?"

"We took a ride out to Vegas." He lifted his hand, flashing a gold band. "We didn't want anything from anybody. And this is what we wanted. So we did it. Tina's parents aren't too happy either, but it's done."

Savage shut her eyes, held herself. "You know this girl a few weeks and you marry her?"

"Ma, I've known her since I started school," Donny said, staring at the beer cans. "We've been pretty serious for the past six months."

"And all this time you haven't told me anything about her," Savage screamed. "And then you go and fuckin' marry her?"

He bent down, picked up a few cans. "I didn't tell you because I knew you'd be like this. And I was right again. You've hated every girlfriend I've ever had. You nitpick them to death. Lori comes over for Thanksgiving and tells you the sweet potatoes aren't cooked enough, and you freak out on her. She cried for a week after that. And it wasn't like she told you you're fat or a drunk. Give me a break. I'm just tired of apologizing for you." He moved into the kitchen to toss away the cans.

"You're tired of apologizing for me? Well, isn't that too fucking bad? A mother is looking out for her son's best interests, and God forbid she embarrasses him."

"Ma, you're out of control."

"*I'm* out of control?"

He gritted his teeth and returned to the living room to pick up more beer cans. "This place is disgusting. Is this what you're gonna do all week?"

"Get out."

"Fine." He threw down the cans. "I was going to give you Tina's parents' number."

"Keep it. You go live your life. Go fuck up. But one day your old mother is not gonna be here. And I just want you to remember that, remember what you're doing now. Remember this conversation."

"Yeah, I will. I'll remember how you spent most of your time trying to make me feel guilty about living my own life. Know what the problem is, Ma? Your love comes with conditions." He shook his head in disgust and left.

"You go back to your slut," Savage shouted at the closed door. "You go back to her. You do it."

Lieutenant Juan Martinez had denied Abe's request for another Field Training Officer. No, he would not rewrite his schedule. No, he would not call around to see if he could swap someone for Rasso. No, he would not do a damned thing. Too many people were on vacation. "Think of it this way, Abe," he had said. "You survive two weeks with Rasso, you can ride with anybody. That's better training than anyone else will give you."

Abe glanced across the cab, where the devil himself sat, picking his nose.

They had just finished transporting a man who had stabbed his girlfriend a couple of times with a steak knife because, as he had put it, "Da bitch never do nuttin' wit' me. Then I finds her ass in bed wit' my brudda." The girlfriend, who had been transported by Doe and Vivas, had wrestled the knife away from him and had managed to slice open his bicep and stab him in the inner thigh. (She'd been going for his crotch.) She outweighed him by about seventy-five pounds, had simply flattened him like a pro wrestler, and had carved him up like a holiday turkey. Turned out that the man had been in bed with the girlfriend's sister, and when the girlfriend started smacking him, he had run into the kitchen and gotten the knife. Between the two of them, they had told quite a tale and had dripped blood all over two rescues. The police were now looking for the sister.

But that call still wasn't as bad as the one Rasso had told Abe about. A black couple had been fighting, and when the husband had passed out drunk on the couch, the wife had boiled a pot of water, had added lye, then had dumped it all over him. The lye had turned his face, arms, and neck permanently white. When Rasso and his partner had arrived, the guy had been standing in the doorway, screaming.

"Well, here it is, Saturday night," Rasso said. "Who will die? Who will cry? Only the cops and the medics know. Tonight, somebody in our naked city will get into a grinder and be pulled from his car in pieces. At least six people will overdose. A half-dozen *cholos* will shoot each other. A few johns will contract AIDs. And you know what? We'll be here to see it all. We're the grand conductors of humanity."

"Man, you are strange. And your statistics are bogus."

"Of course they are. The numbers are much higher."

"Higher?"

"Hey, Abe?" Rasso stared intently. "Sorry about the other night."

Abe nearly ran a red light. "Excuse me?"

"Yeah, I'm sorry I didn't offer you a beer before I told you what a fuckin' numbnuts you are. That was pretty rude of me. Popcorn makes you thirsty, you know? Next time you come over, I'll make sure to be a little more thoughtful." He grinned tightly.

"You need help."

"I know, but the shrinks don't know what to do with me. So what did you say to Martinez?"

Abe paused, finding it interesting that Rasso actually cared. This was the second time he had asked that question. Maybe the guy was worried about his job, though that seemed unlikely. "I told you. I said I just want another FTO because our styles are so different. I made a professional request."

"You know me and Martinez go way back."

"Oh, yeah?"

"He was my son's godfather."

"Oh, really." Now it all made sense. Martinez wouldn't do anything to call attention to Rasso, his old buddy. Abe looked at the man, whose expression soured.

"Engine Ten, Rescue Nine. Engine Ten, Rescue Nine. Code 3 to an ill person. Nine-seven-six Orinta Avenue. Cross street Hubbard. Time out, twenty-two fifteen."

Abe snagged the mike before Rasso could grab it. "Rescue Nine responding."

"Rescue Nine."

"Hey, kid. I'm running the mike."

"Yeah," Abe said, looking away. "I guess you are."

They pulled up in front of a single-family home. Brick face. Professionally landscaped. Big bucks. Rasso wheezed like an old dog as he climbed out of the rescue, rubbing the small of his back. Abe fetched the gear and joined him. The crew of Engine Ten had beat them to the scene, and one firefighter, a middle-aged guy named Brown, came out of the house with a very fit, very worried-looking man of about forty-five with gray hair and beard.

"Got a fifteen-year-old girl inside," Brown said. "Took a half-bottle of Tylenol this morning."

"You the father?" Rasso asked.

The bearded guy nodded. "We didn't know. She just told us a few minutes ago."

Rasso smiled bitterly. "Why didn't you take her to the hospital?"

"Well, for one, I don't feel like sitting in a waiting room for two hours. And I didn't call for the ambulance. The poison center did. My daughter says she's feeling a lot better now, anyway."

Abe pushed past Rasso and entered the house, knowing that his act would draw the old medic away from an argument with the father—who, in fact, had done more than most people. It was not as if citizens memorized the number for poison control, and more people than not failed to post that number on their refrigerator or near their phone.

A glassy-eyed, silver-haired woman wearing an expensive bathrobe stood in the kitchen, talking with the other two firefighters. The girl sat at a table, her head down in her arms.

"Can I get a little room?" Abe said, hoping the other firefighters would leave the house and let him go about his business. This was a delicate case, to be sure, and the girl did not need a uniformed audience of smoke eaters. "Hi, ma'am. I'm Abe Kashmiri." He proffered his hand.

"Barbara Tannenhill. This is my daughter Samantha. Sam, honey, look up and say hi."

The girl raised her head, eyes swollen, face pale. She managed a nod, then glared at her mother. "Why's this have to be a scene? I told you, I'm okay. And I'm not going in an ambulance. That is, like, so ghetto."

"Mind if I have a look in your medicine cabinets?" Rasso asked the father as they entered the kitchen.

"Why?"

"Because I wanna see what else you've got lying around that she might've taken."

"I only took the Tylenol," Samantha interjected.

Rasso winked at her. "That's what you say, sweetheart."

The old man really knew how to make a connection with his patients. No introduction. No sympathy. Just take one look and accuse her of lying.

"I'm sure she only took the Tylenol," said the mother. "She didn't even tell us about taking the pills until now," argued the father, who then regarded Rasso. "Guest bathroom's over here. Half-bath up front. Another off the master bedroom. I'll show you."

"I'll find 'em," Rasso said, then headed out.

"What's the big deal?" Samantha cried. "Why doesn't everybody just leave?"

Abe dropped to one knee, then gently took her wrist to get a pulse. "Samantha, how many pills did you take?"

"I don't know. Like, half the bottle? Maybe twenty?"

"Twelve is a toxic dose."

"What does that mean?"

Rasso's grating voice came from the guest bathroom. "It means, sweetheart, that you've messed up your liver pretty bad. You might even need a transplant."

"Is he serious?" asked the father. "She looks fine. She says she feels fine. It was just Tylenol for God's sake."

"I know that, sir, but the drug kills liver cells, which is what's happening right now If her liver fails. . . ."

Samantha trembled. "Oh my God. Oh my God."

"You're telling me you can kill yourself with Tylenol?"

Abe's tone grew more sober. "Yes, I am, sir."

"Then why is it available over the counter?"

"Shut up, James," hollered the mother. "What do we do now?"

Abe straightened. "We transport. Which hospital?"

The mother swallowed. "Uh, San Fernando. Is there anything they can do for her? Will she really need a liver transplant? No way! That can't be possible."

"They can give her an antioxidant drug called Mucosil and some other drugs that might help repair the damage. They'll also lavage her stomach and probably make her drink some activated charcoal. Anyway, we gotta move. Dad, if you're up to it, you can follow in your own car. Mom, you're in back with Samantha."

• • •

Once they were out in the rescue, Abe leaned toward Rasso. "I'd like to ride with her."

"Good idea," Rasso muttered. "I got no use for these little fuckin' debutantes who wanna kill themselves because Daddy won't buy 'em a new car or let 'em pierce their belly button."

"You don't have any use for most people," Abe said, then climbed into the rescue. "Okay, Samantha. Let me finish strapping you in. Mom, you see that seat belt right there on the bench? That's yours."

Rasso made an ugly face, then slammed the rear doors.

The mother pulled a tissue from her purse, wiped her eyes. "Why didn't you talk to us?" she asked her daughter.

Samantha folded her arms over her chest, shut her eyes.

"Hey, Samantha. I just want to get a blood pressure."

"Whatever."

Abe gently took her arm and wrapped on the cuff.

"She won't even tell us why she took the pills," said the mother.

"Did you break up with your boyfriend?" Abe asked as he pumped up the cuff.

"I don't have a boyfriend."

"Are you mad about that?"

"No. All the guys in my school are assholes."

"Samantha . . . ," her mother warned.

"You doing okay in school?"

"She has straight A's," Mom interjected.

Samantha turned away. "Can we just not talk?"

The mother's eyes widened, then she pursed her lips, shook her head. The rescue jerked from the curb. "I don't know what to do anymore."

"So, Samantha, you're just mad at the world, that it?"

"Yup."

"Me, too. I think I know how you feel."

"No, you don't. Your friends didn't all dump you. You don't have a ten o'clock curfew. You don't have parents who treat you like a baby."

"My parents live pretty far away now. And they were really strict. But you know what? I miss them now. I miss them a lot. And being strict wasn't such a bad thing. Just takes a while to figure that out."

She didn't reply.

Abe sighed and, having made a mental note of Samantha's vitals, he picked up the mike and made the report to SFMC. After that, he just looked at the girl. So young. Her whole life ahead of her.

"Doe!" Vivas shouted. "Are you crazy! Let him go! Wait for the cops."

"He'll be long gone by then!"

The ten- or twelve-year-old Caucasian kid who had just swiped their drug box ducked down an alley between an ice-cream store and an antique shop. Doe hauled ass and came up hard on him, but the kid suddenly turned down an adjoining alley. Five smelly Dumpsters sat in a row, dimly illuminated by a streetlight. A portly Asian man wearing a white chef's hat and carrying a bulging garbage bag emerged from the back door of a restaurant.

"Stop him!" Doe cried.

The big chef came from behind one of the Dumpsters, took one look at the kid, then stepped back. "Hey, I ain't no cop."

Doe swore to himself. "Thanks a lot."

As the kid reached the end of the second alley, he paused, looked both ways, then turned right, heading toward a side street lined with apartment buildings. If Doe didn't catch him within the next minute, the kid could dart into the shadows between buildings.

Damn it! The whole thing had probably been a setup. The guy in his twenties who had fallen to the sidewalk, complaining of chest pain, was working with the kid. And when the two had realized that law enforcement would be late, they saw the opportunity. When Vivas was working a patient, all of her attention was on that patient, and Doe often stood back, serving as her eyes and ears. He had just leaned in to search the "unconscious" man's pockets for an ID when the kid had struck.

All right, you little bastard, you little surfer dude. I'm going to get you. Doe bounded across the rain-slick pavement and narrowed the gap.

Ten yards between them, with the boy slowing a little as he hit a puddle.

Five.

Three.

The kid stole a look back—

As Doe leaped, reached, slammed palms on the kid's shoulders.

Down they went. Hit the sidewalk with a breath-robbing thud and splash.

The drug box went flying, hit the concrete. Doe had unlocked the box for Vivas, and the kid had been holding the lid down with his finger. Drug-filled ampoules and vials, preloaded syringes, 4x4s, and several 500cc bags of IV saline scattered across the walk and grass.

"Don't hurt me," the kid pleaded.

Doe seized the punk by the back of the head, digging gloved fingers deeply into the kid's greasy blond hair. "Hurt you? I oughta kick your ass from here to Ventura." Doe pushed himself up, dragging the kid with him. They staggered toward the fallen drug box. Doe tightened his grip. "You're gonna throw everything back in the box and close it. Hear me?"

"Ow, that hurts."

"This is nothing. Now bend down. Pick it up! Don't test me."

"Hey, dude, I'm sorry. I'm really sorry." He began gathering vials and syringes.

"You're sorry you can't run faster. How old are you?"

"Old enough."

"What? Like thirteen? You ain't gonna make fourteen doing this shit. You live around here?"

"Sometimes."

"Where are your parents?"

"Doesn't matter." The kid finished collecting the fallen drugs and equipment.

"Okay, now seal it." He did, and Doe scooped up the box. "Let's go."

They turned and started down the sidewalk, toward a VPD officer jogging forward. "Yo, Doe," called Lou Fabiothello, an Italian cop with the nose to prove it.

"Hey, Louie. Got a present for you."

"What? No card? No bow? Forget about it." Fabiothello arrived, out of breath. He removed his cuffs and came around the kid. "You give me a hard time, and this'll hurt even more."

"Don't lock me up. Please."

"What are you worried about?" Fabiothello tightened the cuffs. "They don't hang thieves anymore."

Doe inspected the kid's arms for bruises and track marks. Yup. He was a user all right, probably a runaway who had been lured into a gang or into working with dealers, and was, unknowingly, slowly paying off his one-way ticket to the morgue. "What's your name?"

"Chris."

"Or Tom or Joe or Sammy," said Fabiothello, patting the kid down. "Whatever he feels like. And, of course he's got no ID. Just some . . . what's this? Marijuana? Why didn't you try to ditch this?" Fabiothello held up the Ziploc bag.

" 'Cause you'd find it anyway, right?"

Fabiothello chuckled under his breath. "So you're only half a dummy." He led the boy back down the alley, with Doe pulling up the rear.

They reached the sidewalk where Vivas and Doe had found the stricken young man. The guy was gone, and Vivas was talking with Officer Jon Gruger and a few firefighters from the engine. Three pedestrians stood near an antique store and were being questioned by officers from a second police unit. A Middle Eastern woman, the ice-cream store owner who had made the call, was saying that the kid who had swiped the drug box had been talking with some bangers wearing green caps.

Vivas detached herself from the group and came toward Doe. "You idiot! What if he had a weapon?"

"Then I'd be dead. Would you miss me?"

"Your kid would miss you, that's for sure. If you wanna be a daddy, you'd better stop this—" she broke off. "I'm talking to a wall."

He closed his eyes for a moment, felt a sting on his elbow. He touched the pain, and his fingers came away bloody.

"Come on," Vivas said. "I'll patch that up."

"So the other guy took off, huh?" Doe asked, following her back to the rescue.

"He did. I'm yelling at you to stop, and I turn back, and there he is, doing the hundred-yard dash."

"And you didn't follow?"

"Excuse me, but I got a little girl who needs me. No

way am I chasing some asshole junkie. I'll never do that. Got it? What you did was totally wrong."

"Oh, so it's better the kid gets away, and our drugs wind up on the street?"

"You didn't chase him because you thought that. You just figured you screwed up and wanted to cover. But you didn't screw up. The box was right there. You were just checking for an ID, and that kid came out of nowhere. Not you, not any other medic would've seen him. That's exactly what I told Gruger."

"But now everyone's happy."

"Yeah, but maybe it won't come out that way next time. No more risks for you. That's the first thing you have to learn." She unlocked the rescue's back door and climbed inside.

"I can't be me," Doe said, turning around to sit on the tailgate. "Won't be fun."

"Need that box," Fabiothello said, coming over with an evidence bag. "And I'll be back for your statement."

"I'll give it to you now. Residentially challenged youthful offender acquires emergency vehicle drug box without authorization and with intent to misappropriate said county-owned pharmaceuticals. Emergency Medical Services representative gives chase, apprehends youthful offender, recovers box. Details at eleven."

"You're getting pretty good at that. Almost sound like me. Almost. Be back in a sec."

Doe thought he heard a cell phone ring. "Izzy, is that yours?"

"I think so." She pulled the phone from her pocket. "Hello? Yeah? Mama, I told you not to call me at work unless it's. . . . What? What? Oh my God. Where is he? Okay, okay. Don't worry. I'm coming. I'm coming."

Doe hurried into the rescue. "What is it?"

9

Fire Station Nine
Studio City
Sunday, 1:05 A.M. Pacific Time

After they had placed Samantha Tannenhill in Dr. Joanna Boccaccio's capable hands, Abe and Rasso had left the ER, though Abe would have preferred to stay out of service for just a few minutes to see how much damage Samantha had done to her young body. Would she really need a liver transplant from taking all that Tylenol? Abe's curiosity had been piqued. He had found himself worrying for the girl, for the parents, though he knew better.

Of course Rasso had not given a rat's ass. The cranky old man had picked up a couple of cookies in the cafeteria and had met Abe outside, near the ambulance entrance. Abe had cleaned up the patient compartment while Rasso had bitched and moaned about the weather, about Boccaccio treating him so curtly, and about how the young girl needed straight talk and not hand-holding.

They had run two more calls, both minor MVAs, with the patients transported to Valley General. Rasso's mood seemed to improve a little, though his eyes grew more bloodshot. When they returned to the station, he groaned into a recliner, pillowed his head in his hands, and stared blankly at the CNN reporter on TV.

"You're still alive," Fitzy said as he and Abe shared Cokes in the station's kitchen. "Thought you'd be DRT after a couple of shifts with that asshole."

DRT: adjective. Technical term. Dead Right There.

"He's really a nice guy," Abe said, feigning a smile. "Just misunderstood."

Fitzy nearly spit up. "Son, I admire you for hangin' in there. I heard about that suicide call."

Abe lowered his gaze. "Guess I'm hangin' in. Does it matter if it's by threads?"

"Nope. Tell you a story about an old battalion chief. Used to work our district. I won't name names. Anyway, this guy was getting on. Got passed over for promotion. Became your typical bitter old asshole. Rode everybody real hard. Wife left him. Kids didn't want to know him. Dog bit him. We all know this guy. So anyway, we get this big three-alarmer up on Coldwater Canyon. Couple of houses. Big arson job. And this guy decides he's gonna turn over command to a lieutenant and take a line in himself. Maybe he's feeling a little impotent. Who knows? So he takes the line in, and nobody hears from him. His personal alarm doesn't go off. Nothing. Couple guys in the back of the house find him lying on the floor, mask off." Fitzy took a long sip of his soda and looked at Abe. "I was telling you a story."

"Uh, yeah, about the battalion chief."

"God damn it. First your pecker, then your memory. Don't get old, kid."

"I won't. So they find the battalion chief on the floor."

"I've told you this before?"

"No," Abe insisted with a grin. "Come on."

"Where was I?"

"They find the battalion chief on the floor."

"Right." Fitzy brought his bushy gray brows together and shook an index finger. "And you know what?"

Abe checked his watch. "What?"

"The son of a bitch OD'ed. They found some of the pills. He wanted to go out in a blaze of glory but also wanted to make sure he was definitely DRT. Lieutenants covered it up. Reported he had accidentally died in the fire. No autopsy. You know, for the family. And the department."

"Wow, another happy tale. So why'd you tell me this?"

Fitzy looked at him. "There was a point. Where was I going with that?"

"I have no idea. Were you trying to cheer me up? It didn't work. You think I should OD or drive my rescue into an overpass?"

Fitzy snapped his fingers. "I'm saying, you see that old Rasso in there? We're gonna read about him someday. It'll be just like that old battalion chief. Either that, or somebody'll take care of him during a fire. And don't pretend that shit doesn't happen."

"I'm just surprised he's still on the job. I can't believe he hasn't racked up enough complaints and POed enough partners to get fired."

"Well, he's got a few friends in high places."

"He's known the lieutenant for a long time."

"Oh, his buddies go way beyond Martinez."

"How'd he make friends with that attitude?"

"Once upon a time he really was a nice guy. But let me tell you something, son. It's not the fire department's fault that the job got to him. It's his. You can't blame the system. You have to take responsibility for yourself. You have to know when—"

The alarm cut off Fitzy and boomed a harsh wake-up for those sleeping upstairs in the hood. "Engine Nine,

Rescue Nine. Engine Nine, Rescue Nine. Female with leg pain. Nineteen twenty-three North Ryland Avenue. Unit four-thirty-five. Cross street Alamo. Time out, one-fifteen."

"Hey, Rasso?" Abe called.

The veteran did not budge from his recliner.

"Hey, Rasso?"

"Yeah, yeah," he moaned. "I'm coming. Leg pain, huh? Probably some transvestite who cut himself shaving."

The condominium complex, built in the sixties, was freshly painted, with a well maintained pool and professionally landscaped grounds. Abe had been there before. The building catered to elderly folks who insisted on their independence, though occasionally overexertion would strike them down, as it had one sweet old lady Abe had transported a week before. Abe's paternal grandfather would do well in such a place. He was ninety-one, lived in Pakistan, and still did everything for himself. He remained quite lucid and spun tales of his youth that lasted for hours. You never dared cut him short, and planned your visits with him very, very carefully.

Abe took the airway bag and cardiac monitor from the rescue. If Rasso told him that he didn't need the monitor, he'd argue that getting a reading on a geriatric patient wouldn't hurt.

But Rasso simply punched in a code on the intercom. A woman answered.

"Fire department. You call 911?"

"Yes. Yes. Come up."

"You're pretty quiet," Abe said as they entered the foyer and passed row after row of antique mailboxes.

Rasso yawned. "I'm sleeping right now on that recliner. Don't wake me up."

"I'm sure our patient will find that very reassuring."

They rode the elevator. Abe opened his mouth to say something, then looked at Rasso, who leaned against the wall with his eyes closed. *Why bother?* Ding. Fourth floor.

A short old woman wearing plaid pajamas, slippers, and a hair net stood in front of an open door. She was a bag of bones huddled against the hallway's chill. "Over here," she said. "Over here. We have an emergency."

"Nana's got an emergency," Rasso muttered. "Ripped her stocking. Call the ER. We got a level 1."

"You made the call?" Abe asked the woman.

"Yes. For my neighbor, Maggie." She led them into the condo, and Abe couldn't help noticing the stale smell and the decor—if you could call it that.

Maggie had done a lot of traveling and liked to collect souvenirs: ashtrays that said Rocky Mountains, little pencil holders that said Niagara Falls, and hundreds of other trinkets like flags and snow globes and little statues and music boxes. The surfaces of her shelves, bookcases, end tables, and coffee table lay hidden beneath piles of those cheap memories. Two large knit blankets protected an antique sofa and love seat, and plastic runners lay across the rug. Ironically, she didn't want to get her rug or sofas dirty, yet there must have been an inch of dust on her little paperweights and back scratchers and mugs.

Abe, Rasso, and the neighbor reached the bedroom, another study in souvenir hunting gone awry. If there was anything tasteful, it was a picture wall with about twenty black-and-white photos hanging in frames of various sizes. Below them was a four-poster bed on which Maggie lay, propped up by pillows. She was Caucasian, about seventy-five, with greasy white hair; a sizable belly tented up her floral-print pajamas. One leg was heavily bandaged from a recent surgery. She probably had multiple medical problems, judging from the half-dozen or so prescription bottles on the nightstand. The bottle holding one of the drugs, oxycodone (aka Percodan, a powerful narcotic), was still full. Maggie's prescription was for 2mg of oxycodone mixed with 325mg of aspirin, and she had probably not received a dose since her nurse had left. She was sweaty, anxious, and clearly short of breath.

Abe snorted off the stench of mothballs emanating from a nearby closet and approached the woman. He nearly gagged—and not from the mothballs. Maggie had not been bathed in a very long time.

"I've been checking on her since the surgery," said the neighbor. "I heard her moaning, so I came in. She didn't look good. Kept saying 'leg hurts, leg hurts.' She was having a hard time breathing. I didn't know what to do, so I called you. I also talked to her son up in Palmdale. He's coming down."

"Hi, Maggie. How're you doing? I'm Abe Kashmiri. I'm a paramedic. I'm here to help you. Do you understand?"

"Yes," she gasped.

Abe zipped open the airway bag, removed a simple face mask, then attached the tubing. "I'm going to give you some oxygen. It'll help you feel better." He slipped the mask over her head, then opened the valve on the small tank inside the airway bag. He got her pulse: 130; then Maggie winced and clutched her chest.

"She break her hip?" Rasso asked the neighbor.

"Yes. She fell in the elevator. Thank God I was there."

Rasso crossed to the nightstand, glanced at the drugs, then set the cardiac monitor on the bed and switched it on. "She have any other medical problems? Heart problems?" He yawned again.

"Yeah, I think so. I think she had a heart attack last year. I'm not real sure. She doesn't like to talk about it."

"Maggie, does your chest hurt?" Abe asked.

"Yes."

"Can you describe the pain to me?" Abe pumped up the BP cuff. "Is it sudden and sharp?"

"Yes."

Rasso unbuttoned Maggie's nightgown and applied the cardiac monitor's pads to her chest.

"BP's 60/0. Respiration, 45," Abe reported.

"That doesn't sound good," said the neighbor.

"Why don't you pack a few things for her?" Abe said. "She'll need them."

"She has to go to the hospital?"

"Yeah."

Rasso snickered. "Don't say that so causally, junior. She obviously threw a clot, and now she's got a pulmonary embolism. Look at the monitor. She's tachycardic, having ten, maybe fifteen multifocal PVCs per minute. She's hurting. And oh, there goes a lead. She sweat it right off."

A blood clot had blocked one of Maggie's pulmonary arteries, and the strain on her heart caused her to have premature ventricular contractions, a kind of hiccup of the heart. Too many PVCs in a row could be lethal.

Fitzy's voice echoed from their portables. "Engine Nine is on scene."

"Engine Nine," said the dispatcher.

"Hey, Fitzy?" Rasso called on the tactical frequency. "Roll our stretcher in here."

"Copy that."

"No . . . hospital," Maggie said.

Abe stroked the woman's forehead. "It's okay, Maggie. I know you've seen people go to the hospital, and they don't come back. But you have to go. They can help you there."

Her eyes pleaded. "I . . . I'm . . . scared."

"I know you are." Abe took her hand.

Within a minute, Fitzy, Firefighter-EMT Joe Tenpenney, and Firefighter-Paramedic Paul Cannis hustled into the bedroom, leaving the stretcher just outside the door. Cannis helped Abe carry Maggie over to the stretcher, the head of which they had positioned at a 45-degree angle. Tenpenney held the oxygen tank and cardiac monitor while Fitzy braced the woman's hip fracture. Once they set her down, Abe strapped her in and Tenpenney placed the oxygen tank and monitor between Maggie's legs.

Meanwhile, Rasso took a bag of clothing from the neighbor, who declined to go with them (her daughter was visiting in the morning). She agreed to try to reach Maggie's son and tell him they were taking Maggie to SFMC. That done, Rasso stuffed Maggie's prescription bottles into the bag. "I got her stuff."

Fortunately, the elevator was wide enough to accommodate the stretcher. Rasso, Fitzy, and Abe rode with Maggie while Tenpenney and Cannis took the stairs.

Down on the street, Cannis opened the rescue, and they gingerly loaded Maggie as bystanders did what bystanders do: gawk.

"I'll start a line," said Rasso, shouldering his way between Abe and Maggie.

"I'll do it," Abe said, hoping he would once again ride in the back, because Rasso probably had no use for geriatric patients, either.

"I'll take care of her," Rasso insisted. "Get us out of here."

"We'll let Tenpenney drive. I'll stay back here and help you."

"I said get us out of here."

Abe huffed, then headed out of the compartment.

"I'll ride with you," Cannis told Rasso.

"That's all right."

"We usually run two medics and a driver on a call like this," Cannis argued.

"I got it," Rasso yelled. "Close these goddamned doors and let us transport this patient!"

Although Abe was already opening the driver's side door and couldn't see what was happening in the back, he guessed that Fitzy, Tenpenney, and Cannis were staring slack-jawed at Rasso, whose ego would not allow him to accept help.

Abe fired up the engine, slid on his headset. "Ready back there?"

"Get going."

Suddenly, the passenger side door opened, and Fitzy jumped in. "I'll check right for you, son."

"Thanks."

"Your buddy wants to be a hero."

"He's better off working alone. He'd be yelling at Cannis and not paying attention to the patient." Abe hit the lights and sirens, checked the mirrors, then sped off.

Rasso wasn't particularly thrilled that Fitzy had come along for the ride, but there wasn't anything he could do about it except act rude and not permit the old firefighter to help roll in the stretcher. The triage officer waved them on, and Emergency Department attending physician Thomas Louderman, a young and extremely friendly doctor new to San Fernando Medical Center, met them in an exam room.

While Rasso rattled off his report to the doctor, Abe placed Maggie's bag on a nearby counter. Louderman came over for a quick peak at the meds she was on, examining each bottle as he removed it from the bag. When he got to the Percodan, the bottle rattled a bit, catching Abe's attention.

The bottle was only half full.

Louderman set it down and spoke rapidly to two young, female residents as Abe opened Maggie's bag and searched for the missing pills. None there.

One of the RNs got Abe's attention and handed him the cardiac monitor because she had attached Maggie to the hospital's own equipment. In a few moments they would transfer her from the rescue's stretcher to a hospital gurney. Abe put the monitor on their stretcher, then went over to Maggie. "Don't worry. They're going to help you now."

A tear slipped from one of her eyes.

"Shhh. It's okay now," Abe said. "It's okay."

"Hey, kid?" Rasso called. "I'm leaving the run form here." He set the clipboard on the stretcher. "Going for a cup of coffee. Finish fillin' it out."

Abe bit his tongue.

"Don't you ride with Savage?" asked the RN, an amiable, middle-aged black woman. "She on vacation?"

"Yeah. She's pretty tough on me, but she's nothing like this guy."

The RN looked to the doorway where Rasso had just exited. "Not a happy man, is he?"

"Nope."

Fitzy slapped Abe's shoulder. "Let's let 'em work, son."

When he finished with the run form, Abe handed a copy to Charti, who sat at his Medic Controller station. As

Charti was about to make small talk, a shaken-looking Doe came walking toward them, towing a Firefighter-EMT-I named Timothy Avalty, who wore his trademark Buddy Holly glasses.

"How's Vivas doing?" Charti asked.

"Not so good," Doe answered, scratching his shaven head. "What'd you expect?"

Abe raised his gaze to Doe. "What happened?"

"Her ex got beat up and shot. Skull fracture. ICP. Bullet lodged in his chest. Shitty pressure. They hyperventilated and knocked out some of that CO_2 retention. They finally got him into surgery."

"Oh, man! Where is she now?"

"She's up there. But I wouldn't go say hi."

Rasso came up, blowing on his cup of coffee. He eyed Doe. "Hey, asshole. Nice haircut."

"Scumbag," Doe said with a terse nod, then left, trailing his temporary partner.

"Another one of your buddies?" Abe asked.

"Of course. Couldn't you see the love? We're out of here."

As Abe and Fitzy wheeled the stretcher and gear toward the ambulance doors, Abe said, "You ride in the back."

"Something bothering you?"

"I don't know."

They loaded the equipment and pulled out. Rasso sipped his coffee, disregarding the OSHA rules against food in rescue vehicles. "It's Sunday already," he mumbled.

Abe tightened his grip on the wheel. "I was wondering where Maggie's Percodan went. Bottle was full. Then Louderman pulls it out, and half the pills are missing."

The old medic did not flinch. "That bottle wasn't full."

"No, it was full. I saw it. It was right there on her

nightstand, right in my face. You put the bottles in her bag. You put the bag in the patient compartment."

"And you carried it into the hospital," Rasso added. "Now, kid," he began slowly, "if you're gonna accuse me of being a fuckin' thief, then accuse me of being a fuckin' thief. But if I were you, I wouldn't do that." He widened his eyes and leaned toward Abe. "That'd be unhealthy."

Abe took a deep breath, tried to calm himself. "I'm just making an observation. I'm not saying you took the pills. I'm saying it looks like you took the pills."

"You finished, Detective?"

"Yeah. No. There's another thing bothering me. You had to go and check the medicine cabinets in that girl's house."

"Yeah, I did. Funny how they say they took one thing, then you find an empty bottle of something else and, oh, yeah, I took that, too."

"You never said if you found anything."

"I didn't."

"I wonder what would happen if I went over there and asked them if they were missing any of their medications?"

Rasso's eyes narrowed to slits. "Go ahead. But if you keep making accusations like this, I'll have to talk to Martinez about a certain *probationary* medic."

Abe didn't reply. The diesel engine rumbled on. Streetlights blurred by. Drizzle struck the windshield. The dashboard clock lied about the time.

And Rasso took another sip of his coffee.

10

Vivas had said barely three words to Manny's parents, who sat across from her in the small waiting room. They spoke to one another in harsh whispers and occasionally threw a glare her way. Of course they had assumed that whatever had happened to Manny was her fault. No, they hadn't come out and said that, but questions like "Do you have a new boyfriend who might've been mad at Manny?" said enough.

Her cell phone rang. She leaned back, answered. "No, I haven't heard anything yet, Mama. No, he's still in surgery. No, I have no idea when he'll be out. Is my baby still sleeping? Good. Now don't you tell her anything, you hear me, Mama? I'll do that. You hear me? 'Bye."

Manny's father, a short, balding man with lips like tire tread and a gut fighting against his white T-shirt and polyester slacks, removed his bifocals. "So, Isabel, I see you're still driving the ambulance."

Every muscle in her body tightened. "Yes."

"Do you think you're spending enough time with our granddaughter?"

"Don't start with her, Raymond," said Manny's mother.

"You know how she is." Delores Nuva massaged her sore eyes, then adjusted her impeccable blouse for the tenth time. Why she remained with her slob of a husband, Vivas would never know. She removed her compact from her purse, checked her gray hair and makeup, then returned to her Bible—which the hypocrite obviously wasn't reading, because she held it upside down. She was, of course, too busy planning her next attack.

Vivas thought of dismissing Raymond's question, but Delores's "You know how she is" and her husband's scowl and remarks made her tremble with the desire to choke them. "I spend more time with my daughter than most people do with their children," she snapped. "I'm surprised you haven't asked about her until now. Is talking to me that hard?"

"Not at all," replied Raymond. "It's just a waste of time."

"Maybe if you learned a little tolerance. . . ."

"You're going to sit there and tell us to learn tolerance after what you've done to our son?" Delores asked. "I can't believe you even said that."

Vivas clutched the chair. "What did I do to your son?"

"You really want to know? Right now? At two in the morning, while my baby is . . . is lying up there, maybe dying?" Delores's eyes glassed over, and she bared her teeth in anger. "First you tell me what you told the police."

"That's confidential."

"That's my son!"

"Your perfect little son is not so perfect after all. And I don't know what really happened, but I don't think this is something random. No, it wasn't random at all."

"They took his money," Delores countered.

"Maybe they just wanted to make it look like a mugging. We both know why this happened—you just don't want to admit it. You can't deal with the fact that your son used to be in a gang. This has 'gang' written all over it."

Delores slammed her Bible on her thigh. "We can't deal with the fact that our son was tricked into a marriage by a woman who promised to be a mother and wife, then decided to drive an ambulance at all hours of the night. What kind of life is that?"

"I've seen the kind of women who are cops and medics," added Raymond. "And you know what? They don't even look like women. Our son wanted a wife, not a—"

"Not a what? Dyke? Lesbian? Butch? Go ahead, say it. You've been saying it for years. Maybe we should get it all out in the open—once and for all."

Raymond stood, worked a kink out of his back. "Isabel, you have no sense of tradition."

"You have no sense of reality. Maybe your wife cooked and cleaned, but that's not the way it is."

"We tried with you," he said, then waved a hand. "We're done."

"You tried?" She leaned back, held herself from cursing. "You never gave me a chance."

Detective Gerald, a VPD veteran who had questioned Vivas earlier, tentatively entered the waiting room. "Ms. Vivas? Can I talk to you outside?"

"We're his parents," hollered Delores. "You tell us, too."

"It's okay," Vivas told Gerald. "If Manny screwed up, then I want them to hear it."

"You mentioned that Manny loaned one of his friends some money, a guy named Paco. You said he worked with the guy."

"That's what Manny told me."

"Well, Paco was murdered yesterday morning."

"Oh, my God," cried Delores. "They killed one of Manny's friends, then they tried to kill him."

Vivas glanced disgustedly at her ex-mother-in-law, then faced the detective. "You don't think Manny did it. . . ."

"I can't tell you whether we do or we don't. I'm just wondering if he said anything else about Paco. I mean, even the littlest thing. And you're sure you've never seen a guy with a snake tattooed on his forehead?"

"No. And I told you everything Manny told me. The cousin. The auto parts. Where he lived. That's all I know."

"All right, then." He started out.

"My God, why us?" moaned Delores. "Why us?"

"Shut up," Raymond groaned. "And Isabel, you can go home. We'll take care of our son."

"He's my daughter's father. I'm staying."

"We know why you're staying," said Delores. "Don't pretend. We know Manny's been taking you out."

"He told you?" Vivas said, hoping to God that he had.

"No. I went over there to clean up that disaster. I heard your messages on his machine. I don't know what you think you're doing, but my son's trying to get back on his feet after a divorce that almost ruined him. I'm warning you, there's no way in hell that I'll let you hurt him again. And he's crazy if he thinks you and him will ever work out."

Vivas closed her eyes. "Maybe I am, too."

Although Stephanie Savage had called Isabel Vivas at 9 A.M. then at 2 P.M., and now at 4:30 P.M., the medic still wasn't home. Savage knew for a fact that Vivas was not working. Where the hell was she?

And . . . oh, my God. The first responder class. They

had changed this week's class to Sunday night. Tonight. Oh, my God! That was in thirty minutes. Savage stumbled into her bedroom, yanked open the closet door, took out a uniform, and tossed it on her bed. With a happy numbness, she pulled on her clothes. She tied her black work sneakers, then headed for the kitchen. Breath mints. Had to have breath mints. And she couldn't drive. No. She wouldn't be stupid. There was time to catch the bus.

She left her apartment and headed down to the corner to stand in the frigid air with a girl wearing a Wal-Mart smock and a skinny kid in an expensive leather jacket who had a blond, European look about him. The bus arrived.

I'm smart, Savage thought. *I know what I am. I'm smart.* Somebody had to pat her on the back for not driving.

It had been a long time since she had taken public transportation. And it was, after all, very public. Why people kept staring at her, she wasn't quite sure. Couldn't be the uniform; they had seen it before. She offered the old lady in the seat across from her a breath mint. No, Grandma didn't want one. The kid in front didn't want one either. Unfriendly bastards.

When the bus reached her stop, she almost didn't get off. Fortunately, she had told the old lady where she was going, and the woman had reminded her. Grandma looked almost happy to see Savage go.

The walk across the college campus took way too long because there was definitely something wrong with her shoes; she kept tripping. At least she didn't fall, and reached the classroom about ten minutes late. George Solaris was out in the hallway, dancing with one of the CPR dummies as two women from the class sipped coffee and watched him, hardly amused.

Savage gave George a stern look, then went inside. Only seven or eight students were present. The rest were milling about the hallway, waiting for their instructor. Where the hell was Tony? Oh, that's right. He was off. What the hell were they covering tonight? Better check the syllabus. Shit! Tony had those.

Maybe I can wing it.

She scanned the bored-looking crowd as the last few students wandered in. George tangoed into the room, drawing a laugh or two before planting a fat, wet kiss on his plastic partner. He laid her to rest along with her sisters behind the teacher's desk, then took a bow and a seat in the front row.

"Okay," Savage began. "Let's review."

George raised his hand.

"What?"

He motioned her closer.

"What?"

"You got something right here," he said, pointing to the corner of his mouth. "Looks like tomato sauce or something."

"Thanks," she said, then lowered her head and wiped her face. "Okay. Can anyone tell me the proper way to immobilize someone's cervical spine?"

They looked blankly at her.

"How do you secure someone to a long backboard? How about that?"

Vacant stares.

"What's the matter with you people? You got no memories? Don't you understand that we're talking about life and death? Don't you understand that this isn't some bullshit class you gotta take? You could save someone's life. You could be the first person on a scene, and you never know what you're going to walk into. You could be in some shithole that looks like it should've been condemned years ago and find people living there. And maybe one of them is counting on you to save her life. Maybe she's just a little girl. Maybe she's the one who called 911 because she needs you to save her life. And you won't know what to do because YOU DIDN'T PAY ANY FUCKIN' ATTENTION IN FIRST RESPONDER CLASS!"

"I'm sorry," said the old lady in the back, but I have been paying attention, and I resent that language."

George raised his hand.

"Your question can wait," she said, then focused her attention on the old lady. "You resent that language? Then why don't you shut me up and answer the questions?"

"Pssst," George stage-whispered.

"I told you to wait," Savage said, pointing a finger.

"If we had covered that material, I'd be able to answer that question," said the old lady. "But we haven't. Maybe my memory's not what it used to be, but I have notes."

"We haven't covered c-spines?" Savage took a step back to sit on the desk.

She sat.

The desk was farther back than she thought. Down she went.

Laughter erupted from the cops and firefighters in the back. The ceiling collapsed. The lights turned to liquid. Then a face materialized from it all. Wide eyes. Concern. "Steph? Steph?"

She looked at George, then took his hand. For a skinny guy, he did pretty well getting her up. "What happened?" she asked.

"The breath mints ain't working," he said softly. "You are so drunk that it's not even funny." He turned back to face the class. "Uh, Steph's not feeling real good right now. Let's take a break."

A few people in the back rushed for the door while others murmured and shook their heads. Savage thought she heard the word "drunk" at least twice. *Oh, Jesus. What did I do?*

George guided her toward the chalkboard as a few of the firefighters gathered around. "It's okay," George said. "She'll be all right."

"Maybe we should assess her," said one fireman sarcastically. "Airway, breathing, and circulation—just like we were taught."

"C'mon, Steph. Let's go outside." George guided her past the firefighters and toward the door.

"This is ridiculous," said someone.

"No, it's just really, really sad."

Savage ran a hand along the wall to steady herself as they left the classroom. "I'm okay now," she said. "I'm all right. Leave me alone."

"We're just going outside to talk," George insisted.

"Talk about what?"

"About you."

He hurried her toward the end of the hall, then pulled her around the corner, where they stopped. "Stephanie, why did you come like this?"

"Like what?"

"Come on, you're drunk."

"I had a couple of beers."

George smiled sadly. "How big were those beers?"

She looked at him. That was the kind of question she often asked drunk drivers. "George, get out of my face."

"You can't go back in there. Everybody knows."

She shoved him, lost her balance, groped for the wall.

"Why do you care? Just get out of here. Drop this class. Get out of my face."

"I know I got a problem when it comes to hospitals and medics and all that. I'm a psycho. But I got this new therapist, and I'm working on it. I don't know what your problem is, but you're obviously self-medicating yourself with alcohol. I got a car. I'll take you home. Is there someone we can call? That Tony guy? Maybe he can come in and teach tonight?"

Savage threw her head back against the wall. "Oh, God! This is gonna get out."

"It already is out. And you know what? That's what you wanted. That's why you came."

"I could lose my job."

"We'll get you out of here. You just tell them you were sick. That's all. I'll try to cover for you. I mean, I owe you, right? How many times did you try to help me?"

"I'm not driving with you."

"Then we'll call a cab. You got any money?"

She started for the classroom. "I can't do that. I have to get back in there and teach."

"Stephanie, you don't know what you're doing," he said, blocking her path. "Come on. Let's go."

It all hit her suddenly. Donny. The thing. Their marriage. His quitting school. Her ex-husband. Her life. Her lip quivered. Tears fell.

"I'm getting you out of here," George said, then grabbed her wrist.

Once his shift had ended, Doe had driven straight from the firehouse to Geneva's apartment. She had opened her door a crack and had said that she needed "time." Doe had asked her how much "time." She said she wasn't sure, and had told him to go away. He had taken himself and his extra time back home. The shift had drained him, so he had decided to sleep away the rest of his Sunday. At about 7 P.M., the phone wrenched him from a great dream in which he had been windsurfing off the coast of Hawaii. When he answered, a breathy female said, "Tuba's. Eight o'clock. See you there." She hung up before he could tell her no. He had forgotten to get her phone number, and he didn't have caller ID. The best thing to do was go to Tuba's, look her squarely in the eye, then tell her he was involved and not to call again.

But if the meeting would be a simple blowoff, then why was he spending so much time picking out clothes? Why had he bothered to shower and shave? Why had he made sure to wear the cologne he knew she liked?

I will do the right thing. Okay, a little flirting could happen. Hey, I'm a guy, right? But I'm not going to let her control me. Never again.

"Nicole, if I were single, this might be a different story," he thought aloud. "But I'm really involved. I'm going to be a father." He shook his head. "That won't work. She'll say something like, 'If you're so involved, then why did you come?' And I'll tell her that I want to get things straight. And she'll turn that into something sexual and, oh, damn. . . ."

He pocketed his wallet, scooped up his keys, and, feeling as though he should bless himself, set the alarm and left.

By the time Doe reached Tuba's, a sizable knot had formed in his stomach. He checked his watch as he entered the club: eight o'clock, right on time. He glanced up at dozens of silver, white, and brass tubas hanging from the walls and looking for all the world like great mouths threatening to swallow unsuspecting drinkers. The place was owned by a famous jazz musician whose name Doe had forgotten. Every night at closing time, the guy came out and played a solo on his tuba, a sad song that, according to him, would remind you of the "beauty and horror of your own mortality." Deep shit. Not for Doe. He wove his way past one of the bars in the back, heading for his usual stool at the end of a second bar near the VIP lounge. No sign of the target female.

"You think you can just come in here and take that seat?" asked the bartender, a guy of about thirty-five with bushy black hair and an even bushier beard. "You think I'm going to serve you a greyhound like you're a king or something?" the bartender added, pouring Doe's drink. "You barely come in anymore, then you show up, and we're supposed to be friends? What's the problem? You got a pregnant girlfriend who won't let you out?"

Doe put a finger to his lips. "Actually, Jimmy, I'm here to meet someone so I can—"

"But didn't you say you were done with the singles scene? I should've known she couldn't keep a leash on you." Jimmy tossed a cardboard coaster on the bar, then lowered Doe's drink. "But you know what? You're not getting any younger. And she sounded like a real nice girl. And you got the kid on the way. . . ."

"I'm not gonna cheat on her. I just have to put an end to something else."

"I know her?"

"Yeah, you do. It's Nicole."

"Nicole? I thought she went east."

Doe winced. "She's back."

"But she dumped you. So now she wants you? Fickle bitch. Some of them figure out that your pot belly and empty wallet really don't matter. Just takes 'em too long, right? The grass ain't greener."

"You're a poet, Jimmy. So, how am I gonna lose Nicole?"

"You tell her I want her."

"Oh, that'll make her forget about me, Mister Married with Three Kids and Working Two Jobs. And you're the one with the gut and the maxed-out credit cards."

"Easy, now." Jimmy winked, then tapped his wedding ring. "You're forgetting the thrill of the hunt. I'm taboo. They all want me." He shifted down the bar to serve another patron.

Two girls at a table in the VIP lounge giggled, then one bit the other's earlobe. They caught Doe staring, and he quickly turned his head. He hoped there were no lonely divorcees who had fixed him in their sights and would come over and tell him about their hysterectomies or how their fathers died last year or how all they had in the world were their mothers and sisters. Some women would go from "Hi" to the most intimate details in a matter of seconds.

"Playing with your stick again?" Nicole asked, sliding onto the stool next to his.

Doe dropped his stirrer. "Hey."

"God damn it, Jimmy, you're still here?" Nicole asked, all flashing eyes, damp hair, and perfume far more intoxicating than the vodka in Doe's glass.

"I've been waiting for you, sweetheart," Jimmy said, putting his hand on hers. "And now you sound a little like a New Yawka."

"Can't help it."

"Still drinking those frozen margaritas?"

"Damn, this guy's got a good memory," Nicole said, nudging Doe. "Let's do strawberry."

And Doe knew that Jimmy would slice a few whole

strawberries and slide them onto the rim of her glass—because he liked to watch her eat them.

"I can't stay long," Doe blurted out.

"I was hoping we'd have a couple of drinks, get a little tipsy, then we could go back to my place." Her expression grew serious. "You can spank me for dumping you."

Doe shook off the image. "Nicole, don't talk to me like that."

"Like what?" She turned on her innocent schoolgirl face and bit her fingernail. "You mean I can't talk about all the different ways we used to do it? Like when you hung me upside down from that—"

"No, you can't. And you think that's getting to me, but it isn't. It just sounds . . . I don't know. We're just not who we were."

"Oh, I forgot. You're still mad at me for leaving. I can kiss and suck and make it better—if you'll let me." She put her hand on his hip, stuck her finger deeper into her mouth.

He removed the hand. "I have a girlfriend. It's serious. I came here because I wanted to tell you that. You can't be leaving messages on my machine."

"Well, why didn't you tell me about this girlfriend the other day?"

"It was an MVA. I was in a rush."

"You could've told me, but you didn't. And all of a sudden, I feel sorry for your girlfriend because you're sitting here and wanting me, and you're just afraid to admit it. You'll finally come around, but not until after you put her through an emotional nightmare."

"Like the one you put me through?"

She leaned toward his ear. "Maybe you think I'm too confident, but I know you, Doe. I know you more than any other woman you've ever had. I know what you love and what you hate. I know your fears. I know your dreams. There's no one else who can compete with that."

He closed his eyes. "But you left."

"I was stupid. I'm sorry. It just happened. Maybe I forgot that you and I are the same. That's why we belong together. I guess I thought I could fight it by leaving. But I couldn't—just like you can't fight it now." She breathed heavily into his ear. "Don't fight."

He hung there in balance. Fight. Don't fight. Her voice sounded so good. But she lied. She always lied. He jerked back and guzzled his drink. "This is nuts."

"Is it really?"

"What happened to you in New York?"

She smiled at Jimmy as he brought over her drink. "New York?" She took a sip and shrugged.

"You didn't come back just because you felt like it or because you wanted to start something with me. I'm just your entertainment. You're here because something happened there. And you know why I know? Because I know you."

Nicole found great interest in her drink. "New York was . . . different. But you don't want to hear about it. You want to find out once and for all if there's anything left between us. And maybe you're pissed off at your girlfriend for whatever reason—maybe she knows about me—whatever, and you want to vent some anger by proving to yourself that you still got what it takes. You want to show her that you're still a man."

"I don't need to do that."

"You're doing it right now."

He slid off his stool. "Well, now that we understand each other, sort of, I gotta go." He pulled a few bills from his wallet, set them on the bar. "I got yours."

"Where are you going? Home? To sit around? Be

bored? Why don't you just stay here? I promise I won't talk dirty."

"I can't."

Out in the parking lot, Doe reached for his car door.

"Hey, wait a minute," Nicole called. She came over to him, gasping, her eyes glassing over, her voice cracking. "Did I hurt you that much?"

He just looked at her. If she didn't know by now. . . .

"Come on, Doe. Stay." She tugged his arm. "We haven't even caught up. I owe you a round."

"Sorry." He moved to unlock his door, but she wrestled the keys from his hand. As he turned to face her, she shoved the keys down the front of her tight jeans and into her panties. "I can't let you go."

Doe scanned the parking lot. A security guard stood near the building, and yes, he would see Doe strangling the poor, "innocent" woman. He thrust out his palm. "Come on, Nicole."

"Come and get them."

"Don't tempt me."

"What's the matter? Not man enough? I thought so. See you." She turned back toward the bar.

He watched her a second, then rushed up, slid an arm around her waist, and dug into her jeans. She broke into hysterical laughter as he finally rescued the keys.

"Oops. Big mistake." She whirled out of his grip, seized his shoulders, and brought her lips very close to his. He closed his eyes, and . . . and . . . damn it, let it happen.

I've been having *sex with a security guard. Still no word
from Mom, but now her number has been disconnected.
Should I call the police? Should I try to find Drew again?*

"Dr. Boccaccio?"

She looked up from the chart in her hand. A despondent
Isabel Vivas stood there in rumpled jeans and sweatshirt.
"Izzy, any news?"

The paramedic sighed. "Manny's still in a coma. I just
wonder if there is anything else they can do."

"Manny was in some very capable hands. Dr. Masaki's
worked a lot with GSWs."

"Yeah, I keep bringing in patients for him to practice
on. So, do you have a minute?"

Boccaccio glanced to exam room 2, which was open.
"Come on. I know you need a sympathetic ear."

Vivas smiled. Barely. "So you've met my in-laws."

"I didn't want to say anything." Boccaccio closed the
door. "They, uh, really love their son."

"And really hate me."

Boccaccio sighed. "It's the old story. Mommy's little

boy. No girl is ever good enough. I only talked to them for a minute, but they seem . . . pretty traditional."

"You got that right. But what's weird is they don't have a huge problem with female doctors, just paramedics. It's like they think I'm doing a man's job."

"Which is funny, because females are natural caregivers."

"Tell them that."

"Think about it. If a man stays home to raise children, other men think he's emasculated. Mr. Mom doesn't cut it with them. I heard we're living in a progressive society, but those traditions die hard."

"I'd love to find a way to kill them." She snorted. "The traditions, I mean. Anyway, I don't really want to talk about his parents." She leaned on the exam table. "It's my daughter. I still haven't told her. My mom's been driving me crazy. She says we have to let Consuela know, but I'm not sure how she'll take it. I'm really worried about that."

"What did the social worker say?"

"She said that it's better I tell her now, in case something worse happens. At least she'll have time to prepare, though I don't know if little kids even do that. She said it won't come as such a shock."

"But you're scared."

"Yeah. And I'm sick of all this. Sick of the city, sick of all the bullshit. They say it takes something like this to wake you up. Well, I'm awake."

"Bad things happen to good people. You know the rules."

"Remember a few weeks ago when you told me that I can't do this job for my daughter? You said she can't be the reason why I'm a paramedic? Well, you're right. And now with Manny getting hurt, I'm running out of reasons for being here."

"I don't get it. How does what happened to Manny make you want to quit being a medic?"

"It's just this place. I need to slow down. Both of us do. Maybe head north. Find some small town. Get work. Raise our family the right way."

"Wait. You're going to run away? Stay home and cook and clean?"

"I don't know. There's nothing wrong with that. You find ways to make it fulfilling, I guess. Maybe I can work part-time or volunteer." She laughed under her breath. "Listen to me. It sounds like I'm ready to get back together with him. Maybe I won't have that chance."

Boccaccio gazed intently at her friend. "Going up north and settling down? That's not you, Izzy. You'll never last. You're a firefighter. You're a medic. And you need to be here. You need to remember what drew you to the job in the first place. If you can remember that, maybe you won't give up. I'm saying this 'cause I'd miss you."

"Thanks."

"Well, you need to tell Consuela. Right now, I have a little boy who got beat up at school and a resident who's not exactly good with kids. When I get a chance, I'll come up to the ICU."

They stepped into the hall, and Vivas left. Medic Controller Charti Darunyothin came over and drummed a knuckle on his notebook. "Dr. Boccaccio, I have something for you."

"Doesn't sound good. Maybe you should keep it."

"Not this. I know you were trying to find your mother's friend in Vegas. He worked in a casino, but you couldn't find the right one."

"Yeah, sorry about that, Charti. I was just venting. That's my stress, not yours."

"I know, but it's been kind of slow around here, so I got this really comprehensive list of casinos on the Internet."

"You did what?"

"I know, I know. But it's not like anyone found out. Far as the nurses were concerned, I was trying to track down a patient's relative."

She wanted to curse but held herself. "Charti, I didn't ask you to do that, and I don't want you doing anything."

"I promise I won't do it again. But you seemed kind of upset, and I knew I could help you. Anyway, I found him."

"Drew?"

"Yeah. I got the casino and his office number." He tore a page from his book.

"Damn! All right. Can you get Marsha to help Riteman in Exam 1? Tell her I just need her to cover for a couple of minutes."

"You got it." He rushed off.

"Charti? Thanks." Boccaccio thumbed on her cell phone, then slipped back into the exam room. She dialed the number, waited, then a familiar voice with a thick accent came over the line. "Drew?"

"Yes? Who is this?"

"It's Joanna Boccaccio."

"Oh, hi, Joanna. I think maybe I should have called you, but your mother, she tell me no, no, no."

"Drew, what's going on? I've being trying to get a hold of my mother for weeks. I leave messages. She doesn't return my calls. Now her phone's been disconnected."

"Your mother, she's very . . . she got very upset with me, and maybe she thought that me and her were no good."

"You broke up?"

"Yeah, it was only a few days after we come back from visiting you."

"Did she move?"

"Joanna, I don't know."

"So exactly why did you break up? I mean . . . well, I'm not sure what I mean."

"The last time I talk with her, she say maybe she go back to L.A. That's all. I don't hear from her since then. Maybe she's near you."

Rosemary Boccaccio had spent the last eight days at the Motel Six just five minutes from her daughter's apartment. She had barely spoken to anyone since coming to Los Angeles to put distance between herself and Drew. They had been so good together, but then he had found her bank statements and had learned that she was broke. All right, so she had lied to him about how much money she had had, figuring that once she had him, she would ease him into the truth. She had drained most of her excess cash by getting plastic surgery for him, and then the bastard had left her. She kept telling herself that she was better off without him—but without him, she felt so . . . old.

Why had she come back to L.A.? Just to put distance between herself and Drew? Or did she need her daughter's help? No. She felt bad about how she had left it with Joanna, but her daughter had become so conceited and so caught up in her job that Rosemary could barely stand to be around her. How dare her own flesh and blood have a holier-than-thou attitude, and judge her clothes and choice of men? How dare the little bitch?

Eight days in L.A., and all Rosemary had accomplished was a few visits to the supermarket and a single visit to a private physician, who, like the rest of them, prescribed antidepressant medication. She had even managed to have the prescription filled, but the bottle of pills sat in her purse, untouched until now. She had sworn that she would not poison her body with chemicals that would do little more than make her fat. Wasn't there some way to be happy?

Joanna had found a way. Rosemary had followed Joanna in her rental car and had watched her daughter leave a shopping mall with a young security guard. In fact, she had been following her daughter for several days now, just watching, waiting, thinking, trying to decide if she should make contact, trying to decide where she belonged in the world.

Twice she had been stopped on the street by VPD officers. So maybe her dress was a little trashy. That didn't make her a real tramp. Besides, you had to give the young men what they wanted: big tits and tight underwear and high heels. But for some reason, they had not noticed. Well, there had been that one short, fat guy who had stopped her outside the supermarket and had asked for oral sex. One good scream had sent him running.

What was that achy, burning sensation in her stomach? Oh, yes, the pills, washed down with a little booze. Was that really them? Or maybe the burning wasn't real. She staggered out of the motel room and into the gloom and rain. She clicked across the parking lot, toward a gas station on the corner. Car horns blared. Those drivers loved her heels, bra, and panties. Old broad or not, they loved her. She had found them, and felt so young now. She looked at the man holding the gasoline nozzle. A kid, really. Dimples. Really great dimples. She smiled. He did, too. She wiped rain from her eyes, saw mascara smeared across her knuckles. *Damn it*!

"Yo, you all right?"

Who had said that? Not the kid. She craned her head. Another young guy. Handsome. Man in a uniform. Little 76 logo on his breast. Had to love that. He frowned, but probably still wanted her.

"Hi," she said in her most seductive voice.

"Lady, you're—"

He stopped talking. Why? Oh, she was on the concrete, with her head throbbing and the rain coming down so hard that she closed her eyes. It all felt so good now. Her heart beat faster and faster. The rain washed her clean and took her back to those baths as a child, all those baths that made her feel fresh and new, alive with possibilities. One little girl had been reborn.

"Engine Nine, Rescue Nine. Engine Nine, Rescue Nine. Female down. Possible code. Seventy-Six gas station. One-seven-nine-nine-eight Isla Avenue. Cross street Inca. Time out, eleven nineteen."

Rasso glanced sidelong at Abe as they rumbled away from Valley General's ambulance entrance.

"What?" Abe asked.

"Oh, so you've learned your lesson? You're letting me run the mike?"

Abe widened his gaze on the radio. "You'd better get that."

With a groan, Rasso acknowledged the dispatcher.

The rain came down harder, and the wind pitched it toward the rescue like a major leaguer with a bad attitude. Abe leaned into the wheel and tried to concentrate. The wipers squeaked. There were few things worse than code 3 driving; one was code 3 driving in bad weather, and another was code 3 driving in bad weather when you had barely slept for two days.

He could thank Rasso for the insomnia. The guy might

very well be stealing drugs, then taking them himself or selling them. Abe still couldn't prove anything, and his frustration turned him further in on himself. Lisa had wanted to help, and once again, he had thrown up the wall. If she figured out what to do, then maybe he wasn't qualified to be a medic. He needed to handle every situation, and he had to do it alone. Sure, Savage had taught him to depend on your partner because you're so much more powerful as a well functioning team. But it didn't work that way with Rasso. He gave orders. You listened. He did as little as he could and bitched about everything. Bottom line? Abe did not have a partner, and maybe he needed one in Lisa. Maybe talking to her wouldn't be a sign of weakness but would make him stronger. She had been so understanding. He had even asked her why she put up with him, and she had said that she could appreciate how stressful his job was, and that if he needed time, he had it. If he wanted to talk, she'd listen. So why not just tell her? Was it really his ego in the way? Or was he still trying to protect her? He knew his brooding would eventually drive her away. But he worried that if she really learned who he was, she wouldn't just leave—she'd run.

On Monday, Abe had considered going to Samantha Tannenhill's house and asking the girl's parents if they were missing any medications. But what was he supposed to say? "Hi, I think my partner might be a dealer or a junkie, and he may have stolen prescription medication from your house"? Even if the Tannenhills were willing to talk, Abe assumed that they'd get law enforcement involved, which might ruin Rasso's reputation and definitely would ruin Abe's career, because the old man was certainly capable of vengeance. Abe needed hard evidence. Simple as that. Maybe Rasso wasn't selling, and was just addicted to painkillers. Maybe his problem wasn't that bad. But could Abe take that chance? He could send an anonymous tip to Lieutenant Martinez, but that wouldn't fool Rasso.

So Abe would now probe his FTO for faults and worry that the old man might screw up so badly that it would cost both of them their jobs. It was an ironic turn of events: the student scrutinizing the teacher.

"Female down," sang Rasso. "Possible code. Possible nothing. Maybe she got hit by a car. Maybe she fell out of a building. Maybe she slipped on the wet concrete and banged her head. Maybe the MI came on when she saw the gas prices. Maybe she"—he checked the cross street—"clear right. Maybe she's having a baby. Maybe she got raped and escaped from the van while the guy was getting gas. Maybe she— "

"You mind? It's not like I'm driving a rig code 3 or anything."

"What's the matter, kid? You can't do that . . . what the hell they call it? Multitasking, that it? You can't multi-task?"

"Did you steal that old lady's pills?"

Rasso checked the next cross street. "You're clear."

Abe waited. Waited some more. "Did you hear— "

"I heard the question," Rasso barked. "You've been waiting all morning to ask that, huh? Sitting there in the day room, looking at me, wondering if I'm working with some dealer or addict, wondering what you should do."

"That's right."

"And now you come to the point where you just can't take it anymore. Well, you know what, Abe? Too fuckin' bad."

Abe squeezed the wheel until it hurt. "You owe me an answer."

"What is it with me owing you? One day you'll be sitting in this seat and telling some snotnose the same shit."

"I doubt that."

"Tell you what, kid. I don't wanna hear another accusation come out of your mouth. You mention that lady's pills again, and it's gonna be a very long shift."

"It must hurt."

"What?"

"Carrying around all that anger. It must hurt."

Rasso played with the siren.

Abe missed the entrance to the gas station and wound up slamming over the curb. Rasso swore and clutched his neck. Of course the gas station had the requisite quickie mart, and Abe parked the rescue between it and the pumps. Their victim lay about five yards away. Two attendants from the station knelt beside her. They had placed a small umbrella over her head. Judging from her lack of clothes, unnaturally firm bosoms, and proximity to a motel, she was probably a hooker who had been beaten and robbed. Not an uncommon call—especially during lunch hour.

"Rescue Nine is on scene," reported Rasso.

TRO Six echoed, "Rescue Nine."

Abe gloved up, then hesitated.

"Ah, shit," Rasso moaned, "now we get wet. And what're you waiting for?"

"What equipment should I take? I don't want to set up an ER out there."

Rasso smiled painfully. "Shuddup and move."

"You're like a father to me," Abe muttered as he left the cab and jogged to the back of the rescue. He grabbed the airway bag and slipped twice before reaching Rasso, who was already questioning one of the attendants.

"She came walking out of that motel over there and just collapsed," said the skinnier attendant. "She had this." He handed over a plastic prescription bottle.

"Well, they come in threes," Rasso said, then handed Abe the bottle.

"Threes . . . ," Abe mumbled as he read the label. Mental images of Brian's suicide in that bathroom and the stricken expression on Samantha Tannenhill's face burned anew. The woman had been prescribed Adepril, a brand name for amitriptyline, an antidepressant with sedative effects. She may very well have tried to kill herself with her antidepressant medication. Sounded ironic. Was all too common.

Because Rasso had no intention of kneeling on the wet pavement, Abe dropped to his knees and moved the woman's head in the chin-lift, head-tilt maneuver. Her airway looked clear. He checked for breath sounds, though the rain and cars splashing through puddles made them nearly impossible to hear. He observed her chest and tried to feel her breath on his ear. Nothing. He grabbed her wrist for a radial pulse and blood pressure estimate. No pulse. He checked her neck for the carotid pulse. Nothing there. "Full arrest," he told Rasso, then checked her eyes. "Pupils fixed and dilated."

"If it looks like an OD and it acts like an OD, I'm thinking—and this is genius work here—it's an OD," Rasso said.

"High overdoses of this stuff can cause temporary confusion, disturbed concentration, or transient visual hallucinations. Hypothermia, tachycardia, and other arrhythmic abnormalities like bundle branch block are also on the list."

"You read that off a cereal box, Junior?"

"I have a lot of this stuff memorized because—"

"I'm not listening," Rasso sang, heading back to the rescue. He opened both doors. "Start CPR."

"Yeah." Abe had just wanted to prove that he was familiar with the drug, but his timing had been way off.

Rasso glanced at the attendants. "You guys direct traffic to those far pumps until the cops arrive. Can you handle that?"

They nodded.

In the meantime, Abe placed a collapsible pocket mask over the woman's face. He gave two slow breaths into the mask's valve to make her chest rise. After that, he checked for a pulse. Still none. He scooted around to begin compressions. Fifteen compressions, two breaths. He completed the first fifteen, then grabbed the woman's legs, while Rasso slid his arms through her armpits. They lifted her from the pavement and hustled her over to the rescue. Rasso gingerly stepped backward, up, and into the rig. They placed her on the stretcher, and Abe immediately resumed CPR, grimacing at the smell of urine.

"All right," Rasso mumbled. "Now that we got her in our office, let's see if we can bring her back." He dried the woman's chest with some towels, then applied the cardiac monitor's pancakelike electrodes. Once again, Abe checked for a pulse. Nothing.

Back to the mask now. As Abe finished his next pair of breaths, the woman's rhythm came up on the monitor: ventricular tachycardia, v-tach. No doubt about it. A rapid and lethal rhythm that, on the readout, resembled a tight series of peaks and valleys. Only a shock to her heart would get her back.

"Okay, let's hit her with two," Rasso said. "Clear."

Abe made sure no part of him touched the woman's

body. Her back arched a bit as 200 joules of electricity went to work. "No conversion," Abe said.

"I can read," Rasso spat. "Giving her three. Clear."

Engine Nine rumbled into the gas station, and with its whining diesel engine added to the rescue's, to the rain, to the traffic, it felt as though two great hands of noise were reaching into the patient compartment and pressing on Abe's ears. He eyed the monitor. The woman's rhythm had not changed. This time Abe kept his mouth shut and minded his compressions and ventilations. The stench of urine grew stronger.

"One at 360," Rasso said, then wiped rain from his droopy eyes. "Clear."

"Damn it," Abe muttered after the shock did nothing.

Rasso, who had hunkered down near the monitor, stood and reached for the rescue's mike.

"What are you doing?"

"I'm calling for a doc."

"We're not done working on her."

"Come on, she probably took the whole bottle. What is she? Mid-to-late fifties? She's as DRT as they get."

"The practice parameter for pulseless v-tach has twelve steps. You're giving up after three?"

"Hey, fellas," said Fitzy, leaning into the rescue. "What can we do?" Behind him stood Cannis and Tenpenney.

Abe held his gaze on Rasso, who looked at him, then at the woman, the monitor, the other firefighters.

Finally, Rasso rolled his eyes. "Okay, kid. Tube her. Cannis? You get in here and start a line."

"Thank you." Abe added a curse under his breath, then dug frantically through the airway bag, pulled out the tube, stylet, and laryngoscope. He opened the packages, inserted the stylet into the tube, then positioned the woman's head. He moved her tongue aside with the scope, visualized her vocal cords, and inserted the tube. As he did that, Fitzy shifted in tight beside the stretcher and took it upon himself to ready the oxygen tank, the Ambu bag, and the Tube Tamer to secure the tube to the woman's face.

That completed, Abe attached the Ambu bag, then checked with his stethoscope for good placement. Breath sounds on the right and left. He and Fitzy finished securing the tube as Cannis bitched about not finding a vein in the woman's arms.

"Give me that," Rasso said, taking the 18-gauge needle from Cannis. He shouldered his way between Fitzy and Abe, turned the woman's head to one side, and jammed the needle into her external jugular vein, establishing the IV right there.

"That was going to be my last resort," said Cannis.

"Hey, kid, a vein's a vein—and this one's so big you could drive a truck into it. Finish up." Rasso shooed Abe out of the way and lowered himself into the captain's seat behind the stretcher. From there he would direct the whole procedure like an unmotivated Ahab.

Cannis, still a little dumbfounded, attached the tubing and secured the line in place with a Veni-Gard. Fitzy shifted in tight beside the stretcher and took over on the Ambu bag. Abe went to the drug box for a preloaded syringe of epinephrine 1:10,000. He found the syringe and delivered a milligram of the drug into the woman's IV line.

That done, Rasso called clear. They shocked the woman once more at 360.

"Well, well," said Fitzy, his eyes riveted on the monitor, which now showed that the woman's rhythm had converted to a sinus tach of 140. "The old girl's bouncing back."

"Spoke too soon," Abe said, glancing to the monitor. "Back to v-tach."

"A hundred of lido?" Cannis asked Rasso.

The old man shrugged. "It's the county's money. And now that we're committed, you might as well."

Once Cannis had injected the drug into the woman's IV, they shocked her once more at 360. No conversion.

Cannis regarded Rasso. "How 'bout another hundred?"

"Don't ask him. Just do it," Abe whispered.

"You wanna get more lido on board?" Rasso said, honing his sarcasm. "Get more on board. Then we'll pump her with bretylium and mag, and we'll keep shocking her until our battery burns out or our shift ends—whichever comes first. That make you happy?"

Cannis eyed his equipment. "Hey, man, I just asked a question."

A VPD unit came up behind the rescue and drew Rasso's attention. Tenpenney jogged back to update the officers.

"Okay," Cannis said after a minute. "The lido's in. Ready on the monitor?"

Rasso nodded, waited, then received the okay to shock the woman again. "Clear."

Cannis jerked his head away from the monitor. "Shit."

Abe shook his head. "She's in v-fib."

"Of course she's in v-fib," said Rasso. "That's where she was headed all along."

After glancing at his watch, Abe grabbed another pre-loaded syringe of epi from the drug box. "I'll give her another round."

"And I'll shock her again," Rasso said tiredly.

Abe injected the drug. Rasso delivered the shock.

No change on the monitor.

"Okay, we hit her with 350 of bretylium," Abe said.

"Another shock. No conversion. Another 700. Then we move on to the mag."

"She's asystole," said Cannis, reading the flat line.

Rasso huffed. "I've had enough." He adjusted the frequency on the rig's radio. "SFMC, Rescue Nine, copy?"

"Rescue Nine, SFMC, go ahead," answered Charti Darunyothin.

"Request MCEP consult for cardiac overdose patient."

"Copy, Nine. Stand by."

"Why don't you wait until we finish?" asked Cannis.

Rasso leaned down to get in the younger medic's face. "We *are* finished."

Abe couldn't care less what Rasso said. He nodded to Fitzy, who continued his ventilations. Abe had never seen a miracle happen, but there was always a first time.

"Nine? This is Dr. Louderman. Copy?"

"Copy, Doctor. This is paramedic Vincent Rasso. We have an approximately fifty-five-year-old female who apparently overdosed on amitriptyline. Patient was found supine, unconscious, unresponsive. No breath sounds. No pulse. Initial reading indicated v-tach. We shocked her at 200, 300, and 360 without conversion. Intubated. Administered one milligram of epi IV push and shocked her again at 360." Rasso droned on and on, detailing the treatment they had administered, his tone growing more agitated as he concluded: "Finishing up third round of treatment via asystole practice parameter with no improvement."

"Copy that, Nine. Give her two of Narcan and an amp of bicarb. Follow with a megadose of epi, copy?"

"Copy," Rasso said, then repeated the orders.

Abe and Cannis prepared and delivered the drugs. The Narcan would bind the narcotics and reverse the effects, and the sodium bicarbonate would reverse the acid levels of her blood—not that either "improvement" would really help if her heart didn't start beating again.

"Administered two of Narcan, an amp of bicarb, and a megadose of epi," Rasso said. "Monitor shows asystole."

"Copy, Nine. Check her blood glucose. Copy?"

"This is bullshit," Rasso said, his thumb off the mike. "Now he's just covering his ass." He keyed the mike. "Copy. Checking blood glucose."

Cannis administered the test. The woman's level came back at 150.

"Still asystole on the monitor?" Louderman asked.

"Affirmative. Still asystole."

"Okay. Cease resuscitation efforts. Call time of death at twelve twenty-one."

"We got the order, gentlemen," said Rasso. "Let's clean up and get the coroner down here."

Fitzy stopped his ventilations and stared down at the woman. Abe joined him.

They come in threes.

"Hey, kid? Smell that? Wasn't just rain you were kneeling in." Rasso winked, then whirled to face one of the cops, who had hustled over from the motel.

Sure, Abe knew that cardiac patients often lost control of their bladders, and maybe he had knelt in the woman's piss and had been smelling his own pants, but at the moment, he didn't care. *I'll never be that cold. I'll never be that cold.*

"Got an ID," the cop told Rasso, who took one look at the woman's license and recoiled.

"What is it?" Abe said, getting to his feet.

"Look at that last name," said Rasso, handing him the license.

• • •

The young man had been shopping at his local hardware store when a display had collapsed on the distal portion of his right ring finger. He said he was a writer and was very concerned about his ability to type. Boccaccio sealed the laceration with glue, saved his career, and was just saying good-bye when Charti paged her to the radio.

"What now?" she mumbled, then left exam room 3 and trudged down the hall.

"It's Nine," said Charti from his Medic Controller station. "I was going to get Louderman, but they wouldn't talk to him anymore. Sorry."

"He just pronounced an OD for them, didn't he?" she asked, accepting the mike.

"Yeah. And Nine's probably still on scene."

"What? Do they want a second opinion? Give me a break."

"I don't know. They wouldn't say."

"Nine, SFMC. Dr. Boccaccio here. Copy?"

"Copy, Doctor. This is paramedic Vincent Rasso."

"Go ahead."

"Uh, do you know a Rosemary Boccaccio?"

Boccaccio flinched. "Yes, she's my mother."

Static. Then, "Stand by."

Back at the 76 station, Rasso lowered the portable. "Well, I know one doctor who's about to have a bad day."

"She'll find out one way or another," Abe said. "We should tell her. It'd be better than a call from some stranger. We worked on her mom. We were here when she died."

Rasso folded his arms over his chest. "Ain't our job."

"Look, I've only worked with her for a few weeks, but from what I've seen, she's a really good doctor and treats us pretty damned well. I say we should do this. If you don't want to, I will. I bet she'd appreciate it."

"Nine, you copy?" came Boccaccio's voice from the portable. "Did something happen to my mother? Nine, you copy?"

"SFMC, Nine here," said Rasso. "Stand by." He shrugged. "You wanna tell her? Tell her."

With the frequency already set on his portable, Abe keyed the mike. "Dr. Boccaccio? This is Paramedic Abe Kashmiri."

A level 1 trauma case was just coming into the ER, and Boccaccio strained to hear the radio above the commotion behind her. "Abe, is something wrong with my mother?"

"I'm very sorry, ma'am, but we just got an ID on our overdose patient. Name is Rosemary Boccaccio."

She fell against the counter. Charti sprang from his seat and grabbed her arm. *Mom? Mom was their patient? No. No way. But didn't Drew mention that....* "Say again, Nine?"

"Our patient was Rosemary Boccaccio. I'm looking at her license right now. Address is nineteen forty-four Alpine Avenue, Las Vegas, Nevada."

After the divorce, Boccaccio's mother had insisted on keeping her married name as a way to remind Joanna that it was her father who had "torn up the family."

"Doctor, do you copy?"

"Yeah. Jesus, yeah." She trembled violently and blinked off the oncoming tears. "Do me a favor, Abe? Transport her here. Please."

"We'll call for permission, ma'am. I'm sure it won't be a problem. I'll update you on our ETA en route. Nine, out."

"Dr. Boccaccio, I'm so sorry," said Charti. "I'm so sorry. If there's anything—"

"God damn it, there's nothing," shouted Boccaccio. "There's nothing at all." She tore free and ran toward the bathroom.

12

"Well, how about that? Another animal hospital gets robbed," Rasso said as the dispatcher called Rescue Seven to the scene. "Didn't Ten get the last call?"

"I think so," Abe answered, straining to see in the storm. The damned defroster was making that chugging noise again. He slowed toward a red light.

"These bangers got it all worked out. They set up their local lab to cook up their meth so they can bypass the big bosses in Mexico, and they make a few extra bucks with Special K. The boss here makes more in an hour than we'll make in a month."

"You sound jealous," Abe said.

"Don't fuck with me, kid. I know where you're going with that. I'm just making a comment—not dealing drugs."

Abe pushed his headset's microphone away from his mouth as the light turned green. He thought of poor Rosemary Boccaccio lying in the back of their rescue. She had taken a bottle of pills, had staggered half-naked into the rain, and had made it to a gas station, where she had collapsed on the filthy pavement. Because there had been witnesses to her fall and subsequent death, and no indications of foul play, a VPD sergeant—along with Lieutenant Martinez—had allowed Rasso and Abe to transport the body as a special favor to Dr. Boccaccio. Most of the time, a large metro fire service like Valley would not do that. The county medical examiner would investigate the scene and transport the body to the county morgue.

What a week! Too much death. Rasso had probably brought it with him, and Abe was supposed to deal with it. All the books gave you pointers on handling the dead and dying. You were supposed to familiarize yourself with the stages identified by Dr. Elisabeth Kübler-Ross. Patients began in denial, then moved on to the anger stage (why me?) until they began bargaining in an attempt to postpone death. Finally, they got depressed, worked through that, then accepted their fate—often before their families did. Of course, the process never went that smoothly, nor were the stages neat little categories. Sometimes patients experienced more than one stage at the same time, never advanced, or skipped a stage. There were no hard-and-fast rules when dealing with the families. You were, however, supposed to be alert to their needs, even while they screamed at you. You needed to listen with sympathy, never offer medical opinions beyond your scope, make good eye contact, and use a gentle voice—most of which ruled out Rasso as a candidate for consoling Dr. Boccaccio.

They reached one of SFMC's rear entrances, the one closest to the morgue. Abe jumped out and went to the back doors while Rasso spent half a minute getting out of the rig, muttering something about the rain and his back.

"Gotta love this weather," said the cop, a stocky black woman with a touch of gray, who had ridden with them to continue her death report.

"You serious?"

"You're too young to remember some of the real droughts we've had."

"Guess so." Abe unfastened the stretcher, then waited for Rasso to help him lower Rosemary Boccaccio to the concrete. They had covered her from head to toe in blankets. Before they even got her through the doors, Dr. Boccaccio rushed to them, with two RNs just behind. Boccaccio removed the blanket and chewed her lip as she stared at a face that, despite being decades older, closely resembled her own.

"All right, come on," said Rasso, waving the RNs out of the way. "No one needs a show. Let's get her to the morgue." He shoved the stretcher forward, and Abe glared at him as they rolled the body into a narrow, dimly lit hall festooned with pipes and broken by large, metal doors on which hung rusty warning signs. The only people who frequented this part of the hospital were maintenance personnel tending to the boilers and electrical systems. Ahead lay a service elevator.

Boccaccio stayed with the stretcher, keeping one hand on her mother's shoulder while one of the RNs did likewise on Boccaccio's shoulder. Though the doctor's eyes were swollen, she displayed remarkable control. "Why'd you cut off her pants?" she asked, her voice husky and broken.

"We didn't," answered Rasso, his tone even and anything but sympathetic. "Found her like this."

"The amitriptyline might've given her some hallucinations," Abe said, knowing all too well that Boccaccio was probably feeling as embarrassed as she was grief-stricken. Excuses might comfort her. "I'm really, really sorry. Whatever you need. Whatever I can do—"

"So she was unconscious, unresponsive when you found her? She didn't say anything?"

Abe shook his head.

"She spoke to one of the witnesses before she collapsed," Rasso said. "Told him hi, and that was it."

Boccaccio whispered the word: "Hi."

Once they were inside the elevator, the doctor stroked her mother's cheek. Her remarkable control began to falter.

Abe glanced to Rasso, who failed to hide his yawn. The two RNs kept close to Boccaccio, and she thanked them for coming.

Another doctor, the one who would perform the postmortem, was waiting outside the morgue's double doors. In her fifties, with dark hair razored short and graying at the roots, she slid an arm over Boccaccio's shoulder and took her inside, ahead of the stretcher. "Oh, Joanna. 'Sorry' just isn't enough. You stay with me now. We'll take care of her together."

Rasso took his hands off the stretcher. "I'll meet you out here."

That was odd. The cold stone should feel right at home in the morgue.

Thanks to George Solaris—son of the famous TV star, frequent flyer, and hospital fetish boy—Savage had made it home okay from her first responder class on Sunday evening. George had called for a cab and had even helped her all the way to her apartment.

When she had awakened the next afternoon, she had found a note from him saying that he hoped she felt better and that he had called Tony for her and had explained that she was sick. He had even left his number. With a shudder, she realized that he now knew where she lived and had even been inside her apartment. Angel? Weirdo? Savage wasn't sure, but she now owed him big time. And a semigood thing had happened on Monday. She had run out of beer and had been too weak to drag her ass down to the market, but thoughts of a drink had kept nagging at her. By nightfall, her thirst had driven her into the shower, into fresh clothes, and into the beer aisle. Two six-packs had turned Monday evening and most of Tuesday into a numbing blur.

Vivas still wasn't returning Savage's calls. What the hell was the matter with her? Savage thought of dropping by, but remembered that Vivas was working now. With a deep sigh, she aimed her remote at the TV, shut it off, then checked the kitchen clock. She had about an hour to kill before first responder class. She was about to get something to eat when the phone rang. It was Tony. He sounded funny.

"Yeah, Tony. Listen, I'm so sorry about Sunday. I think I got food poisoning or something. My equilibrium was off. I felt sick to my stomach. It was a real mess."

"I covered for you," he said. "And I have the rest of your classes covered. Steph, I'm sorry, but I don't think I'll need you right now."

"What? You're firing me?"

"It's nothing personal. I just have all the help I need."

"Bullshit! You were just telling me how so many people bail on you at the last minute. I'm the only one who's reliable."

"No, now you're one of those people who bail on me."

"I was sick."

"Really? Some of the students were saying that you didn't look sick. You looked . . . drunk."

"I wasn't drunk."

"Well, at this point, that doesn't matter. You know how

the rumors fly. And I can't have anyone working for me who has a problem. We'll let things cool down for a while. Then maybe in a couple of months, I'll bring you back."

"If you don't let me work now, it'll be even worse."

"Steph, I'm an old man. And I've been exactly where you are right now. You can't bullshit an old bullshitter, right? You got problems. You brought them to work. I can't have that. Sorry."

Ten minutes later, Savage hit the streets in her dying pickup. She couldn't sit alone in that damned apartment. Every time she passed a supermarket, she thought of stopping. *I'm not stupid enough to drive drunk. I'm not.*

She cruised by Fire Station Nine and repressed a chill as she wondered whether anyone there had learned about the first responder fiasco. Tony hadn't been lying when he said rumors fly, and Savage felt too nervous to stop and say hello to her colleagues. With a whole lot of free time to burn, she headed over to Fire Station Ten, hoping she would catch Vivas and Doe and find out why Izzy was avoiding her.

"No, Izzy isn't here," said Doe, seated in a recliner. He glanced up from his magazine. "Haven't you heard?"

Savage tensed. "Heard what?"

"Her ex got beat up and shot. He's over at San Fernando. She's been there since Saturday night."

"Oh, my God."

"Yeah," Doe said. "He's still in a coma. She's over there with his parents and his sister."

"I don't believe this. It always happens to the good people, right? Jesus, this is terrible."

"Yeah, it is. So I'm riding with Avalty here for this shift. They were talking about having Troft ride with me until Izzy gets back. That could still happen."

"If that happens, only one of you will come out alive."

"That's what I told Greenwell."

She checked her watch. "Well, I'm heading over to the hospital."

"Tell Izzy I said hi. Tell her we're all pulling for her."

"I will." She headed for the door.

"Hey, Steph, how're you doing?"

She froze. "I'm fine."

"You sure?"

"Yeah, I'm sure. Why?"

"Just asking."

She looked at him. Did he know? Should she ask him?

"Long vacation, huh?" he asked, breaking the tension.

"Yeah. Too long."

"Last time I was off for two weeks and didn't go away, I spent most of my time around here. You believe that?"

She nodded. "We don't just take our jobs home. They *are* home. And that's scary."

"Yup. Tell Izzy I'll be by in the morning."

"Okay. Maybe I'll see you next week," she said, then slipped into the cool, damp air.

Doe switched his gaze from the door to Avalty, whose thick glasses had slid down the bridge of his nose. "Glad you kept your mouth shut."

"She didn't sound drunk to me."

"She wasn't. But now Martinez will be gunning for her. I wonder what happened. Maybe something with her son. She's always talking about him."

The alarm went off.

"Finally," Doe said, then listened to the call: a female down, shots fired. "Let's go, buddy. Hot one. Put on your vest."

"What about you?"

"Don't worry about me. If bullets start flying, I'll stand behind you."

Avalty grimaced. "Thanks a lot. So, are you ever gonna finish telling me what happened between you and Nicole? You get the keys back. She jumps on you. And then what?"

Savage entered Manny's room in San Fernando Medical Center's ICU. She had been in this room many times before, following up on patients she had brought in. The familiar beeping instruments, glowing screens, and dozens of wires and tubes that she usually ignored now meant pain for someone close, for another firefighter, for a friend.

Vivas's eyes widened in recognition. She rose and rushed to hug her. "I got your messages. I've just been . . . it's just. . . ."

"Shhh. I know. I know." Savage released her friend, then spotted the older couple and the pretty girl in her mid-twenties seated across the room, near a colorful collection of floral arrangements. Savage smiled politely. The girl returned a grin. The couple managed a nod.

"Stephanie, these are Manny's parents, Delores and Raymond," said Vivas. "And this is his sister, Luz."

"Hi." Savage searched for a chair, found none. "I just made it. Visiting hours end in a few minutes." She tossed a look to Manny, whom she had met only once. His chest and head were heavily bandaged. He was intubated, on a ventilator, and very pale. "Any change?"

Vivas shook her head. "It's the usual waiting game. And it's driving me crazy. Masaki won't make any promises that he'll come out of the coma."

"They never do."

"At least we're getting the royal treatment. Charti and the RNs downstairs sent those flowers over there. They've been buying us lunch and dinner." Vivas sniffled, cupped a hand over her mouth. A tear broke free from one eye. "It's not supposed to happen to us, you know?"

"Yeah."

"Did you hear about Boccaccio's mother? They brought her in this afternoon. She ODed on amitriptyline."

"God damn!"

"It gets worse. Your rookie partner Abe and old Rasso were first on the scene. They worked on her for a while. Then they called to have her pronounced. Brought her back here so Boccaccio could see her."

"And I thought I had problems," Savage said. "Now we wait for one more."

"That's right. One more makes three. I hate that."

"So Stephanie, how do you know Isabel?" asked Delores. "From work?"

"Yeah. But I work out of Station Nine. We've run a lot of calls together."

Raymond's brow shot up. "Oh, so you're a fireman, too?"

"That's right. The politicians have taken to calling us Fire Service Technicians," she said, grinning slightly over the label. "But most people just call us firefighters. I'm also a medic like Izzy. And right now I'm a Field Training Officer."

"I see," he said, clearly unimpressed, then pushed his pudgy frame to the edge of his seat and adjusted his Sears Flex slacks. He regarded Vivas with a tired look. "Now here's something I've been trying to tell my ex-daughter-in-law for years, no offense to you, but not all female firemen are as large as her. Let's say I get stuck in a burning building. I pass out. How's some ninety-pound weakling woman supposed to pull me out? So I die because some female politician or some committee somewhere wants equal rights for women and forces fire departments to hire them. You can't tell me that doesn't go on. Oh, it's all unofficial, and affirmative action or not, it goes on. They *encourage* females to apply. Try to tell me they're as capable as the men. I know how that works. And I don't understand why we can't just say that there are some jobs better for men, some jobs better for women. What's wrong with that?"

Vivas gently placed her hand on Savage's shoulder and steered her toward the door. "Let's go downstairs for a cup of coffee."

"Well, it was nice meeting you," Savage said.

Raymond barely looked up. "You, too."

Out in the hall, Vivas said, "Oh, my God. I am so sorry."

Savage laughed. "That man is a trip. My husband would have to be a goddamned prince for me to put up with that."

"You didn't even get a piece of Delores. Once they're both going, forget about it."

"What's their problem?"

"They're like overachiever parents, and it just drives them crazy that their son didn't marry the perfect little homemaker. It's like they have no conception of the real world."

"And it sounds like they're so stuck in their ways that you'll never change them."

"God knows I've tried."

They paused at the elevator doors. "I don't get it. How can they hate you so much?" Savage asked. "I mean, it's you. Not an evil bone in your body. Treat your daughter like gold. You try to do the right thing."

"Doesn't matter who it is. No one's good enough for Manny."

They chatted for about a half hour in the hospital's caf-eteria, then Vivas headed back up to the ICU. Savage had carefully maneuvered their conversation away from talk-ing about her son—for whom, of course, no girl was good enough. Subtle or not, Vivas had made her point, and as Savaged headed home, she considered how much of Donny's new "life" she was willing to accept. Could she welcome the thing into her house? A mother's love was supposed to be unconditional. Donny had told her hers wasn't. Was that true? Was she really being just like Vi-vas's former in-laws? No, she wasn't that extreme. Was she?

On her way home, Savage took a shortcut through a seedier part of the valley, knowing very well that she would pass the tenement where that little girl had clung to her leg and had begged to be rescued. Had HRS done something about the situation? Or was that poor baby still living in filth with her junkie mother? Savage had resisted the temptation to go back and find out. It wasn't her place. She knew that. So she told herself that she would just cruise by.

Or maybe not.

While stopped at a light, Savage checked her wallet. She had about fifty bucks in cash. Maybe she would give it to that mother, urge the woman to buy the child some good clothes. Yes, in a fantasy world that might work. The mother would use the money to buy drugs. Maybe Savage could buy the clothes and give them to the girl. All she needed was the correct size.

Why I am obsessing on this? Is it just guilt? This is not normal. It was just a call.

Within five minutes she turned down a side street on which plywood walls of graffiti failed to keep crack heads out of the long row of abandoned shops. The apartments above looked different without the rain and darkness to mask some of their filth. The peeling paint and taped-up windows were still there, but twilight revealed the drab whites and faded browns and streaks of dirt.

Across the street was another apartment building, a five-story brick structure built quite a few decades ago, with several boarded-up windows and wisps of smoke rising from it and fading into the breeze. A VPD unit was parked next to the building, its lights off, both officers still inside, one writing a report.

Savage reached the corner, turned left, then parked in front of a broken meter. She thought of getting out, but five young males—two white, three Hispanic, all wearing green knit caps and baggy pants and T-shirts—came bopping down the street, listening to a hip-hop tune in their heads. Savage pretended to search for something in her glove compartment as they passed. At least her old pickup truck didn't draw much attention.

Get out or not? She wasn't in a safe neighborhood, and she had little protection, although that VPD unit was right there. If she got into any trouble, she could alert them—if they hadn't driven off. She took a deep breath and stepped out of the truck.

As she mounted the rickety stairs, a shimmer caught her eye. She reached between the first and second steps and withdrew an empty vial with a dog-eared label. Ketamine. She swore, tossed the bottle, and warily continued up.

A black woman in her thirties who weighed no more than eighty-five pounds was just setting down a garbage bag as Savage reached the landing. She looked up, then blinded Savage with her penlight. "How many times we got to tell you DEA idiots that we ain't cookin' no crank here? Go somewhere else." She shooed Savage with a scrawny hand, then spun and padded down the hall.

"I'm not an agent," Savage said, then followed her inside. The hall looked just as dirty as she remembered it, and the scents of urine and trash seemed even stronger. She reached apartment 5, its missing door number barely visible in the shadows. Surprisingly, she did not hear any loud music thumping from within. She knocked. Knocked again. A third time. A fourth.

This is stupid. I'm not going to change anything here.

Maybe HRS had done something. Maybe the mom had finally figured out a way to better herself and help her children. Maybe they had received some assistance and had moved to a better part of town. Savage felt her way along the wall and shuffled back toward the stairs.

"What you want?" came a thin voice as she neared the landing. It was the little girl's mother, and seeing her, backlit by dim apartment light, triggered the name: Shonica. She swung beaded hair out of her eyes, and, without much flesh and bone to support them, her jeans seemed to stand up on their own.

Savage moved cautiously back into the hall. "I came to see how you're doing. See if you needed anything. Do you remember me? I'm a paramedic. I was here about a week ago. A Sunday night."

The skinny woman who had taken out her trash emerged from a nearby door. "They can't harass us like this, Shonica," she said. "I'm gonna call the po-lice and get their asses removed again."

"I said I'm not an agent. I'm just here to see if you needed any help."

"Help? From you?" Shonica said, her eyes bugging. She left her doorway and started toward Savage.

"How're your kids doing? The last time I was here, your son was sick and your daughter wanted to leave. There has to be something you can do to get out of here. I know it's not gonna happen overnight, but there's gotta be something. Maybe I can help you."

"You fuckin' bitch!" the woman screamed, then charged at Savage, drawing back a fist.

The other woman rushed up behind Shonica, and she, too, was ready to strike.

Dumbfounded, Savage drew back, caught her running shoe on something, and fell onto her rump.

Shonica dropped to her knees and sent fists through the shadows.

"Whoa, whoa, whoa," Savage yelled. "If you don't want me here, I'm leaving." She caught a fist just as Shonica brought it down.

"You get out, hear me?" hollered Shonica. "Get out!"

Savage shoved the woman, then scrambled to her feet as the neighbor smacked her across the face.

"Jesus Christ, I just wanted to help," Savage said, cupping her flaming cheek. She reeled from the blow and shuddered with the desire to slug the woman. Only the tears in Shonica's eyes held her back. "I'm a public servant. And that's assault."

"And what do you call what they did?" shrieked the neighbor.

It took a few seconds for Savage to piece it together. "Where are your kids, Shonica?"

"Just get out!"

"You got no right to come in here!" added the neighbor.

Savage held up her palms. "Look, I'm sorry. Maybe I can help you. I have some friends who are social workers.

We can get you cleaned up, get you out of here."

The neighbor waved her fist. "We want you to go! Now go!"

"Hey, what's up out here?" A bearded white man in his forties, wearing dozens of gold chains, rings on every finger, and hoops in his ears came from Shonica's apartment, scratched his bare belly, yawned, and squinted.

"Nothing's up," Savage said, gritting her teeth. "I was just leaving." She slowly backed up, turned, then reached the stairs.

"Don't come here, bitch!" called the neighbor.

"Oh, don't worry," Savage answered, "I won't."

Back at her truck, Savage brushed off a tear. Shonica's children had been taken away—and rightly so. But Savage understood the pain of being separated from a child. She understood far too well.

B occaccio's father finished saying good-bye to the funeral director, then skirted a puddle in the parking
lot and came toward the Jeep, where Boccaccio sat waiting for him. Thank God for Dad. Boccaccio had no idea
what you did to arrange a funeral. And what about a will?
Did Mom have one? Dad wasn't sure. Frightening truths
had revealed themselves as she and Dad had investigated
what had happened to Mom prior to her death. She had
sold everything but her clothes and jewelry box and had
broken the lease on her apartment in Las Vegas, according
to a woman who had known Mom and had worked for
the property management company. If Mom had a will,
they couldn't find it—not that the few hundred bucks in
her checking account really meant anything. She had three
maxed-out credit cards and had cashed in her life insurance policy. A couple of pay stubs indicated that she had
worked as a hostess in a topless bar just off the Vegas
Strip, and some of her mail confirmed that she still owed
money for her surgeries. The last check she had written
was for the examination and scrip for amitriptyline.
Everything Mom had left in the world now sat on Boc-

caccio's living room table, and Boccaccio had cried as she had stared down at the pathetic collection, a meager testament to a life that could have been much more fulfilled.

The rest of the day would be spent placing dozens of phone calls to relatives, making more arrangements, and tying up loose ends. Mom's rental car needed to be returned, and her motel bill needed to be paid. They would head over to the motel now. Boccaccio would pay the bill, then Dad would follow her back to the rental car agency.

He buckled his seat belt and sighed. "I got her a nice coffin."

"I'm sorry," she said, having told him that she just couldn't go inside and select her mother's box.

"It's a nice one."

"I'm sure it is."

"She left some fuckin' legacy, didn't she?"

"Dad. . . ."

"I knew this would happen. Saw it coming for years."

"What? That she'd OD?"

"She used to blame her problems on everyone but herself. It was all our fault, even though we tried to help her. She got her revenge by sticking us with the bill. What a piece of work!"

Boccaccio had never seen her father so bitter. Sure, he would pass a cutting remark now and then, but he usually made allowances for Mom's "condition." Boccaccio remembered how just a few weeks ago he had told her that he should have been more forceful with Mom. He should have said, Okay, you're screwed up and these are the drugs you need and you're going to take them. He had said that it wasn't anyone's fault. The world had grown too complex for them.

"Right now I'm hating her so much," Boccaccio said.

"And then I think about her out there at that gas station, lying there, and it's like I failed. The whole 'if I were a better daughter' thing gets to me."

"You're the best daughter any parents could have: pretty, smart, successful. Sometimes at night I ask God why he blessed me with you. And let me tell you something. Your mother wouldn't have made it into her sixties. She could never cope with aging. I tried to help you deal with her, but to be honest, I knew in my gut that you'd be wasting your time."

"Now we'll never know." She blinked at the soreness in her eyes and fixed her gaze on the road. "I've just been so busy, you know? I was thinking that maybe if—"

"Have you been listening to me? Don't go blaming yourself."

"Dad, why are you so mad? Is it just the money?"

He yanked off his glasses, raked fingers through his curly gray hair. "The money means nothing. I care about what she's done to you. She and I agreed that no matter what happened with us, we'd try to give you the best. We'd be there to support you. But she didn't come through—even in death. Pissed? You bet your ass I am."

They came up on the motel where Mom had stayed, but Boccaccio pulled into the 76 gas station.

"The tank's full," Dad said, reading the gauge. "Oh, don't do this, Joanna."

"I want to see where my mother died."

He raised his brows. "You promised."

"Yeah, I did." Boccaccio pulled in front of a pump, hopped out, then went into the quickie mart.

A kid with dark eyes, a hoop in his nose, and sideburns down to his earlobes stood behind the counter. "Help you?"

"There was a lady here yesterday. She, uh, she collapsed out there somewhere."

"Yeah, that was pretty wild." The kid looked to the parking lot. "You another detective?"

"No. I was just wondering if you saw what happened."

"I was in here the whole time, but I saw it. She walked up in her underwear. Pretty crazy. Anyway, she just kinda fell down. Then the ambulance came, and they were working on her inside the fire truck. Then they took her away. I heard she died."

"She did. Can you show me where it happened?"

"I leave this counter, I get fired. But if you look out there . . . see that pump? She was right there, maybe ten or fifteen feet ahead."

Boccaccio saw the spot, nodded, then went outside.

Dad leaned on the Jeep, arms folded over his chest. "Ready?"

She glanced blankly at him, then crossed to the pump. A tiny scrap of a paper that had soaked onto the pavement lay just to her left. She hunkered down, peeled it up, and realized it was a piece of a Veni-Gard wrapper, perhaps the only evidence that medics had been there and that a woman had died. She tucked the scrap into her pocket, then looked around, trying to see what her mother had seen. Billboards. Streetlights and signs. Apartment buildings. A row of towering palms. And cars. Lots of cars. As final views went, it wasn't much. Boccaccio placed her hand on the asphalt, feeling its coarse surface and the heat surging into her skin.

"Joanna. . . ."

Her hand became a fist.

"Joanna. . . ."

And the fist struck the pavement.

"It's time to go."

She regarded her father, his sad face blurry through her tears. "How could she do this to us?"

"I don't know." He took her wrist.

During the next few hours, they returned the rental car, placed a funeral announcement in the newspaper, and stopped off at SFMC so that Boccaccio could make sure the place hadn't fallen apart. She told the ER director and her nurses about the wake and funeral, then left with a stack of sympathy cards and a pair of floral arrangements she had found on her desk.

I don't have a mommy anymore.

Back at her apartment, Dad made the calls. Mom's two brothers were catching the red eye. They lived in Seattle, about an hour away from each other. One taught elementary education at a community college, the other worked for the DMV, where he took license photos and billed himself as the Northwest's worst photographer. Uncle Ridley was a real character, a genuine flower child/bachelor and militant environmentalist who occasionally got into scuffles with the law. Boccaccio hoped he could cheer her up. Dad also called his two sisters, but Boccaccio didn't expect them to come. They had always hated Mom, and it would be a cold day in hell before they coughed up the bucks to fly in from Virginia. Dad let them off the hook with a gentle "Oh, it's no problem." When he had finished calling everyone he knew, he looked up and asked, "What about the boyfriend?"

Still in a daze, Boccaccio just looked at him.

"The boyfriend. What's his name? The greasy guy in Vegas."

"Drew," she said. "Yeah. I left a message on his machine last night. I just told him to call. It was urgent."

To her surprise, the phone rang.

Dad tipped his head. "Speak of the devil?"

"Hello?"

"Joanna? Where you been?"

It was her mall security guard, Jose Santiago. He had left three messages on her machine. "Hey. Sorry I haven't called back. I, my uh, my mom passed away."

"Serious? Oh, man. Joanna, I'm so—"

"Sorry. Yeah, I know. And I'll need lots of time to work through this, so if I don't call back, don't worry. It's not you. Okay?"

"Let me help you. What do you need? I'll take time off if I have to. Just tell me what I can do."

"It's all right. I'm fine. Just, I guess, be patient. Can you do that?"

"Whatever you want. Just let me know."

"I will. 'Bye, Jose."

"Who was that?" Dad asked.

She glanced longingly at the sofa, then went to it and dropped. "That was this young guy I'm fucking."

Dad cringed. "Joanna. . . ."

"I don't know what's wrong with me," she said, closing her eyes.

The phone rang again.

"Want me to get it?"

"No," she said, then bolted to the receiver, where she read the caller ID screen: John Smith. For a moment, she couldn't place the name. Oh, it was Doe, probably calling to say "I'm so sorry." She answered, and Doe's usual jovial tone had sobered:

"Hey, Doc. I don't mean to bother you. I just want to let you know that everybody at Ten is thinking about you. If you need anything, we're here."

"What are you doing later?"

"Uh, nothing, really. I'm not back on until Friday morning. What is it?"

"Why don't you come over? We'll get an early dinner."

"Uh, yeah," he said tentatively. "Sure. I mean, are you sure?"

She gave him directions and told him not to be late.

"Another friend?" Dad asked.

She leaned back on the sofa and draped an arm over her eyes. "Yeah. Another friend."

Boccaccio's phone continued to ring about every fifteen minutes. She screened the calls and answered only a few. Dad went home to take care of some errands. He said he would return if she needed him, but she insisted that he take a nap. She would meet him at the funeral home later. She took a shower, tried to make herself look as presentable as possible without making it obvious that she had gone to great lengths; of course, that involved trying on way too many outfits. She paced the apartment, listening to her parakeet chirp and the muffled sound of Mrs. Stone's TV next door. When would that stubborn woman get her hearing aid fixed?

Doe finally called on the intercom downstairs. Boccaccio buzzed him in and waited for the ring at the door. It was a long wait. She opened the door.

He looked his usual self: damned good. He was a classic, all right. Blond, blue-eyed California surfer boy with a dangerous gleam in his eye and a gorgeous ass. He survived on junk food and adrenaline, and stood in stark contrast to most of the pale-faced intellects of Boccaccio's world. Some of her colleagues' greatest risks involved getting sunburned on the golf course. Boccaccio loved it that Doe had pursued her, and she had rejected him not because he was—in his estimation—a lowly medic but because she knew his playboy antics. And she knew herself too well, knew her weaknesses, knew just how quickly and deeply she would fall for a guy so bad for her. She also didn't think she could have a relationship *and* a career. How were you supposed to find the time? She had watched too many of her colleagues suffer through bitter divorces. But each time Doe had asked her to go waterskiing, she had imagined, in the wee hours, the wind rushing through her hair, the spray catching her eyes, and the tingle of his hands on her. After a day of boating, they would fall into bed, feeling giddy, sun-worn, and . . . young.

He was reckless.

He was very much alive.

And when he had told her that his girlfriend was pregnant, she had been surprised at how much that had bothered her. She had lied and said she hoped it worked out for him. She had cursed herself for not giving in to him sooner.

"Hi, Doctor," he said politely, then offered her a card and glanced at the floor. "I don't want to say 'sorry' because I guess you're sick of hearing that."

"I'm sick of you calling me Doc for what, four years? It's Joanna when we're not around the residents. And if you don't want to say 'sorry,' then just tell me you're not. Tell me you didn't know my mom, so you don't really care that she died. You just feel bad for me because I had a death in the family."

He gave a slight grin. "I think I like 'sorry' better."

"Come in," she said, then started for the kitchen as she opened the card. "What're you drinking? I have everything."

"You pick."

She read the sympathy card with mild interest, then

returned to the living room with two bottles of water.

He thanked her, took his bottle, then wandered farther into the living room, eyeing her modest furniture. "I thought you'd have a house."

"Yeah, I know I'm throwing my money away on rent, but I don't want the stress. I can barely keep up with this place. And I'm not here much. Still, I know I'm stupid."

When he reached the window, he peered behind the blinds. "Well, you got a decent view of the pool."

"Are those two sisters down there again? They have some issues with tan lines. My next-door neighbor is always calling the manager about them."

"Yeah, I think they're down there, but they got their suits on—not that that really matters." He left the window. "How 'bout the tour?"

She gave a slight shrug and waved him into the spare bedroom, where a wall of bookcases buckled under the weight of hundreds of medical texts. Papers, magazines, junk mail, and videotapes cluttered her desk, and somewhere in there was a laptop on whose hard drive was stored a half-written article she had started over a week ago and should have finished by now.

"This doesn't look quakeproof," he said, testing one of the shelves.

"Yeah, I know. I'm a disaster waiting to happen."

"The other bedroom's over there?" he asked, gesturing to the hall.

"It's a mess."

"I have this lady who comes once a week. She's really good and doesn't charge much. I think she's an illegal, but I can give you her number."

"Why don't you give me yours? I don't have it."

"Yeah, okay. Remind me before I go. And, uh, thanks

for inviting me over. Wasn't too long ago that you turned me down for just a cup of coffee."

She let that hang and drifted back into the living room. "Tell you the truth, I don't feel like going out. Mind if we order in?" She sipped her water.

"Sure. Whatever."

"You like Chinese?"

Thirty minutes later, Doe slowly scooped out a small portion of chicken lo mien and fried rice while she dug into the heaps on her plate.

"You're scarfing that down like Izzy does when she cheats on her diet," Doe said.

"Oh, sorry," she said with her mouth full. "I'm so hungry. That's terrible news about her ex-husband."

"Her ex, your mom. When it rains, it pours. And shit, it's been raining a lot lately. I heard we're going to get hit again."

Boccaccio cleared her throat. "My mom's going to be lying in a coffin tonight. I'm supposed to go there and look at her and listen to everyone moan about it. I don't want to go."

"So don't."

"I can't let my dad go alone."

"Then go. Or maybe you should just tell him that you don't want to be there."

She batted her eyelashes, her expression pleading. "Would you tell him?"

He raised his palms. "Hell, no. I got enough problems of my own. You keep yours. I'll keep mine."

Though she saw an opportunity to ask him about his girlfriend, Boccaccio thought better of it. If he was feeling any guilt about coming to her apartment, she didn't need to remind him. "So, now that you've seen how I live, you still think I'm a snobby doctor? I bet your apartment is much nicer."

"A little bit, but you've focused all your energy on being the best doctor you can be. Shit, if I got hurt, I'd pay extra to have you working on me."

Boccaccio began to nod, but her thoughts returned to her mother, to the impending wake, to what the woman had done to her. The tears came quickly.

Doe suddenly rose, came around the table, and hunkered down. He put a hand on her shoulder. "Hey, it's okay."

She took his hand and brought it to her cheek. His touch felt so good that she nearly sighed. Without thinking, she leaned forward to bring her lips to his.

"Doc?" he said tentatively.

"Uh-huh?"

"What are you doing?"

What am I doing? Oh, my God. What am I doing? She wrenched his hand away.

He looked at her, more concerned than upset. "Doc?"

Suddenly ashamed, she turned away.

"Doc, it's all right."

"I can't believe I just did that." She couldn't face him.

But he shifted to find her gaze. "I said it's all right. I mean, it's not all right, but things happen, you know? In the past week or so I've been having the best and the worst luck with women. My timing is always wrong."

"I know the feeling."

"Hey, forget about it. I have a pregnant girlfriend who's all upset and an ex-girlfriend who's driving me nuts. I'm the last person you want in your life."

"I'm having sex with some mall security guard. He's just a kid, really."

"I didn't need to know that."

"And you didn't have to tell me about your stress. So it sounds like you're keeping the baby."

"Yeah. I've even been thinking about marrying her. But with my ex back in town, I'm having second thoughts. And I came this close to really cheating on Geneva, although she'd call it cheating."

"Geneva's the one who's pregnant?"

"Yeah. And Nicole's the ex. I went to a bar to tell Nicole to stop bothering me. Anyway, out in the parking lot, things got—"

"Some women love to scream."

"Oh, she wasn't screaming. She started kissing. I didn't know what to do. It felt so good, you know?"

Boccaccio shivered.

"Anyway, I pried her off, tried to get her mad. Called her names. Anything I could do. But she told me that I'm already hers, and no matter where I am or what I do, I'll always be thinking about her."

"Are you?"

He returned to his seat. "Yeah, I guess I am. I don't know if I'm still in love with her, if I want to get rid of her, if I want to kill her, or what." He grinned. "I actually came here because I figured you needed company, and I thought I'd get a little advice along the way. I usually lay the heavy stuff on Izzy, but she's got more than she can handle right now. The guys at the station just want to hear about the sex. I need a woman's point of view on this."

Boccaccio had trouble looking up. His confession, spoken so sweetly and honestly, eased her nerves. "Doe, I'm sorry."

"Hey. Two people alone in an apartment, going through some problems. This has sex written all over it. If the old me were here, I'd be doing stuff to you right now. Serious stuff. But you know what's sad? I wouldn't care if you had just lost your mother. I'd use that to get you into bed, and I wouldn't think twice. We know how people respond to stress; we see it every week. Feed, fight, flee, and fuck. That's how they respond, and when you're the one under the stress, it's hard to see what you're doing. I'd take advantage of that. It'd be real easy, right?"

"Maybe I shouldn't answer that."

"It's about timing. Mine's wrong. So's yours."

She picked at her lo mien. "And it's probably best that we're just friends. If we had a relationship, then broke up, you'd still be forced to deal with me at the hospital. It would be awkward, and we'd be living that whole pathetic cliché."

"Yeah," he said.

But only halfheartedly.

Their gazes met. *Damn it!*

"You know, if you want, I'll come to the wake."

"If I go, I'd like you to be there. But if we showed up together. . . ."

"Yeah, that's just what I need. Geneva already thinks I'm boffing my ex. If she thought me and you were doing something . . . man, I don't wanna think about that."

"And I don't want to give my RNs something to talk about, although I've heard some of them think I'm a lesbian."

"Izzy gets that a lot. So does Savage. You give a woman some power, and right away some people think she's got a penis and likes women, because only men have power."

"You surprise me. I always thought you had a problem with female authority."

He chuckled under his breath. "It's not the female part that bothers me. I love women. Too much."

"Not necessarily a bad thing. So, lover boy, what are

you going to do with your ex? I mean, how'd you leave it with her?"

"She's still out there. I get tense every time the phone rings. I'm telling you, I'm like one of those gazelles on the Discovery Channel—you know, the slow guy near the back of the herd, the one you just know is gonna buy it."

"What does she do for a living? She's not a medic, is she?"

He rolled his eyes. "She's a medic. At least she's not assigned to my station. But it's not like I can avoid her. She knows everything about me. I mean, we were together for a long time. I'm talking years. That was before I went on my dating rampage. And I keep telling myself that I should get rid of her, but there's something holding me back. If I could figure out what it is, I'd be all right. So, Doc, what's the prognosis?"

"All right, she's a medic. Sounds like she's pretty aggressive. You told her about Geneva?"

"Yeah."

"And that doesn't bother her?"

"Nope."

"Is she spontaneous? Does she like to take risks?"

"Oh, yeah."

"Does she act childish sometimes? When you look at her, do you say, There's a woman who never wants to grow up?"

He nearly leaped from his chair. "Exactly. That's her to a T. It's like you know her."

"No, I know you."

That struck him silent for a minute. He drank his water, stabbed a piece of broccoli. "I once told Geneva that I really liked myself and didn't want to change."

"But you're going to be a father."

"Yeah, a father."

"And you're thinking about marriage. So when you look at Nicole, you're seeing everything you'll have to give up."

"Damn! Maybe you're right."

"Probably not." She smiled. "But it sounds like a good line of bullshit, doesn't it?"

Abe finished inventorying the rescue's drug box, then handed the log to Rasso, who was shaving his gray stubble with an electric razor. The veteran medic scribbled his name, then crossed to the bay door nearest the driver and yanked it open. "You finally got the tanks right, but I don't like the way you secured this mask. Fix it."

"It's my mask. What do you care if it gets broken?"

"I need you alive so you can sacrifice your young heart while saving me."

"That's a pretty big assumption."

"Listen, Allah, get your ass over here and fix this."

Abe's mouth fell open. "Was that a racial slur?"

"Racial slur? Where are your witnesses?" Rasso waved an arm across the apparatus floor, where the engine and squad crews inspected their vehicles. Anything they might have heard was muffled by idling diesel engines.

Abe tensed, stowed the drug box, then trudged to the bay as Rasso took himself and his buzzing razor inside.

The last couple of days had been uneventful, and Abe wished they would get a good call to distract Rasso. Not much had happened after they had dropped off Boccaccio's mother. Abe had asked Rasso about remaining outside the morgue. "I don't go in there," was all the old medic would say.

Surprisingly, they had received only two calls, minor MVAs, during the last eight hours of that shift. Rasso had alternated between sleeping and criticizing Abe for cleaning up the rig too slowly. Meanwhile, the man himself had done absolutely nothing because his back hurt. Again.

After moping around for most of Wednesday, Abe had gone to Lisa's apartment and had spent several hours playing with her daughter and keeping mostly to himself. Lisa had tried her best to lift his spirits, but nothing seemed to work. He recognized the forces that were acting on him, but he felt helpless to react. Dealing with stress had never been so difficult. Recent events had gotten too deeply under his skin, and Rasso only drove them deeper.

On Thursday, Abe had met Lisa for lunch at the bookstore. It was the first time he had visited her at work, and of course she had introduced him to her entire staff. Though he felt a little awkward, he realized that it made her happy to show him off. From the start, her feelings had been blind to his lack of a degree and his Middle Eastern heritage, and she had listened to him when he talked about work. Most guys wouldn't care about that, but Abe felt comforted that he had her approval. Sure, he didn't need it and had never asked for it, but she had taken him as he was. She didn't want to change him. He should be falling to his knees over having such a woman in his life, but he couldn't find that feeling anymore. He didn't deserve any happiness.

People were dying out there.

Lisa had invited him over for dinner that night, but he had declined. Friday shifts were always a bit hairy. He needed a good night's sleep. She had been disappointed, but understood. Before they had hung up, Abe had been on the brink of talking, but the guilt of revealing his vulnerability had returned. He had to handle his own problems. Macho or not, he had to prove that to himself. Funny how he had no problem going to the stress debriefings and venting to colleagues and perfect strangers.

"What are you looking at?" Abe asked as he shuffled into the day room.

Paul Cannis craned his head away from the computer monitor. "Reading up on Special K overdoses. I figure we're gonna get a bunch of those pretty soon. Wanna see?"

"Maybe later. I need an overdose of caffeine." Abe moved straight into the kitchen, snatched a Coke from the refrigerator, dumped his change into the can, then drifted over to the conference table, where Fitzy pored over a copy of the L.A. *Times*. Meanwhile, Rasso made a rough landing on one of the recliners, tossed his head back, and began shaving his Adam's apple.

"So Steph is back soon, huh?" Fitzy asked, not looking up from his paper. "This shift your last one with your buddy?"

"Yeah, at eight tomorrow morning, he's back to his slow station and out of our faces." Abe sat next to the old firefighter and lowered his voice. "I haven't had a chance to ask you—what do you think about Steph?"

"Nothing to think."

"You didn't hear?"

"I heard."

"That doesn't look good."

"She knows."

"What will they do to her? Anything?"

"She'll get the warning. But you know what, son? Once you've been at this for a long time, people make allowances. Look at your buddy. He's got friends in high places who won't bust him out because they know they'd be just like him if the same shit had happened to them. So they cut 'em slack, just like they'll cut it for Steph. I ain't sayin' it's right. It's what happens. But I know her. If she thinks she can't handle it, she won't work."

"Then why'd she try to teach when she was . . . sick?"

Fitzy sighed. "I don't know. So who told you?"

"Tenpenney ran into Doe, who heard it from another guy at Nine who knows a cop who was there."

"Whores for gossip—all of 'em. Everybody's got problems. Everybody."

"Yeah, they do. Hey, remember the first time we met, and you told me how seeing MVAs and death and everything doesn't get to you?"

"You get pretty used to it after twenty-six years."

"You said you used sex as a defense mechanism."

"I did?"

"Yeah, you said it makes you feel invincible."

"I did?"

"You said you never once woke up in a cold sweat."

Fitzy's bushy brows came together. "Well, shit, son, I was lying."

"I know. Sex doesn't work. I've tried."

"You want to know what I really do? I used to think it was the worst thing, but I take it all home."

"Really?"

"Yeah. You look at Tenpenney and Cannis. They come in here wearing their street clothes and change into their uniforms. They draw the line, and if that works, more power to 'em. But some people can't do that. Some people can't hold it in. You oughta know that by now."

"I guess so."

"See, look at this crap," he said, slamming a knuckle

on a headline. "MVA yesterday on the Five. Car gets cut in half, and two people die because some asshole in some body shop put a Mercedes back together with duct tape and shitty welds to rip off the insurance company. God, I'm glad I won't be on this planet for much longer."

"Feel better now?"

Fitzy winked. "You're damn right."

"Ladies and gentlemen," called Lieutenant Martinez from the doorway of his office. "The hepatitis C kits are in. Anyone who wants a test can see me. I also got a copy of that IAFF video, which I want everyone to watch."

"Lieutenant, sir," Fitzy began in a mock serious tone. "I already know I'm dying, thank you."

"What about that Centers for Disease control thing I read?" called Tenpenney from the office. "They said routine testing was a bad idea."

"What about all those rescues some of us old-timers pulled without wearing gloves?" the lieutenant countered. "It only takes one exposure. And remember this: you can go ten, twenty, thirty years and not even know you got it. They catch it early, maybe they put it in remission."

"I don't want to know," Fitzy said. "There's enough bad news right here in the paper." His sentiments were echoed by Cannis and Tenpenney.

"Listen up. The department strongly urges you to test yourself. It's not mandatory yet, but you can bet it will be. So you best get it over with now. That's all." Martinez returned to his office.

Abe left his seat and crossed to the recliner beside Rasso's. "C'mon. Me and you. We'll take the test."

"Get out of my face, kid." Rasso's gaze did not move from the TV. A weatherman warned of more rain.

"You afraid?"

"Of what? I've always been careful."

"Don't you want to know?"

"Listen to old Fitzy. If he's got it . . . if I got it . . . it's already too late. I ain't wasting my time."

"Yeah, you're right. Most people don't get it on the job anyway. They get it through IV drug use and . . . what was that phrase I read? Yeah, they get it though 'lifestyle choices.' "

"Look at that. More fuckin' rain."

"I wonder if those kits detect anything else."

"Like what?"

"I don't know. Maybe painkillers and antidepressants."

Rasso gave a series of grunts and got to his feet. "Let's go outside. I need to show you something in the rescue."

"What I'd do now?"

Once they were on the floor, Rasso yanked open the rescue's back door and waved Abe inside.

"Don't tell me it's not clean," Abe said.

Rasso shut the doors, turned back—

And seized Abe by the shirt collar.

In one powerful and fluid motion, he drove Abe down and pinned him to the bench seat. "Listen, you little motherfucker, I warned you about fuckin' with me. We got one more shift together, and that's it. You shut your fuckin' mouth. Or I will hurt you, young man. I will."

"And I'll have your fuckin' ass thrown in jail, you fuckin', washed-up, piece-of-shit motherfucker. Come on, old man! Come on! You're gonna hurt me? Fuckin' do it."

Rasso just hung there, panting, swallowing spit. Then, as though a mental switch had been thrown, he released Abe and shuddered through a chuckle, a chuckle that broke into booming laughter.

"You think this is a fuckin' joke?" Abe hollered.

"No," Rasso managed, calming himself. "Maybe you do know something about pain."

Abe's heart thundered as he watched Rasso open the door and hop out. He lay there for another moment, chilled over the notion that he had wanted Rasso to hurt him, that he needed punishment from someone other than himself.

The first call came in at eight-forty. Sick child. Respiratory problems. ETA, just three minutes.

A blond woman in her late twenties waited for them at the door. She looked exhausted and undernourished, and she might very well have slept in her wrinkled T-shirt and athletic shorts. "He's in the bedroom," she said, then rushed inside.

Not much of an apartment, Abe thought. Small living room. Cheap, you-assemble furniture. Sparsely decorated.

On the other hand, all kinds of action figures, puzzles, and board games cluttered the bedroom they entered. A computer was on a student desk in one corner, and a TV with a PlayStation game sat on a credenza opposite a twin bed with a Star Wars comforter. Posters hung on every wall and ran the gamut from Pokémon to, believe it or not, a picture of Einstein. A machine about the size of a small television, with an inflatable vest and attached tubing draped over it, stood beside the bed, not far from a tall oxygen tank. In the middle of this chaos sat a dusky-skinned boy of seven or eight, his longish hair tangled, a simple face mask covering his nose and mouth. He was wearing pajamas and leaning forward on a stack of pillows. Sweat beaded on his forehead as he struggled with breath after raspy breath.

Rasso accidentally kicked some kind of mechanical dragon thing as he approached. "He's got CF?"

"Yeah," the woman barely answered. "He's was doing his aerosols. And then. . . ."

Abe rushed to remove a non-rebreather mask from the airway bag. The little boy had cystic fibrosis. Studies showed that some people lived into their thirties with the disease, but this boy looked bad. Really bad. The disease affected his lungs and digestive system. His mucus was thicker and stickier than normal, and led to chronic infections of his lungs. The mucus also blocked enzymes from being released by his pancreas, making him unable to digest food properly. The boy had inherited the disease from his parents. There was no cure.

"What's his name?" Rasso asked, his tone remarkably soft.

The mother shielded her eyes, but the tears slid past her fingers. "Billy."

"Hey, Billy. Hang in there. We're gonna transfer you to our oxygen tank, and then I'm gonna carry you down to our rescue truck. That all right?"

The boy nodded.

Abe shivered as he imagined holding his nose and breathing through a cocktail straw. The boy was more than likely end-stage, and had returned home to die. His mother was giving him the supportive care he needed and dreading this day. Billy might never return home from the hospital.

With the non-rebreather mask ready to go, Abe slipped off Billy's mask and made the exchange. Rasso scooped the boy into his arms, and Abe followed close behind, keeping slack in the oxygen line. The mother asked them to take Billy to Valley General. Her voice reflected chilling, otherworldly peace.

Fitzy and the rest of the engine crew arrived, jumped

down, and were ready to lend a hand as Abe and Rasso hurried outside and toward the rescue.

"Abe? You're in back with me," said Rasso. "Tenpenney? You're driving."

Abe adjusted the stretcher to keep the boy upright as Rasso gently set him down. In the meantime, Fitzy helped the mother into the rescue and showed her how to buckle in to the bench seat, then shut the doors.

Billy started crying as the rescue pulled away from the curb.

"It's okay, big guy," said Rasso. "You hang in there." He turned to Abe. "Let's start a line."

The boy already had a Hickman catheter in place on his chest, in the superior vena cava. This central line had been established at the hospital and had been left in his chest to allow easy venous access. All Abe had to do was attach his IV line to the catheter to get fluids into the boy. While Abe prepared the IV, Rasso set up to administer albuterol via the nebulizer. The boy would inhale the drug, a bronchodilator, which would ease his pain, if only a little.

They could do no more for him.

Abe established the line, and Rasso handed Billy the nebulizer. The boy handled the device without fear, like an old pro, though something in his gaze said that he knew he didn't have long.

"That's right, Billy. You got it now," Rasso said, his voice remarkably soothing. "Don't cry. Okay? Don't cry. Your mom's right here. You gotta be strong."

"I'll need to call his father," the woman said, after Abe finished getting Billy's medical history from her.

"Soon as we get to the hospital," Rasso answered.

The mother's gaze went distant. "He's in Tucson. He,

uh, he's never been good with this. I don't know if he'll come."

Rasso nodded. "It's hard." He moved to the radio, dialed VGH's frequency. "VGH, Rescue Nine. Copy?"

"Nine, VGH. Copy."

"En route to your facility with, uh. . . ." Rasso lowered the mike. His eyes glassed over. "You wanna finish this?" He struggled to keep his voice even.

"Uh, sure," Abe said, then exchanged places with him.

Rasso took the boy's hand in his own. "That's right, big guy. Just keep breathing it in. You're doing fine. You're doing fine."

Abe relayed the information, then finished the call with the usual "ETA code 3, approximately four minutes. Any further questions or orders? Negative. Nine out."

Rasso muttered a curt "Thanks."

After they had delivered Billy to Valley's emergency department, Rasso found a nurse who was familiar with Billy's case and asked how long the boy had.

"A couple of weeks. Maybe. It's sad. I can't stand to see children die. It's the worst part of the job."

"Yeah." Rasso leaned against the wall.

Another nurse claimed her attention, and they walked off.

"Run form's done," Abe said, holding up the clipboard. "I gave them their copy."

Rasso turned back to the curtain covering the exam area where Billy was, a faraway look in his eyes.

"Ready?" asked Abe.

Sans gesture or word, Rasso headed for the exit.

"Guess I'll clean up," Abe said, assuming Rasso would do nothing.

Out at the rescue, Rasso climbed into the patient compartment and assisted Abe with the inventory and trash.

"I'd better duck," Abe said. "Lightning's going to strike with you helping me."

Rasso busied himself with the log, and when he was finished, they pulled out and returned to the station.

Tenpenney and Cannis greeted Rasso. He said nothing, went to the recliner, sat.

He stayed there for the next several hours. Very quiet.

S avage surveyed the apparatus floor, her gaze wandering past the turnout gear, the lockers, and the decades-old calendar from the year the station had opened.

If the station had a voice, it would call her name.

Abe was outside, washing down the rescue, while Fitzy, Tenpenney, and Cannis dried off the engine. Their efforts might be for naught. Swollen black clouds descended over the valley. Savage watched the engine crew, contemplating if she should go over and say hi. No one paid much attention to her, or if they did, they carefully hid it. She held her breath and headed inside. The office was empty. Out in the day room, Vincent Rasso lay snoring on one of the recliners. Good. At least he and Abe had not killed each other. She had feared the worst.

"Hey, Steph?" Lieutenant Martinez called from his office.

"Sorry I couldn't get down sooner. I've been busy trying to buy a new truck. It's like a full-time job to get a good deal." She settled into a chair.

He came around the desk and sat beside her. His voice dropped. "What's going on?"

She looked away. "I don't know."

"Are we back to square one again?"

"No. I'm okay."

"You were doing so well. What happened?"

Her cheeks felt warm, her palms sweaty. "My kid. He's driving me crazy."

Martinez stroked his mustache. "Last I heard, he was pulling straight As down in Florida."

"He quit school. Moved here. Married some . . . some girl. I don't know where he's living or what he's doing." She knuckled her tired eyes. "All these years I've been killing myself for him. And he takes it, and he throws it all away. So that's what's going on."

He breathed a deep sigh of frustration. "You should've called in sick for your class."

"I know." She shook her head over her own stupidity. "It wasn't easy coming here."

"We all got problems. You know mine. I know yours. So what if a few other people know? You admit it, you do something about it, and you move on. But you're not ready to move. You're stuck."

"I'm not stuck. I just feel like I wasted my life on that kid."

"We raise 'em to leave the nest. You teach 'em as good as you can, then you let go. If it makes him happy, you should be happy. You're at the point where you should just give him a little advice. You shout at him, you'll lose him. And I know you, Steph. You've been shouting."

"I just can't believe I raised a person to be that selfish."

"He's doing what he thinks is right for him. Not for you. For him."

"And killing me in the interim."

"You can't lay a guilt trip on him. You need to talk.

Let him spill his guts. You spill yours. Figure it out from there."

"If I could find him. He wanted to give me his number. I blew him off."

"You need to find him—for him, for you, and for your job. I'm serious. This time you only got one strike."

"I know. I won't let you down."

"I'm gonna make sure you don't. You're coming to the meeting next week."

"AA doesn't do it for me anymore. And I can't afford therapy. Twelve steps. A hundred steps. Doesn't matter."

"That's because you haven't made a real commitment to getting better. I'll help you do that."

"I don't know. Maybe I'm just another statistic. Typical drunken firefighter. I'm a joke."

"No, you're one of the best damned medics I've ever worked with. I won't see you waste that. I won't."

"All right, I'll go. Thanks." She averted her gaze and moved toward the door.

"See you next week. I'll remind you about the meeting."

"Okay." She closed the door.

As she turned to head outside, a coarse voice split the air. "Savage."

She whirled to face Rasso, who stood behind her, rubbing his eyes. "What do you want?"

"I wanna talk to you about your rookie. He really sucks. Have you taught him anything? Or do you just tell him to stick his thumb in his mouth and shut up?"

"I'm thinking 'fuck you,' but I won't even waste my time." She tried to get past him.

"So you're having trouble with your son, huh?"

"You listened? You nosy bastard!" She tried ducking right, but once more he blocked her. "You'd better move"—she flicked her gaze to his groin—"or little Vincent's gonna get hurt."

"That's assault."

"That's painful."

"Okay, you can go. I just wanna tell you something. Instead of bitching and moaning about your little boy quitting school and getting married, you should think about how lucky you are. You had a chance to teach him what you know. Even if he takes it and pisses it away. At least you had a chance."

"All right, I'll think about that. And I'll think about you sitting in your apartment drinking yourself into a blackout. You'll never change, Rasso. Your scars will always be deeper." She shoved him aside and yanked open the door.

"Hey, maybe we should go out some time. I'll show you those scars."

She grimaced at him, then left.

Still, he wasn't half bad-looking, and misery did love company. . . .

"Manny, can you hear me?" Vivas whispered.

His eyes slowly opened. "What time is it?"

"I told you not to talk. Your throat's still sore from the tube. You're gonna be okay. The swelling in your head has gone down." Vivas leaned over the bed and touched his cheek. "Your mother will be back in a few minutes. She'll do the talking for all of us."

He closed his eyes. "No."

"Manny, I've been thinking. Remember when we first got married? When were thinking about heading north? Well, I love you. I think we still have something. But not here."

"Okay."

"Don't talk. Just nod. I know moving won't change that much, but it's still a change. And I think that's what we need. Maybe we're running away. I don't care. I just think that whatever's going on with you won't stop. Next time they'll kill you. And I don't want my daughter to lose her father."

He opened his mouth. She covered it with her hand. He nodded.

"Your buddies from Sears came by yesterday. Brought you all those flowers. Your boss is a pretty nice guy."

"Uh-huh."

"There he is," cried Delores. She paraded into the room, arms outstretched, eyes wide. "Just like I told you all. He came back to us. I knew it. I was right. I was right all along."

Vivas retreated from the bed, giving her mother-in-law a wide berth.

Delores pinched her son's cheeks. "And Manny . . . we brought you a present."

Manny's father waddled into the doorway, with Consuela at his side and Vivas's mother just behind.

"Daddy?" Consuela gripped her grandfather's leg.

"Go on, honey. It's all right," said Mama. "Remember what we talked about? Go say hi to Daddy."

Consuela's head shrank into her narrow shoulders.

"Come here, my baby," Manny rasped.

"Daddy!" Consuela ran to the bed.

Vivas homed in on her mother. "Whose idea was this?"

"We told her. She's ready," Mama said in a harsh whisper. "Now shuddup and let your daughter see her daddy."

"I wanted to take this slowly."

Mama's expression stiffened. "You are."

"Daddy? Are you okay?" Consuela crashed her elbows on the bed.

"Yeah, but I can't talk too much. It hurts."

"Okay. I miss you, Daddy."

"I miss you."

Vivas blinked away her tears. Mama slid an arm over her shoulder. "You don't realize what you have until you almost lose it," Mama said softly.

"I wish I could get my hands on the bastards who did this." Delores shook a bony fist, posing no more threat to a gang than a bag lady armed with an unread Bible.

"Vengeance is mine, sayeth the lord," Mama said.

Delores shrugged. "I wouldn't mind helping Jesus kick a little ass. Look what they did to my boy."

"Can everybody leave for a minute?" Manny asked. "I wanna talk to Izzy."

"How many times do I have to tell you?" said Vivas. "Don't talk."

Manny glared at his mother. "I need a minute."

"All right, all right. We'll go outside for a little while," she sang sarcastically. "C'mon, Consuela. You can meet a real nurse."

Once everyone had filed outside, Vivas turned her puzzled expression on Manny. "What?" She raised her index finger. "But don't talk."

"I have to. So you wanna go up north? Let's go. You want me to choose? I choose *our* family. Maybe God's trying to tell me something, right?"

"Maybe. I just want you to be sure."

"Are *you* sure? You'll quit your job?"

"I can still be a medic up there."

"And Sears isn't going out of business any time soon." He pulled her down to him.

They kissed, and it felt . . . true.

•   •   •

"Uh, Doe? We could lose our jobs for this," said Avalty as he removed his Buddy Holly glasses and cleaned them on his shirtsleeve.

"How you figure?"

"You got the other guys in their uniforms, and that's all well and good because they're not on duty—but we are. We're not supposed to be here. If the lieutenant finds out about this. . . ."

"Shuddup. Let's go."

Doe hopped down from the rescue and joined the other nine firefighters who were walking toward Cuts Plus!, a small hair salon in a meager strip mall. The drizzle had just started, so everyone hustled a bit and, one after another, marched inside.

Bringing up the rear, Doe cocked a brow as every head in the place —mostly female heads—turned to regard the impressive assembly of firefighters decked out in dress blues. He popped on his hat and called, "Geneva?"

She came from behind a curtain in the back. Her jaw dropped. "Oh, my God! What are all these. . . ."

Although she finished the sentence, Doe couldn't hear her. He, along with the others, had started singing The Temptations' "It's the Same Old Song" along with the boom box that Avalty had brought inside.

All right, so Doe had stolen the idea from a half-dozen films. Lame idea or not, Geneva was blown away—especially when Doe dropped to one knee and sang the part about having a different feeling since she'd been gone.

When he finally went in for the kiss, the firefighters and patrons cheered. Even Geneva's boss, a heavyset woman with dark roots who had looked irritated by the disturbance, choked up.

"I still don't trust you," Geneva whispered in his ear.

"I'll work on that."

•   •   •

Joanna Boccaccio ducked into the limousine and sat next to her father. She rolled down the window and stared across the cemetery as the last of the mourners huddled against the rain and dodged puddles on the way to their cars. She thought back to the service, just a few hours ago, and how the priest (a handsome Catholic too young to be wearing the robe—what a waste) had made the lies about her mother's life sound so believable. He had even called her a dedicated wife, mother, sister, and citizen. Boccaccio had refused the opportunity to say something about Mom, but Dad had stood and told a story about the day Joanna had been born and how Rosemary would have liked the service. His remarks had been straightforward, charged with only a little emotion, and, thankfully, short. The whole thing felt extremely awkward. Everyone gazed pityingly at her, the poor young woman whose mother had killed herself.

"Close that window, Joanna. You're getting soaked."

She turned to her father. "Who cares?"

He reached across her and hit the button. "I do."

"So now we go have lunch," she said in a monotone. "It's what people do when someone dies. They eat lunch."

"What are you talking about?"

"I don't know. I hope the food's good."

"You kidding? I had Jerry's Famous cater it. The food will be very good."

"Dad? I, uh, I hate Mom."

He took her hand. "You don't hate her. You just hate what she did. I think deep down your mother was a good person. I wouldn't have married her if she wasn't."

"I hate her."

"You'll get past that. I've been working on it myself."

"I'll never forgive her. Never."

"Some people don't deserve forgiveness. You got your murderers and your rapists and your child molesters. They can rot in hell as far as I'm concerned. But I don't think your mother ever meant to hurt you. She just couldn't see what she was doing. And because of that, you should forgive her."

"I don't see how."

"Maybe you need to remember that her death is now part of your life. You choose to learn from it or let it ruin you. I know you feel like she burned you in the worst possible way. I feel like she burned me, too. But it happened. And we have to find the positive in all this. We have to remember that we both loved her."

"I can't."

He squeezed her hand. "If you forgive her, you can."

16

Lieutenant Martinez stood by the door, waving everyone out of the day room. "Let's go, let's go, let's go!"

"Confirmed structure fire, Abe," Tenpenney called excitedly. "Explosion. Fully involved. Probably got some hazmat."

"And some trauma, too." Abe rushed for the door.

"You know what I don't like about explosions? You never know what's burning in there. If I get cancer, I'll know why."

"You hens finished?" Rasso hollered from behind. "You'll be eatin' hazardous materials if you don't move."

"That's no threat," answered Tenpenney. "I've eaten Fitzy's five-alarm chili—and I'm still alive."

That drew raucous laughter.

Fitzy, who had started climbing into the engine, glanced back. "Tenpenney, you bustin' my balls again?"

"Nah. They broke twenty years ago." Tenpenney bounded into the compartment.

Meanwhile, Abe slammed the rescue door shut, popped

on his headset, then buckled in. "Shit, man. It's really coming down."

"Yeah," said Rasso. "Maybe the rain will put out the fire."

"So we won't have to do anything?"

"Work's overrated, kid."

"Maybe so."

Okay, engine started. All lights on. Siren on. The colossal squad vehicle pulled out first. The engine came next, tearing through the squad's exhaust.

Abe clicked on the wipers as they left the apparatus floor. Rain drummed on the cab's roof.

"This part I don't mind," Rasso said. "Nice little rush of anticipation, but when we get there, it's like a couple hours into Christmas morning. You've opened all the presents and you're thinking, This is it?"

"Don't know about that. Explosion. Confirmed structure fire. Pouring rain. Bad neighborhood. I'm pumped."

Rasso thought a moment. "Kid, I didn't take those pills."

Abe just glanced at him.

After another moment, the old medic cleared his throat. "So, this could be our last big call together. You gonna miss me?"

Flashing his tightest frown, Abe answered, "Yeah. I'll miss your sense of humor. . . ."

Doe jogged to his rescue, jerked open the officer's door—

And there sat Michael Troft, curly-haired wiseass who considered himself more than God's gift to women and paramedicine. Troft was the gift giver himself, a paragod par excellence. The perfect skin, a product of expensive salon treatments; the perfect hair, trimmed weekly and gelled into place during a two-hour morning ritual; and the perfect teeth, capped by an expensive dentist with celebrity patients, told you all about Mr. Wonderful without his uttering a word.

Of course, Troft loved to hear himself talk. "Hi, Pooh Bear. You're driving." He grinned. "Seniority. Ain't it a bitch?"

"God damn it," Doe spat, then glanced back to Avalty, who sprinted for the engine. "Hey, Timmy? He swear you to silence?"

"Sorry, Doe. He's buying me lunch next shift for not telling you." Avalty waved, then climbed aboard the apparatus.

"I wasn't supposed to be here this morning, but there was a little mix-up," Troft said with a malicious grin. "Izzy's out and I'm in. Don't look so surprised. You knew this was coming. Just like old times. Now move it, sweetheart. We're gonna miss the prom. And by the way—the new bald look? It ain't you."

Doe slammed the door in Troft's face, then charged around to the driver's side. As he buckled in and donned his headgear, the paragod forged on:

"Nicole and I went out to dinner last night. Did you know that? Did you know me and your old girlfriend were . . . well, I'm sure you got a picture in your head right now. Did you know that she told me she never had a real man? She couldn't believe she wasted so much time on you. Did you know that?"

"I don't care. And I'm happy for you, believe me. You two deserve each other."

"Really? I was hoping you'd have a problem with it. I know she kept a pretty tight leash on you before she cut it. I heard little Doe got his heart broken."

"You get her off my back, and I'll buy *you* lunch."

"You're lying, my misguided apprentice. She's just

fuckin' me. She wants you. And you want her. All she did was talk about you."

"I don't want to know."

"She told me you'd be like this."

"What? She paying you to nag me?"

"No, she's banging me. Much better."

"Just get out of my face."

Troft tilted his head from side to side, working the stiffness out of his neck. "I don't know, Doe. She's a real gymnast. You're crazy—unless you got another girlfriend."

"I'm surprised Nicole didn't tell you."

"She told me you were trying to punish her for leaving you. You're thinking you'll get burned again. But according to her, she's pretty serious."

"Yeah, she's serious. Madly in love with me while she's screwing you."

"She was probably thinking about you while she was doing me. Doesn't matter, though. I wasn't thinking about her."

Doe started to say something, but an update came over the radio. Confirmed structure fire. Big fire. Multiple alarms. VPD units on scene. Stations Eight, Nine, and Ten responding. Move-ups in progress. Battalion Six also responding, which meant that the lieutenants from each station would stress under the scrutiny of the battalion chief. Big fire. Big operation: two aerial ladder trucks, three engines, three rescues, and one squad truck equipped to handle hazardous materials.

"Well, Pooh. Sounds like we bought ourselves some fun in the rain."

Savage opened the refrigerator door, stared at the beers, closed the door.

How many times had she done that? Ten? Twelve? She still hadn't taken a beer. . . .

But she knew she eventually would. You could play all the mind games you wanted. You could change brands because you thought you'd drink less. You could pretend that only one drink wouldn't hurt you. You could keep telling yourself that tomorrow you would really quit. You could drink so much that you'd black out and forget you had drunk so much.

And you would wind up exactly where she was: trying to make it through the day.

She thought of calling the lieutenant, calling someone—anyone—who might understand. Thank God the intercom rang.

"Stephanie, it's George Solaris. I'm downstairs. Thought I'd come by and see how you're doing. Buzz me up?"

George Solaris? She blanked on the name. Oh, God, George. Hospital fetish George. Son of famous TV star George. What the hell did he want? Buzz him up?

"Hey, how'd you get my address?"

"Don't you remember? I called you a cab. Came home with you. Made sure you were okay. You gave me your address."

Damn! She remembered now. What the hell? She could kick his ass if he tried anything. "Okay, I'm buzzing you in."

As she waited for him to ride the elevator, she saw that her soap had been interrupted by a special news report. Big structure fire in the valley. Aerial views from a news chopper showed thick clouds of smoke fighting up through the rain. And that building looked familiar. The doorbell rang.

George beamed at her, then smoothed out his Valley

Fire Department paramedic uniform. "You like?" He twirled like a runway model.

"What are you doing now, George? Stealing more uniforms?"

"Stealing? I don't steal. This was a gift from the same buddy who gave me the T-shirt."

"Impersonating a public servant is a felony, I think."

"Oh, I'm not impersonating anyone," he said, skirting past her and taking a seat on the sofa. "I just like the feel of cotton."

"You're going to get in trouble."

"I already am in trouble. So are you."

"Look, if you try anything, I'll kick your ass."

He grinned. "You think I came here for sex?"

"Uh, let's see, George. You're a pervert. Of course you didn't come here for sex."

"I was thinking maybe we could make a deal."

Savage raked her hair out of her eyes. "George, I'm not making any deals."

"Just hear me out. I've been thinking a lot about you."

"I told you, I'll kick your ass. You know I can."

"We're in the same boat, me and you. I keep telling myself that I can stop doing what I'm doing. But I can't. Know the feeling?"

"George, go back to your mommy's mansion."

"First thing is, *you* have to want to change your life. If you don't want to help yourself, no one else can do anything about it."

"I'm getting counseling from a nut," she said, glancing skyward. "Why is my life so screwed up?"

"Make a pact with me. And make a promise to yourself that you're gonna change. I'll do the same thing. We'll watch each other's backs. For a long time, I owed you. You always tried to help me with my problems. Then I

got a chance to help you. Now it's time we help each
other."

She threw her hands in the air. "What's it gonna take
to get you out of here?"

"Just that promise. That's all."

"Okay. Whatever. I promise to change."

"And so do I."

Savage went to her door, opened it. "Now the first thing
you're gonna do is go home and take off that uniform.
And then you're gonna find a job instead of living off
Mommy's money."

He stood. "I'm gonna do it, Stephanie. And so are you.
I'll see you next week."

"Okay, George, okay. *'Bye.*"

After he left, Savage couldn't help but smile. He was
a nut—a nut who had made a lot of sense.

Abe's hazardous materials operations course had covered
such areas as decontamination and personal protective
equipment, regulatory requirements for patient decontamination, procedures to follow for patient decontamination,
introduction to disaster planning, and using available reference materials such as material safety data sheets, ship-
ping papers, and chemical reference manuals. However,
all the training in the world meant nothing unless you
could react swiftly and adapt to your situation.

Even a few blocks away from the fire, black smoke rose
over the neighborhood and stained the gray sky. The light
ahead turned green, courtesy of their Opticom unit, and
Abe barreled through the intersection, with Rasso calling
clear on the right.

They pulled up behind Rescue Ten, which idled at the
curb about a half-block from the building. VPD units had
already cordoned off the street and evacuated residents

from the nearby buildings. The two ladder trucks were pulling into position to raise their booms and suppress the fires on the third, fourth, and fifth floors.

"Rescue Nine is on scene," Rasso reported.

"Rescue Nine."

The second Abe opened his door, a nauseating, sulfur-like stench brought his hand to his nose. "Oh, man."

"Sorry, kid. Must've been that cheeseburger."

"Damn! What's burning?"

"You haven't figured this out? C'mon. This wasn't no faulty gas line." Rasso opened the bay door and pulled out his fire hat. "Yeah, I remember doing overhaul once in a building a lot like this one. I picked up this soda bottle, and my gloves started melting. What I'm saying, kid, is that you're looking at a meth lab explosion. These *cholos* use pool acid, brake fluid, lye they find in drain cleaners, acetone, denatured alcohol, cold tablets, and they filter the shit with cat box litter. What's burning up there is all of that and more."

"And we bitch about Fitzy's cooking. . . ."

"Yeah, they'll let it all burn up, then send some guys in with Level A suits for overhaul."

Abe went to the back. The airway bag, drug box, and monitor were already stowed on the stretcher, so he just hit the release and called for Rasso to help. They removed the stretcher, then wheeled it and the gear down the sidewalk.

Lieutenant Martinez stood just ahead, near the hood of Engine Nine, along with the two lieutenants from Eight and Ten, as well as the battalion chief, who was an exceedingly busy man at the moment: "All right, let's see if we can knock this one down quick. We'll set up a decon corridor in the warm zone out in the street. I want the treatment sector by that staircase, staging over there, for-

ward staging over there, and rehab on the corner. I'm on
tac one. Go."

Martinez lifted his portable. "Fitzy, you, Tenpenney,
and Cannis get weighed. You're going in."

"Copy that," Fitzy answered.

"Rasso, you and Abe are over in treatment. You got a
lady there with a laceration on her head. The medics from
Ten will work rehab with Rosenberg and Dunhill." Martinez cocked a thumb at the squad vehicle, where Rosenberg and Dunhill pulled out the large awning from the
driver's side of the truck. Doe and another guy were already setting up over there. They would establish the rehab sector beneath that awning, outside and upwind of the
hot zone. Firefighters would log in and submit to a medical evaluation. If they checked out, they'd be filled full
of liquids, fed if they were hungry, given fresh oxygen
tanks, and sent back into the hot zone. The "two-cylinder
rule" dictated that after going through a pair of thirty-
minute air tanks, firefighters had to report to the rehab
sector. Heat-related emergencies did occur, and the rehab
crew would work on fellow firefighters who had developed heat cramps, exhaustion, stroke, or worse.

"You get that first victim over there and start setting
up," Rasso said. "I'll swing the rescue around so we can
get out through that side street."

Rain splashed on Abe's pants as he ran across the
street. Stripe-jacketed firefighters stood in sharp contrast
to the glossy black pavement and building's dull brick.
Three great bands of fire flickered overhead, unbothered
by the rain. Even from across the street, the fire's incred-
ible heat warmed Abe's neck.

"Here comes a medic now," said a cop who held his
umbrella over a lanky black woman seated on the staircase—the same staircase Abe had climbed a few weeks

prior. He recognized a second woman as the mother who had refused treatment for her son. Abe wondered if she'd remember him.

"Hi, I'm Abe Kashmiri. What happened to your head?"

The woman pulled a bloodstained 4x4 gauze bandage away from her temple. "When the place blew up, something must've shot out at me." She glanced to the cop. "He gave me the bandage."

"You look familiar," the other woman said, rain dripping from her beaded hair.

"So do you." He turned to the injured woman. "What's your name?"

"Crystal."

"And I'm Shonica. You were here, weren't you?"

"Maybe. We run a lot of calls."

"Hey, Crystal. That bitch who came here the other day? This is her partner. Yeah, I remember him. He broke Slip's radio."

Crystal's brows came together. "Get away from me!"

"What?"

"You heard me," she spat. "I don't want you touchin' me. You people come here and take my sister's kids away from her. I don't want nothing to do with you. Nothing!"

"You have to go to the hospital. You need stitches," Abe said, focusing on her wound.

"Not with you."

"Problem over here?" Rasso called, marching up.

"He can work on me," Crystal said, then glanced angrily at Abe. "Not you."

Rasso closed his eyes, and a forced calm worked into his tone. "Get me a four-by-four."

Doe looked up from his drug box, and right there, just a few yards away, Nicole Cavalier wriggled into her air tank's harness. Doe's gaze found hers, and he couldn't help but go over. "Thought you'd be riding the rescue by now."

"Last shift," she said, a hint of melancholy in her tone. "Haven't run one of these in a long time. Then again, I hate recovering corpses—especially in the rain."

"Nicole, I just. . . ."

"Hey, it's okay. I was just going to use you again. You know how I am. But you . . . I don't believe it. You finally grew up. I wouldn't have bet on it. Maybe you can teach me."

"Maybe. But the homework sucks."

That drew a faint grin. "When I was in New York, I met this guy. Got pregnant. Had a little girl. I don't know, Doe . . . I couldn't do that whole family thing. I just gave up. Ran away. He's got her now. How could I do that?"

"It's a feeling, like claustrophobia or something. Like you can't breathe. I was there."

She shrugged and put on her mask. He helped her finish checking the O_2 supply, then gave her a hard pat on the shoulder. She picked up her sledgehammer and started for the hot zone.

Twin jets of water struck the burning building from its north and east sides. Flames recoiled, then lashed out at the spray. Smoke grew thicker and belched more heavily from the roof. Nicole wiped off the soot and mist that dappled her mask, then entered the structure with Fitzy, Tenpenney, and Cannis from Station Nine. Down the street, reps from the DEA, Valley PD's drug task force unit, its gang unit, and two guys from the Environmental Protection Agency pored over documents on the hood of one guy's car. Nicole pushed inside, following Tenpenney and Cannis. Fitzy kept close behind her, shoving his pike pole into the nearest wall and checking for flames.

Cannis held up his thermal imager to scan through the thick smoke. Fitzy stopped to glance through his own imager. Cannis signaled them on. They reached an intersecting hall, with apartment doors to the left and right. Tenpenney and Cannis took the left.

Nicole tried the first door to the right: open. They shifted inside. She busted out the windows to help ventilate the unit while Fitzy began the search. They checked closets and cabinets for small children. It was hard not to notice the squalor. Rugs were soiled. Dirty clothes were piled high next to leaking paper bags full of trash. Roaches scattered as doors opened. The bugs were the only ones home. Fitzy gave her the high sign. They rushed on to the next unit.

"Got one," cried Cannis from Nicole's portable clipped to her belt. "Male. Geriatric patient. Unconscious, unresponsive. Bringing him out." While he and Tenpenney delivered the victim to firefighters waiting outside, Nicole and Fitzy finished their sweep of the first floor, then moved back to the stairwell.

Because the third, fourth, and fifth floors were engulfed, they would have only a few precious minutes to check for victims on the second floor before the battalion chief pulled them out. The rumble from above already hinted at an unstable structure.

As they neared the second floor landing, Fitzy lowered his pike pole and imager, then hollered, "We got some victims over here!"

Two Hispanic males in their twenties lay supine on the floor, one near the stairs leading to the third floor, the other near the opposite wall. Judging from their positions, they had tried to make it down from the third floor, had collapsed on the staircase, and had tumbled down to the landing. Both wore green knit caps, and the nearer one's chest had been torched into a horrible bed of full-thickness burns that caused the most extensive tissue damage. His skin had a dry, leatherlike appearance, shifting from white to brown to charred black near the waistline. He had a snake tattooed over his eyebrow. The other guy had partial thickness burns to his arms and hands. Splotches of blistering red skin would've had him howling had he not succumbed to the smoke. Fitzy grabbed the first guy's legs. Nicole reached under the guy's arms, and they carried him down the stairs and out to the waiting crew. One out. One to go. They went back toward the stairs.

Though both "unlicensed chemical engineers" might already be dead, Nicole and Fitzy would risk their lives to get them out. You weren't supposed to judge your patients, but Nicole had never met a medic who didn't. To keep your job, you kept your opinions to yourself and treated all patients equally—and sometimes that was the hardest part.

Back up the stairs a third time so they could finally make their sweep of the second floor. Tenpenney and Cannis joined them, fanning left again, as Nicole and Fitzy worked a careful path to the right. Fitzy paused and drove his pike into the hallway's ceiling, then tugged off a piece of Sheetrock. A bit of smoke came from the hole. The fire was up there, but it hadn't made it down to the floor yet. Good. They went to the nearest apartment door, which hung half open. Fitzy took the bedrooms. Nicole smashed open the windows, then searched the living room and small kitchen. Nothing.

One by one they inspected the other apartments and came up empty. They called a primary all clear, then the call to evacuate sounded.

"Wait a minute," Nicole shouted to Fitzy, though she couldn't see him through all the gray smoke. "One more door here."

"Forget it! Let's go!"

A muffled bang came from inside.

"Couple seconds! Come on!" she urged him. "I heard something."

There it was again. This time much louder.

Nicole tried the door. Locked. Drew back the sledge-hammer. *Bang*! The door split open near the knob and creaked inward—just as Fitzy came up behind her.

"Holy shit," she whispered.

The ceiling above the unit's living room had collapsed to form a flaming cascade of debris. Flames danced along exposed studs and darted behind thick pieces of Sheetrock and blazing plywood. As Nicole and Fitzy watched, a cof-fee table from the unit above slid down the collapsed ceil-ing to crash and heave a cloud of burning embers. Barely visible behind the cascade was an entertainment center whose cheap veneer bubbled off. The TV it supported had melted down like a candle. Something flashed from just above the unit, then—

Bang!

" 'the hell was that?" hollered Fitzy.

Another pop sounded.

With all the smoke and crackling flames, it took Nicole another moment to realize that a box of ammunition lay on top of the entertainment center. That ammunition was now cooking off.

"Oh, shit! Fitzy we have to—"

A sound like machine-gun fire drowned out her words. Fitzy dropped to his knees as she turned from the noise. Then a red-hot poker jammed into her lower back and shoved her to the floor.

17

"We got two personal alarms inside," reported Tenpenney on the tactical frequency. "Fitzy and Nicole."

Abe glanced to Rasso, who had finished bandaging Crystal's laceration. "You hear that?"

"Yeah, I heard it," Rasso said. "Don't have an MI yet. They might've tripped, and it wouldn't be the first time a PASS device went off by accident." He faced Crystal. "How's that feel?"

"It's all right. So let's go to the hospital."

"We'll need to wait for a little while."

"Why? To see if your buddies are okay while I'm bleeding over here?"

"You just need a few sutures. You'll be okay. Might be somebody who needs to go to the hospital a little bit more than you do. Just a few minutes longer, and we'll be on our way."

"This is bullshit."

"Yes it is, ma'am. I totally agree. The customer is always right. It's bullshit that I'm standing out here in the rain and watching some building burn because some

punks had their lab blow up in their faces. It's bullshit
that some innocent people are probably dead because of
them. Bullshit. Definitely bullshit."

"Take me to the hospital. Right now!" Crystal lifted an
index finger and bobbed her head with rage. "Take me to
the hospital, or I'm gonna do something. Maybe I'm
gonna get that cop over there and have you locked up for
not doing your job."

Abe pressed his portable to his ear and tried to tune out
Crystal's bitching.

"What do you got, Cannis?" asked Lieutenant Martinez.

"Okay! Okay! Found 'em. I don't know what happened. Looks like some penetration to their coats. Bringing them out! Bringing them out!"

Doe and Troft were held back from the hot zone by
firefighter-EMTs Rosenberg and Dunhill. When the call
had come in that Fitzy and Nicole had gone down, both
medics had abandoned the rehab sector and had run toward the building's main entrance, where four more firefighters waited. Of course that had been a stupid thing to
do. Of course there had been nothing they *could* do but
wait outside, out of the hot zone.

"Where the hell are they? Come on, come on," Doe
said as he leaned past Dunhill and glimpsed the entrance-
way.

"There's one now," said Troft.

"Doe? Troft?" came Lieutenant Greenwell's voice over
their portables. "You're out of rehab. You got Fitzy."

Tenpenney and Cannis carried Fitzy into the middle of
the street, to an area set up as the decontamination corridor, with two kiddie pools inflated for scrubdowns.
There they lowered Fitzy onto a blanket, then removed
his mask, air tank, and turnout gear. They shoved those

items into red biohazard bags as Fitzy groaned and cursed. Cannis said a few words to the decon officer, a tall black woman named Precious, then he and Tenpenney stood in the kiddie pools while other firefighters scrubbed them down. They were being shifted to the treatment sector.

"Hey, we got him," Doe called as he and Troft hurried over. Doe hunkered down next to Fitzy and pulled on a second pair of gloves. "Hey, buddy. How're you doing?"

"I'm just fucked," Fitzy groaned, looking cyanotic, his face pale, cool, and clammy, his lips light blue. He struggled for breath. "I didn't . . . become a fireman . . . to get shot. Burned, yeah. But not . . . shot."

"Cannis thinks a box of bullets cooked off up there," said Precious. "Maybe nine millimeter."

"Well, he took one right there," Troft said, noting the bloodstain on Fitzy's left shoulder.

"Aw, shit," Doe muttered as he pulled out his trauma shears and began cutting away Fitzy's shirt. "Hey, Fitz? Does it hurt anywhere else?"

"Yeah, my left leg. And I took one . . . in the nut. What am I gonna tell . . . all my girlfriends?"

"There it is," said Troft. A small, oval hole with an abraded edge oozed blood onto the old firefighter's chest.

"Fitzy, we gotta roll you a little to check for an exit wound," Doe said. "It's gonna hurt."

"Fuck. It already . . . does."

Fitzy gasped as they shifted him.

"No exit wound," reported Troft as he finished pulling away Fitzy's shirt. They were looking for a starburst pattern without an abrasion. "Hey, Rosenberg, get me a board."

"You want a collar, too?"

"Nope. Just the board."

The EMT nodded and charged off.

Doc began cutting a long line up Fitzy's pants leg.

"All right, everybody shut up," Troft ordered. He put on his stethoscope and listened to Fitzy's lungs. Doe knew that would be damned difficult, given all the background noise. Troft squinted in concentration. "Sounds absent upper left, very diminished lower left. Present on the right."

After pushing away the pants material, Doe studied Fitzy's leg. "Looks like the one in the groin just nipped your thigh, so your nuts are all right," he said. "Probably a few vessels damaged. The one in the leg just glanced your calf. I've scraped my leg on coral and got more damage."

"But the one . . . up here's gonna . . . kill me," Fitzy added.

"Here's your board," said Rosenberg.

"Okay, let's roll him," Troft said.

Fitzy stiffened. "Here comes . . . more . . . pain."

Troft knelt near Fitzy's chest while Doe positioned himself next to Troft, at Fitzy's knees. They straightened Fitzy's arms. Troft held the left shoulder while Doe held the wrist. They slowly rolled Fitzy onto his side just enough to allow Rosenberg to slide the long backboard under Fitzy's back. They lowered him onto it. Doe fastened a strap around Fitzy's waist. "Fuck the other straps," Troft told Doe. "Okay, let's load him." He unclipped his portable. "Lieutenant? I need a couple more EMTs. Copy?"

Rosenberg helped Doe place Fitzy on the stretcher, then they rolled the old firefighter to the rescue. Once they got him inside, Doe quickly recorded a set of vitals.

Timothy Avalty ran up behind the rescue. "Hey, Doe, Louis is gonna drive. What do you need?"

Troft hustled up behind Avalty. "Lest you forget that I'm riding seat, Mr. Avalty. Get in there and set up to bag him. You got vitals yet, Doe? Or are you just standing around?"

Fuck you. "Pulse is 150. Respirations, 30," Doe reported. "BP, 80 palp. Blood's pushing his heart and his collapsed lung to the right. His trachea's moving."

"Hey, Avalty, get a tube ready," said Troft.

"You see Nicole?" Doe asked Avalty as the younger man climbed into the rescue.

"Just now. Rasso and that rookie are taking her."

"How was she?"

"Dunno." Avalty dug into the airway bag and began pulling out an oxygen line and bag valve mask. Then he went for the laryngoscope and endotracheal tube.

Doe removed a pair of 1000cc bags of normal saline from an overhead cabinet.

"Hey, Doe," Fitzy said. "Go ahead. See how . . . she is."

"Sorry, Fitzy, but he's staying here," said Troft as he shut the rescue's doors. "She's in pretty good hands."

"Yeah, she's with a rookie and a burnout," Doe said with a snort.

Troft grabbed the headset. "Louis, let's go!" Then he glanced wide-eyed at Doe, who looked away and began setting up the large-bore IVs.

Fitzy needed fluids, and Doe needed to concentrate on that. The firefighter would begin to show signs of shock, with a falling blood pressure and a diminished level of consciousness. Once he passed into decompensated shock, only one more stage of decline was left—death.

"Fitzy, my boy, you're bleeding out into your pleural space. I bet that round clipped your left subclavian," Troft said as he applied a big trauma bandage to Fitzy's shoulder.

After mumbling a few words, Fitzy closed his eyes.

"Stay with us, Fitzy," urged Doe.

"He's going under," Avalty said.

Doe got his first line in, withdrew the needle, attached the tubing to the catheter, opened up the line. "Come on, Fitzy. You're a stubborn old fucker. Hang on." He applied the Veni-Gard, then started his second line.

"Rasso, I can't . . . I can't feel my legs," said Nicole Cavalier, lying on a blanket in the middle of the street. Abe knelt at her right side, Rasso at the left. The building still blazed behind her, and the wind swept smoke and rain into Abe's eyes.

"Ready?" Rasso asked Abe.

They rolled Nicole onto her side. She had been hit in the low thoracic spine. No evidence of an exit wound. Abe suspected that the round had shattered one of her kidneys, and it had come dangerously close to her spinal cord. He was no doctor, but she could be paralyzed.

Paul Cannis, who had stripped out of his breathing gear, brought over the long backboard.

Nicole shivered. "Rasso, I'm scared, man."

"Scared? With us treating you? Honey, you've got the best of the best. Well, maybe not with the kid here, but he's learning from the best."

An odd look came over her face. "I don't want to go to the hospital. And where the hell is my purse? God damn it, where's my purse? I need my keys. I'll drive myself home."

"We'll drive you home," Abe said, helping Rasso log-roll Nicole as Cannis positioned the backboard.

Working soundlessly and in concert, they fastened the backboard's straps to immobilize Nicole's spine, lifted her, set her on the stretcher, then moved swiftly but cautiously back toward the staircase and the rescue idling nearby.

"Hey, where you going?" cried Crystal, coming out from beneath her umbrella. "You taking her before me?"

"Cannis? You're driving," Rasso said, then looked to the skinny woman. "You're gonna ride up front in the ambulance. You give us a hard time, I'll make you wait for another ride."

"I want Shonica to come with me."

"Not gonna happen. You coming or not?"

Shonica twisted her lip. "Don't go with this mother-fucker, Crystal."

Rasso finished helping Abe get the stretcher loaded, then waved over the cop. They moved out of Shonica's earshot. "Get this bitch out of my face." He turned to Crystal. "Shonica's not coming. Are you? You got one second to decide."

Crystal moved toward the rescue.

"Crystal? Where the hell you going?" asked Shonica.

"My head's hurting. I'm going. Have Snufa or Kat give you a ride."

Rasso took Crystal by the wrist and led her toward the cab, where he told her to buckle in to the officer's seat. A moment later, he returned to the patient compartment.

"Her pressure's 110 palp. Just got her on the monitor," Abe said, glancing at the reading of 136. "Respirations are 20."

"Where are my keys?" Nicole moaned, her eyes narrowed to slits, her skin growing cold and clammy.

"I have 'em," Abe said in a soothing tone as he rapidly prepared two large-bore IVs. "Don't worry. Your keys are right here."

"Okay, Cannis, let's whistle her in," Rasso ordered into

the headset, then leaned toward Nicole. "Whoa, whoa, whoa, kid. She's losing consciousness."

Doe had once told a rookie that tubing someone inside a moving vehicle is like threading a needle in a typhoon. Well, that might have been an exaggeration, but it still wasn't easy. You suddenly became aware of every bump in the road. He visualized Fitzy's cords, waited a second to see if the pavement would even out a bit more, then slid in the tube. Placement seemed good. He withdrew the stylet, attached the BVM, then listened a second before Louis, up in the driver's seat, jammed on the brakes.

"Jesus H. Christ," Troft yelled, crashing into Avalty and knocking him into the side door.

Ignoring everything around him, Doe listened again for breath sounds. "Okay, Timmy, you're on this bag." Doe slid out of the captain's chair and let Avalty assume his place, behind Fitzy's head. Doe got another set of vitals and wrote them on the back of his glove.

All right. Fitzy was still bleeding out, and his pressure was dropping, but at least they had him bandaged and tubed, and fluids were going in. The rest was up to Louis, a firefighter-EMT with about a year's experience. Doe reached up and switched the rig's radio to SFMC's frequency, hoping to hear an update on Nicole.

"I'll call it in," said Troft, misinterpreting the act. He grabbed Doe's hands, read the vitals, glanced once more at the monitor, then thumbed the mike. "SFMC, Rescue Ten. Copy?"

As Abe slid an endotracheal tube past Nicole Cavalier's vocal cords, he listened to Troft make his report. Fitzy was unconscious, unresponsive, bleeding out, pressure dropping. Just a short time ago they had been joking about his cooking.

"She's Doe's ex-girlfriend," said Rasso, shifting his glance between the monitor and Nicole. "Did you know that?"

"Most of the women I meet around here are Doe's ex-girlfriends," Abe said, then paused to check for breath sounds. Damn it, he couldn't hear them. He tried again. Okay. He began securing the tube while Rasso squeezed the bag.

"Yeah, I've worked with her a few times. We never got to ride rescue together."

"You're riding with her now."

"Yeah."

"Okay, I got the bag," Abe said. "You wanna call it in?"

"Got it. I'll bet Doe's waiting."

"What the hell's taking them so long?" Doe asked, scowling at the radio.

"SFMC? Rescue Nine. Copy?" came Rasso's voice through the small speaker.

"Nine, SFMC. Copy," answered Charti.

"En route to your facility with two patients. The first is an approximately thirty-eight-year-old female, BLS stable. Patient was found A/O times four and suffering from a laceration to her right temple that will require sutures. Second patient is an approximately thirty-two-year-old female firefighter suffering from a single GSW to the lower thoracic spine, with possible spinal cord and kidney injuries. No exit wound. Patient was initially alert and oriented but is now unconscious, unresponsive. GCS is 5. Vitals are BP 60/0, pulse 170. The patient is intubated. Large-bore IVs established in each arm with NS running in each. Updated ETA code 3 is approximately eight minutes. Copy?"

"Copy, Nine. Trauma team will be standing by."

Doe and Troft just looked at each other for a second, before Troft snapped out of it and thumbed the mike. "SFMC, Rescue Ten. Copy?"

"Ten, SFMC. Copy."

"Updated ETA, approximately two minutes. Updated vitals on our patient are as follows: BP is 72 palp, pulse is 154. Copy?"

"Copy, Ten. Standing by."

"And tell Gunga to key open that door for us and clear the hall. Copy?"

"Copy that," said Charti, sounding a little surprised. It wasn't Troft's place to give orders about how the ER should receive a patient, but then again, they weren't transporting the average patient.

"Ten out."

"Fitzy, a lot of people are gonna be pissed off if you kick the bucket, you fuckin' bastard," said Doe, taking the old firefighter's hand in his own. "You can do it, old man. You can do it."

Avalty shoved his Buddy Holly glasses higher on his nose, and squeezed the bag.

Trauma Surgeon Yokito Masaki and two residents on his team were waiting for Rescue Ten outside the ambulance entrance. Whenever cops, firefighters, or medical personnel were injured, a heightened sense of urgency came over the ER. Even if you didn't know the victim, both of you knew the darker side of humanity more intimately than the average citizen. That common ground reminded you of your own mortality.

Troft held up the IV bags while Doe and Avalty rolled

Fitzy out of the rescue and lowered the stretcher's legs. Doe expected Troft to give the doctor a rapid report, but the doc simply waved them forward. "Let's roll right into C booth," he said. "Charti gave me your last update."

Doe grinned a little. It was nice to work with a doc who was so on the ball, especially when you were bringing in a fellow firefighter.

"I got it from here," Troft said. "You want to wait outside for Nicole?"

"I'll see him through," Doe said, a bit taken aback by Troft's sympathy but keeping his gaze riveted on Fitzy. "Thanks."

Once they hit the booth, the usual well-orchestrated chaos began. Masaki decided to crack open Fitzy's chest right there, get a rib spreader in, then clamp off the subclavian. Doe found himself drifting back toward the hall as Troft and Avalty gathered up the backboard, monitor, and airway bag.

In the meantime, off-duty firefighters from stations Nine and Ten began descending upon the ER. Doe bumped into three people he knew from Nine who asked about Fitzy. He gave them a quick update, then broke into a jog toward the ambulance entrance at the end of the hall.

He went outside, expecting Nicole's rescue. Nothing. Then, just above the din of falling rain, came a siren. Louder now. Louder still. Headlights. Diesel engine. Rescue Nine. Air brakes hissed. The siren died.

Doe charged to the back of the rescue. Abe jumped out first, while inside, Rasso released the stretcher. A thin black woman with a bandaged head sat in the officer's seat, repeatedly asking what would happen now. She called for Rasso, who ignored her and helped Abe guide the stretcher, along with Paul Cannis, who finally told the woman to follow them inside.

"How's Fitzy?" Abe asked.

"Cracking him open now. Hopefully they'll stop the bleed and get him up to surgery."

"Coming through," Rasso said as a couple of EMTs from a private ambulance company dodged aside.

Another trauma surgeon, a beefy woman of forty named Hollander, met them about halfway up the hall. "What's going on with her?"

Rasso issued a precise report even as he gasped for air. They rolled Nicole into a trauma bay and pulled the curtain. The shouts of orders, the beeping of monitors, and the clatter of equipment faded. For a second, only Doe and Nicole were in the room.

"Hey, man, come on," said Troft as he took Doc by the back of the neck and forced him outside. "You don't need to shove your face in it. She'll be all right."

"I swear to God, she's got no luck," Doe said under his breath. "Damn!"

"Yeah. Damn shame. Let's go. We have to clean up and get back in service. Get our minds off this."

"That's not funny."

"I know."

"You know? Then you're an idiot. We're gonna get relieved and debriefed. We're not going anywhere."

"I'm not sitting around a hospital all night."

"That's Nicole in there. Oh, I forgot. She was just a quick lay."

"Hey, we all got our way of dealing." Troft gestured around the hall. "If I'm not gonna work, then I'm gonna get permission to go home." He reached for his portable and started for the exit. "And Doe? We still have to clean up for the relief crew. Your ass is mine until Greenwell gets here."

Firefighters crowded the two private family rooms allocated to relatives and friends of Fitzy and Nicole. Abe elbowed his way into the room reserved for Fitzy's people. He and Rasso had turned over their rescue to two medics, Morgan and Wong, who had been called in. Rasso said he was going for coffee and would catch him upstairs. Abe stood in the back of the room and was practically interrogated by the other firefighters. He gave them a detailed account of the fire, of how Fitzy had been pulled out, and of everything they had done en route.

An hour later, Dr. Masaki came into the room and reported that the most serious shot had entered through Fitzy's left shoulder, had hit the top of his left lung, had struck the left subclavian, had barely missed his aorta, and had come to rest behind his breastbone. They had repaired the damage to his lung and vein, and the old firefighter was now in stable but serious condition. He would live. Fitzy's wife buried her head in Masaki's chest and thanked him. The trauma surgeon gave her an awkward hug, dug his feet deeper into his clogs, then escaped before the scene grew any worse.

Abe checked his watch. What had happened to Rasso?

"Geneva? Hey, it's me," Doe said, standing outside the waiting room for Nicole.

"Are you okay? I saw the fire on TV."

"I'm all right. Guy I know from Nine got shot when some ammo cooked off in the fire. Guess who also got shot? Nicole."

Silence for a moment. "Is she dead?"

"Doc just came in and told us she lost a kidney and

her spinal cord got shocked. She'll be paralyzed for a few days, but she'll be okay."

"Really. So I guess you got relieved?"

"Yeah."

"Are you going home? Because if you are, why don't you come here instead?"

"I'll probably be here for another hour or so, then I'll go back to the station and get changed. I won't get there until about nine."

"That's all right."

"You sure?"

"That's fine. And Doe? This is going to sound terrible, but when you just told me about Nicole, I felt glad. Like she got what she deserved. That's horrible, I know. I'm sorry."

Doe hesitated. "I'll see you tonight."

18

Joanna Boccaccio lay in bed, squinting at the long shadows that quartered the ceiling. Rain tapped on the windowsill, and the occasional crack of thunder rattled the window. She had forgotten to wrap up the leftover pizza, and the scent of pepperoni drifted in from the kitchen. She rolled over, closed her eyes, and suddenly felt very, very old.

Mom, tell me how I'm supposed to forgive you.

No cold breeze rushed into Boccaccio's bedroom. No ghost answered.

She pushed deeper into her pillow and thought about what a fool she had made of herself at the lunch. Three drinks on an empty stomach had turned her into a babbling idiot. She had insulted half her relatives, then had retreated to the asylum of her hospital clique, residents and nurses who allowed her to act like an ass. Her mother had just killed herself, and poor Joanna had an excuse to get wasted—though shouting across the room that her mother had been a selfish, fucking bitch did push the limit of her father's patience.

Feeling her legs grow sweaty, she threw off the blanket

and let the air cool her naked body. The headache had come on several hours ago, but the thought of taking something—the thought of pills—made her sick.

"Joanna?"

She rolled over and faced her mall security guard. He lay there, the blanket pulled up to his navel, his youthful form glimmering in the clock's dim light.

"Joanna, are you all right?"

"You have to go."

"I do? But I thought—"

"You have to go."

He sat up, glanced at the clock. "Serious? Do you know what time it is?"

A thunderclap sent chills across her back. The rain tapped louder on the sill. "Please . . ."

"What did I do?"

She turned away. "Nothing. I just need you to go."

"I'll go sleep on the sofa. I don't want to leave you alone."

"You can't stay. You just can't."

"All right," he said through an agitated sigh. "I'll get dressed."

He moved smoothly through the shadows, sliding and zippering and buttoning. Finally he said, "I'm gonna go now. I'll call you tomorrow. You should lock the door."

"I will."

The bed creaked as he braced himself, leaned over, and gave her a peck on the cheek. " 'Bye."

Boccaccio listened to him leave. He would keep his word and call her tomorrow. He would get her machine.

"What're you doing here?" Abe asked, yawning. He crossed into Station Nine's day room. "Figured you went home."

Rasso was in the kitchen, pouring himself a cup of black coffee. "Nah."

"Why didn't you come up? You know Fitzy's gonna be all right. So's Nicole."

"I heard."

Abe practically fell into a recliner. He would rest a moment, go up to the hood and change, then head home to bed.

"So what do you think, kid?" Rasso asked, coming up behind Abe. "You still think you want to do this?"

"Yeah. So I can be just like you."

Rasso snickered. "That's right. Just like me. Whistling down a freeway to hell. Tell you what. Maybe I'll stick around to keep showing you how it's done. With old Fitzy out of the loop for a while, they might ask me to stay on for another, oh, I don't know, couple of months?" He moved in front of the recliner, smacking his lips as he lowered his coffee mug.

"You wouldn't want to do that," Abe said, growing edgy at the thought. "You'd be riding the engine most of the time."

"Oh, no. I'm senior medic. They wouldn't keep me there. Martinez would have me riding with you and Cannis."

"Stephanie wouldn't let that happen."

"She wouldn't have a choice. But I'm just bullshitting you. No one's asked, and I'm not sure I'd want to come. I've put my time in at these busy stations. Can't say I mind running only a few calls per shift."

"I'll remember that when I get old."

Rasso made a face. "Well, asshole, I'm gonna leave." He returned his mug to the kitchen, then lifted his duffel bag and left the day room, heading for the apparatus floor.

Abe rose, feeling compelled to go after the man and

thank him. But for what? Two weeks of hell? The only thing Rasso had taught him was how to deal with a hard-core asshole. Then again, maybe that was something valuable. Abe still didn't know if the guy was an addict or not, and he worried that someone—a patient—would find out the hard way. He still wondered if he should go to the lieutenant, but maybe Fitzy had been right about the higher-ups making allowances. And because Abe still had no hard evidence, he would just be branded a snitch.

Upstairs in the hood, Abe opened his locker. A small envelope fell to the floor. Someone had shoved it under the door. Something bulky was inside the letter, and the handwriting looked familiar.

My brother (a bigger asshole than me) gave me this for putting up with him for all these years. So here's your medal for spending two weeks with me. Pin it on your ass. Let these other losers know how many times I kicked it.—VR

"Hey, what's that?" asked Tenpenney as he tugged open his own locker.

Abe pulled out a heart-shaped medal hanging from a piece of blue silk. The medal had a purple enamel background with a gold border and a gold relief bust of George Washington. Abe held it up. "I don't know."

Tenpenney gaped. "You don't know? Jesus. . . . Let me see that." He took it into his hands and examined it as though it were rare and expensive. "This is a Purple Heart. You gotta die or be wounded in combat to get one of these. My dad's got two of them. Where'd you get it?"

"It was a gift."

"Nice gift," Tenpenney said, awed. He returned the medal. "Hang on to it. It really means something."

The medal shimmered a moment before Abe tucked it into his pocket. *You took those pills, you bastard.*

"What's wrong with you now?" Tenpenney asked.

"Nothing."

Friday had turned out well for Stephanie Savage. She had made it through the day without a drink, and that evening she had purchased her new, white Ford F-150 pickup. All right, so buying the truck was a superficial way of making herself feel better, but she did need transportation. The dealer gave her old pickup last rites and a meager trade-in allowance.

Savage tugged on her jeans, slipped into her sandals, and excitedly grabbed her keys and purse. In a few minutes, she'd be down at Station Nine, enjoying a cup of coffee and showing off her new wheels. She locked the door, was about to walk away. The phone rang. Aw, hell. She stuffed her key back in the lock and went inside. "Hello?"

"Ma, it's me."

Savage opened her mouth.

"Before you say anything, let me talk."

"Donny—"

"I want you in my life, but you have to deal with the fact that Tina is my wife and that I'm living here and going to school here and this is the way I want my life."

"But Donny—"

"Her parents have really helped us, and so has Dad. You're the only one who has a real problem with this now, and I really wish you'd do something about it, because I don't want to alienate you, but you're not giving me—"

"Donny—"

"—much choice. I don't understand what the problem is. I don't understand."

"I'm the problem."

"What?"

"I'm the problem. I still think what you're doing is stupid, but you're right. It's not my life."

"Oh, no. Here comes the guilt trip."

"No guilt trip. You're my son, Donny. I sacrificed a lot for you, but I'm not supposed to get anything in return."

"Really?"

"Really. I have to be here for you—even if I don't like what you're doing. It's just hard to keep my mouth shut."

"Maybe what I'm doing is stupid, but I gotta try. And you know what? I think I turned out pretty good, Ma."

"Yeah, you did." She swallowed, told herself not to cry. "I don't want to lose you."

"I know, Ma. Why don't you meet us for lunch? Okay, so no one's ever going to be good enough for me. But why don't you give Tina a chance? Will you do that for me?"

"Okay, Donny. I'll try."

Early Saturday evening, Doe showered and went by the hospital to catch Nicole before visiting hours ended.

"What's the matter with you?" he asked as he approached her bed in the ICU. "You look like you got shot."

"Hey," she whispered.

"I brought you some of those mints you like," he said, then dropped the bag on her rolling table. "Maybe they won't let you have them. You want me to hide 'em or something?"

"No."

"So, they all come by to see you today?"

"A few people from the station. Troft, of course. He's a pain in the ass. Hey, it's the weekend. Shouldn't you be out with your girlfriend?"

"A buddy gets hurt. It's not like it hasn't happened before and I haven't been here before. She knows how it is, and she knows where I am."

Nicole nodded slightly, then blurted out, "Doe, thanks for coming." A tear fell, and she rolled her face into the pillow, embarrassed.

"Hey, you don't do that, Nicole. You never do that."

"I know. I'm just so fucked up. I can't stay, Doe. When I get out of here, I have to go back."

"To New York."

"Yeah."

"You're doing the right thing."

"I'm scared."

"So am I. I'm gonna be a dad. But you just can't walk around feeling nervous. You have to say when it happens, it happens—and you'll worry about it then."

"My daughter's father . . . he's, uh . . . I don't know what he's going to do."

"It'll take some time, but he'll come around. I wouldn't want to raise a kid by myself. Bet he doesn't, either."

"What if he won't listen to me?"

"Then you'll deal with that. You're strong. I'm not worried about you."

"You should be. I came all the way out here, tried to get back into my old life. I wasted all this time."

"You didn't waste anything. You came here, and you figured out what you want. Definitely not a waste."

"You know, you're making it hard to leave."

"You want me to call you a fuckin' whore and walk out?"

"No," she said with a smile. "Just let me close my eyes,

and you give me one soft kiss. When I open my eyes, you'll be gone." She took a deep breath, shut her eyes.

He gave her the kiss, then pulled back and waited.

She opened her eyes, saw him. "Jerk! You were supposed to leave." She banged him in the head with the bag of mints.

"What kind of corny soap opera shit is that? *When I open my eyes, you'll be gone.* . . . If you weren't in that bed, I'd kick your ass all the way back to New York."

"Yeah, you probably would."

Abe and Lisa curled up on her sofa and watched forty-seven cable channels (Lisa liked to surf). They had just put her daughter to bed, had turned off *The Bananas in Pajamas* video, and finally had some time alone. "You still haven't asked me about my shift," he said.

"No," she said cautiously. "And I'm surprised you haven't said anything. It was all over the news. I was looking for you. I saw the trucks from your station."

"I don't want to take the job home."

"You are the job."

"I don't know about that."

"You want to talk. You're just afraid—otherwise you wouldn't bring up your day."

"I'm not afraid."

She slid up to him, rested her head on his shoulder. "Yes, you are. How was your shift? How were the past couple of weeks?"

"Busy."

"You think if you tell me all the gory details I'll leave? Come on. You've already told me some stuff."

"I don't think you'll leave."

"Liar. You didn't care as much in the beginning. You opened up, figuring you had nothing to lose. Maybe you were testing me to see if I could take it. Now, all of a sudden, you're worried. I'm hoping that's because you care."

"I do. It's just . . . if I can't deal with this myself, then I don't belong in this job."

"If you deal with it alone, *then* you don't belong in the job. You know how good it feels to vent. You go to the debriefings. Why can't I help?"

"One of the people who got shot, old Fitzy at my station, he told me he brings the job home to his wife."

"And what's wrong with that?"

"Some stuff's better left at the station."

"But you're not leaving it at the station. You're carrying it around. It's here with us, right now." She tapped his heart. "All those people you have to deal with. . . ."

Abe sprang off the sofa. "You want to know who's here? Little black girl living in a slum who grabbed my partner's leg and begged us to take her away from her junkie mother. *You* stand there and try to tell that girl No. Then there was a depressed guy named Brian, about our age. I was talking to him, and he was right there on the other side of the bathroom door, and I was telling him how to get rid of stress. He told me he knew a good way—he put a fuckin' bullet in his head. Turned out he was HIV-positive. You know who else is here? Fifteen-year-old girl named Samantha Tannenhill. She tried to kill herself with half a bottle of Tylenol because her friends dumped her and her parents treat her like a baby. How the hell did she get to that point? And there's a little old lady named Maggie who collects snow globes and ashtrays and shit from all over the country. She threw a clot and had a pulmonary embolism. She was taking Percodan, and I think my partner might've stolen some of her pills. But I didn't say anything. Maybe I should have. And those pills get me thinking about Rosemary Boccaccio, the mother of a doc at San Fernando. She downed a bottle of amitriptyline, wandered out to a gas station, and went into arrest right there. We worked her and worked her. Then we got to tell the doc that her mother had died. That was fun—but not more fun than when we took Billy to the hospital. He was about seven. End-stage cystic fibrosis. You should've seen his mother. That was way too fuckin' sad. You know, some medics say that seeing all that pain and suffering makes you immune. You get crass and joke about it. But I'm not laughing anymore."

"No, you're not," Lisa said, getting up to rub his shoulders. "This is a different kind of medicine."

Tuesday morning.

What a weekend.

Doe pulled the rescue outside of Station Ten, then hosed down the crimson-and-chrome beast. Isabel Vivas came walking over, out of uniform and looking a little upset. Manny was getting better. What bothered her now?

"When you coming back, Izzy?" Doe asked. "You know it's a matter of life and death, right? You know I can't ride with Troft much longer, right? You know that, right?"

"Sorry, Doe. I gave them my two weeks' notice, and I'm taking those weeks as vacation."

"What?"

"I've been thinking about this for a long time. That bastard with the snake on his head? The guy who shot Manny? Well, he finally died last night, so there's no more reason to wait around."

He gave her a hard look. "Thanks for sharing."

"Sorry."

"Yeah, well, I guess I wasn't always the best listener. And I never did tell you about Nicole."

"So we're even."

"And now you can leave." Doe reached into his wash bucket. "First shift, and I find out my partner's bailing on me? Damn, this is gonna be a shitty week." He furiously worked his sponge across the rescue's hood.

"Don't you want to know what I'm going to do?"

He tossed the sponge back in the bucket, realizing he was being a selfish bastard about the whole thing. He softened his tone. "Yeah, I do."

"We're moving up north. All of us. Probably take a month to get everything squared away and for Manny to get well enough. I'm just tired of it here. I want to know what a blue sky really looks like. I don't want to worry about my daughter getting shot at her day care."

"C'mon, Izzy, that shit goes on everywhere. You can't run from it."

"No, but I don't have to live in the middle of it."

"You'll try to get work up there?"

She nodded. "The lieutenant's looking into a few things for me. I'm not sure I can ever stop being a medic, but I'd like to work out of a nice, slow station."

"That doesn't sound like you."

"I know. Maybe that's what's good about it."

"As long as you're happy, right?"

"Yeah." She closed her eyes.

"Oh, man, don't do that," he said as tears lined her cheeks. "I don't know what it is with me. I talk to women, and they cry."

She broke into a smile. "I'm gonna miss you."

"I'll come up and visit."

"You'll bring your family."

His eyes widened. "Whoa. I guess I will."

"I haven't even met Geneva."

"Tell you what. Before you go, we'll all have dinner."

"Sounds good."

"Doe, you're not finished with that rescue yet?" Troft barked from the apparatus floor.

"I'd better go," said Vivas.

"Yeah," Doe answered, whirling to face Mr. Wonderful. "We're about to get a call. Fireman down at Station Ten. Respond code 3."

"Hey, Steph," Tenpenney called. "The lieutenant wants to see you and Abe in his office."

Savage glanced worriedly at Abe, then they left the conference table.

"Tuesday morning, and we haven't even had a call. How did we get in trouble already?" Abe asked.

"I'm sure this is about me," Savage said. Her breath shortened as she entered the office. Abe came up beside her and gripped the back of a chair facing the lieutenant's desk.

Martinez cupped his hands behind his head and leaned back. "Morning, Steph. Abe. You two eat bad burritos or what? You look sick."

"What's up?" Savage asked.

"Well, we're doing all kinds of community relations work this week. Got a couple of middle school classes coming on field trips and some students from first responder classes doing ride-alongs. You got one coming in today. Apparently this guy requested you."

"Oh, no," Savage said. "What's his name?"

"Hey, George," Martinez called. "You can come in now."

"Good morning," came a familiar voice from the doorway.

"It can't be him," Abe groaned.

The frequent flyer, hospital fetish boy, and TV star's son wore black polyester pants, a plain white dress shirt, and a Texas-sized, shit-eating grin. "I told you I'd see you next week," he said to Savage.

"Come on, it's my first day back from vacation," Savage pleaded with the lieutenant. "I had lunch with my son and his wife, and I've been feeling really good lately—if you catch my drift. Don't do this to me."

Martinez stood and waved a hand. "This is just what you need. Our buddy George here is gonna keep you honest for the next twenty-four hours. It'll be good for you to cover your protocols with him. Keep the skills sharp, right?"

"But sir, you know this guy. You know how he is," Abe argued. "He'll get in the way."

"I'm just an observer. I know I can't touch anything or talk to patients. I know that," George said. "I won't be any trouble."

Savage crossed to Martinez and muttered in his ear, "What am I supposed to do if he gets a woodie in front of a patient?"

"Throw a blanket over him. No problem."

The alarm sounded. Chest pain. Auto body shop.

"Yes! Got a good call already," George said.

"A good call?" Abe asked. "Could be anything."

"You behave, now, George," Martinez warned. "Authorized or not, I can still pull you off that rescue."

"You won't have to."

Out on the apparatus floor, Savage yelled for George to strap into the captain's chair in back as she hopped into the cab. Abe was already inside, firing up the engine and siren.

"Can you hear me?" George asked over his headset.

"Yeah, we hear you," Abe said. "Just shut up."

"I love the sound of a siren in the morning," George said breathlessly. "And on such a glorious morning, with the sun shining, the birds chirping. . . ."

Savage just looked at Abe. Talk about long shifts!

As they turned onto Haven Street, they passed a yellow house where two little boys always played in the front yard before their mom drove them to school. Savage grinned as the boys spotted the rescue, clutched their hearts, then crumpled to the wet grass.

About the Author

Peter Telep received a large portion of his education in New York; spent a number of years in Los Angeles, where he worked for such television shows as *In the Heat of the Night* and *The Legend of Prince Valiant*; then returned east to Florida. There he earned his undergraduate and graduate degrees, and now teaches composition, scriptwriting, and creative writing at his alma mater, the University of Central Florida.

Mr. Telep's other novels include the *Squire Trilogy*, two books based on Fox's *Space: Above and Beyond* television show, a trilogy of novels based on the best-selling computer game *Descent*, four books in the film-based *Wing Commander* series, the adaptation of the Warner Brothers film *Red Planet*, and *Night Angel 9*, the first book in this series, as well as *Night Angel 9: Something for the Pain*, book three of the trilogy. You may E-mail him at PTelep@aol.com, visit his Web site at www.earthnetone.com, or contact him via the publisher. He is always excited to hear from his readers.